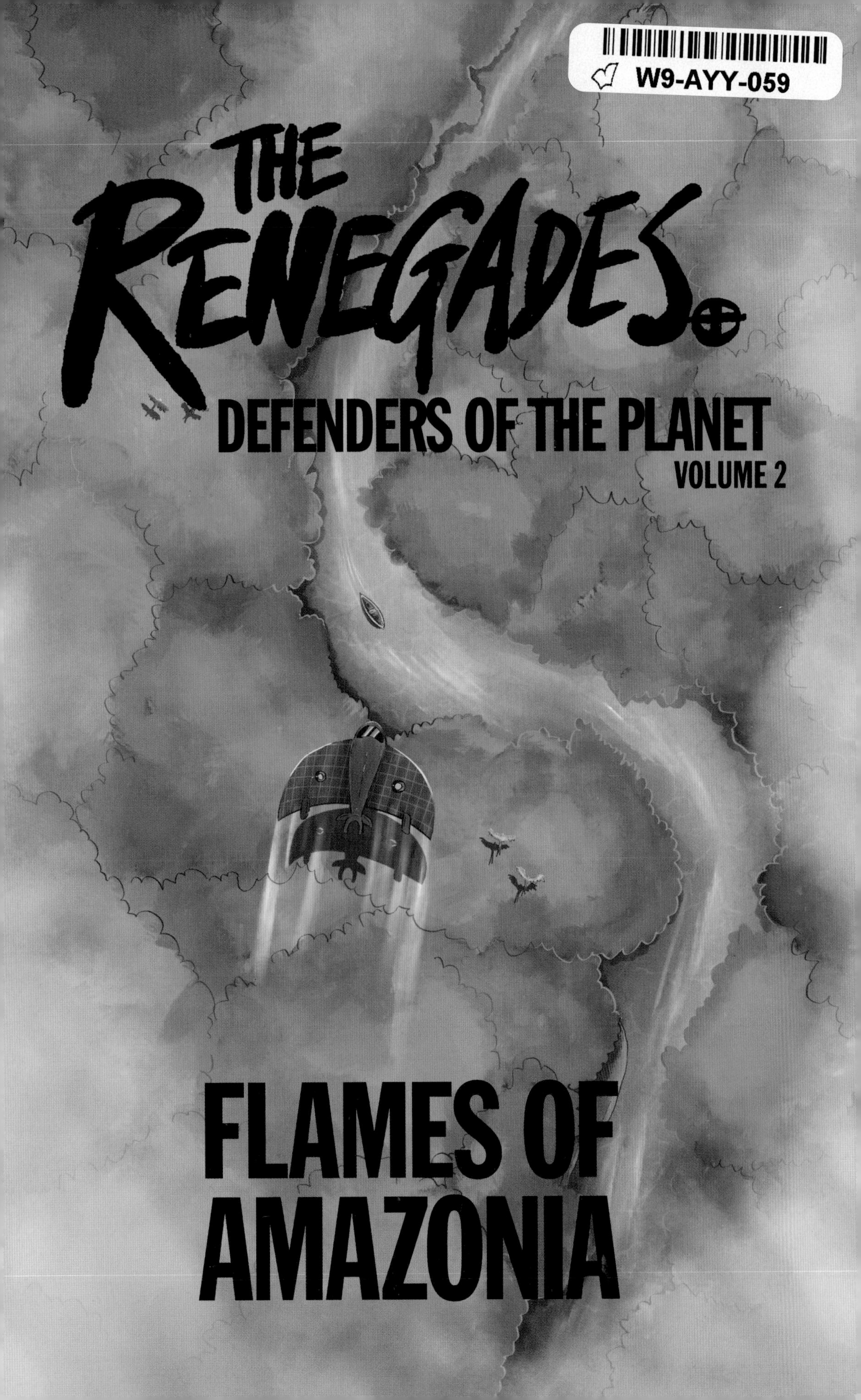

THE RENEGADES

DEFENDERS OF THE PLANET

VOLUME 2

FLAMES OF AMAZONIA

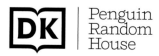

DK LONDON

Editor Vicky Richards
Designer Kit Lane
US Editor Heather Wilcox
Managing Editor Francesca Baines
Managing Art Editor Philip Letsu
Production Editor George Nimmo
Production Controller Sian Cheung
Jacket Designer Surabhi Wadhwa-Gandhi
Jacket Design Development Manager Sophia MTT
Publisher Andrew Mcintyre
Associate Publishing Director Liz Wheeler
Art Director Karen Self
Publishing Director Jonathan Metcalf

First American Edition, 2021
Published in the United States by DK Publishing
1450 Broadway, Suite 801, New York, NY 10018

21 22 23 24 10 9 8 7 6 5 4 3 2 1
001–323219–May/2021

Published in Great Britain by Dorling Kindersley Limited.

A catalog record for this book
is available from the Library of Congress.
ISBN 978-0-7440-3674-9 (Paperback)
ISBN 978-0-7440-3675-6 (PLC)

Printed and bound in China

For the curious
www.dk.com

MIX
Paper from responsible sources
FSC™ C018179

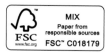

This book was made with
Forest Stewardship Council™ certified paper–
one small step in DK's commitment to a sustainable future.
For more information go to www.dk.com/our-green-pledge

THE RENEGADES.

DEFENDERS OF THE PLANET

VOLUME 2

CREATED BY JEREMY BROWN, KATY JAKEWAY,
ELLENOR MERERID, LIBBY REED,
AND DAVID SELBY

FLAMES OF AMAZONIA

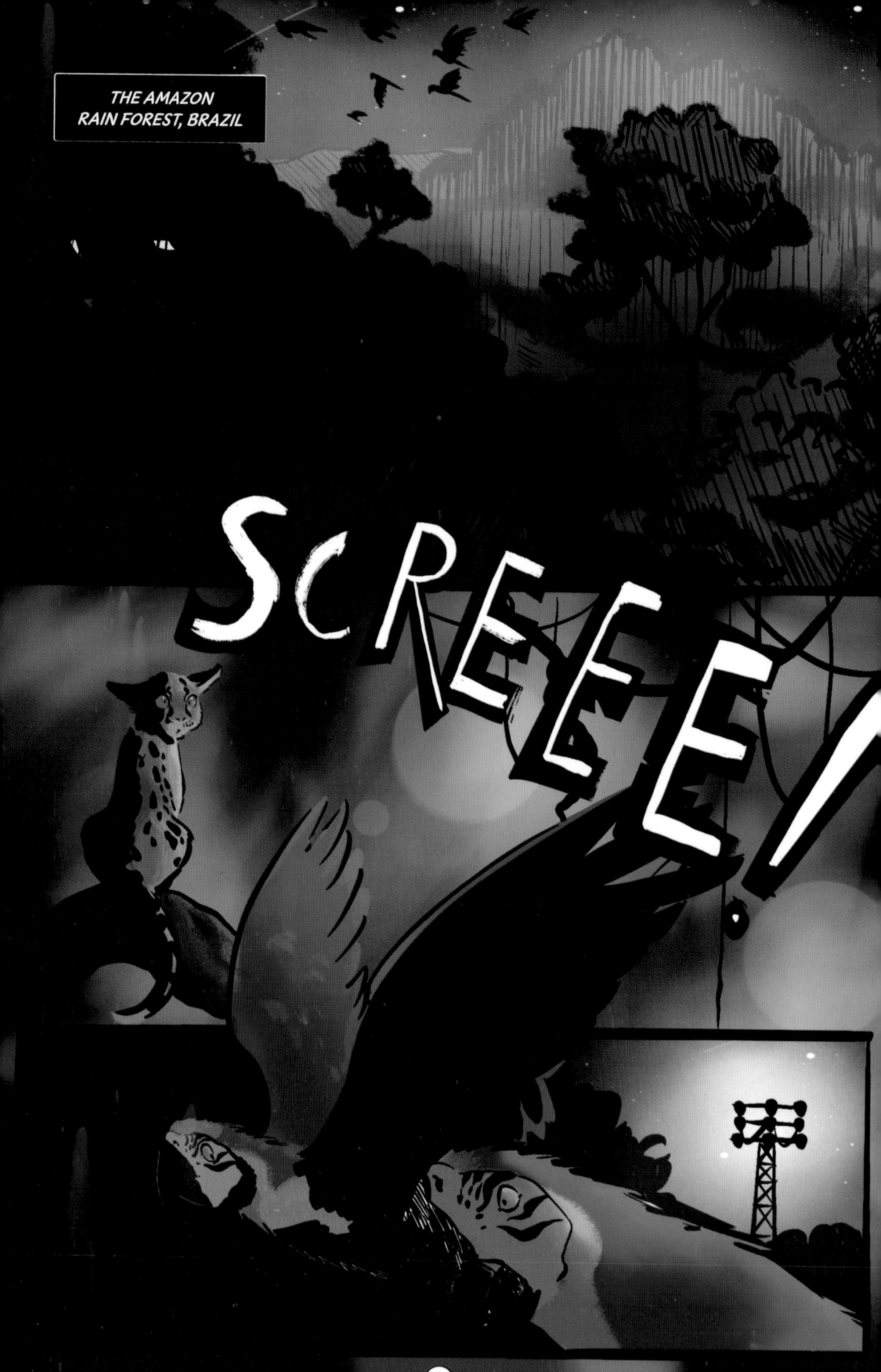
THE AMAZON
RAIN FOREST, BRAZIL
SCREEEE!

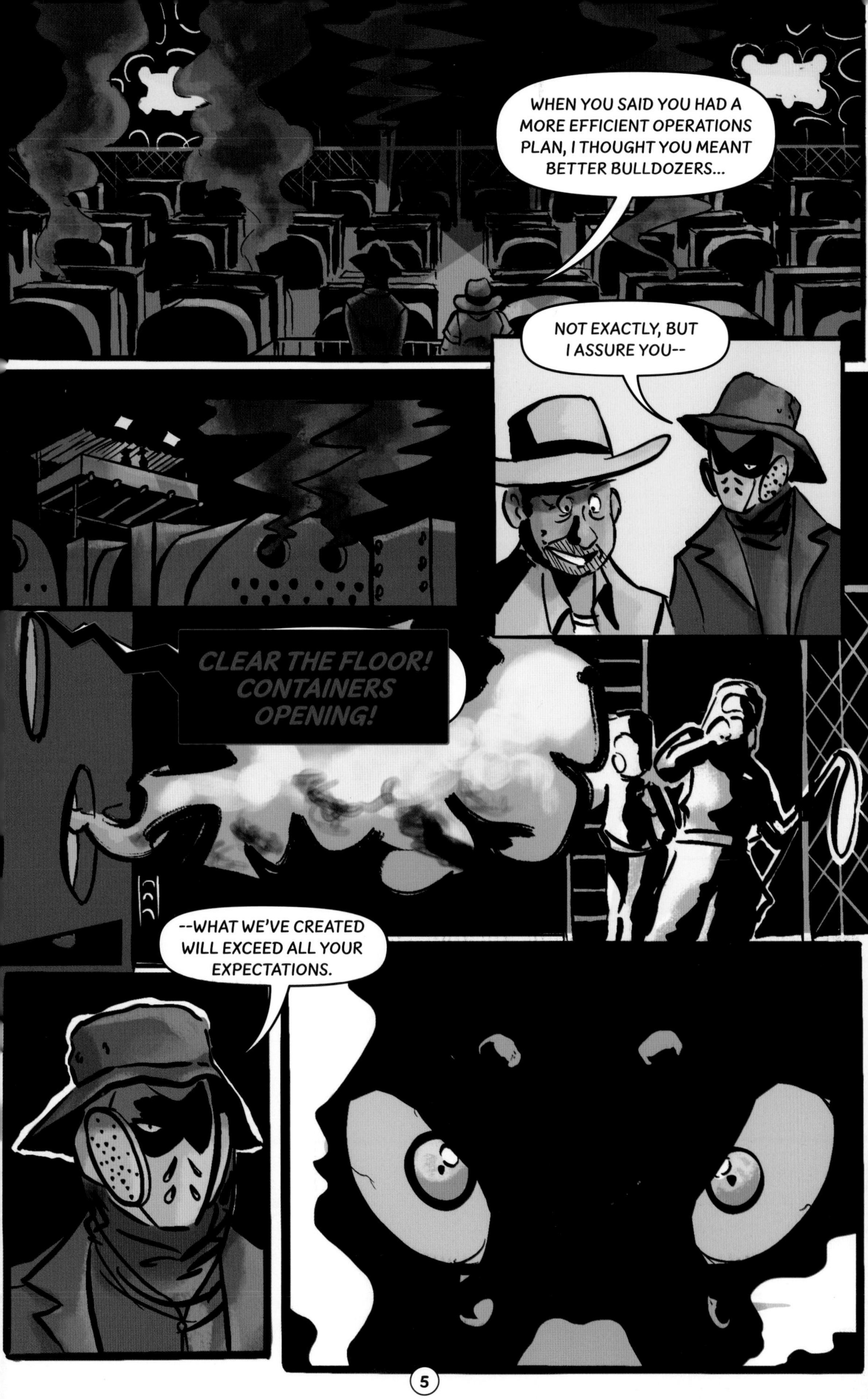

WHEN YOU SAID YOU HAD A MORE EFFICIENT OPERATIONS PLAN, I THOUGHT YOU MEANT BETTER BULLDOZERS...
NOT EXACTLY, BUT I ASSURE YOU--
CLEAR THE FLOOR! CONTAINERS OPENING!
--WHAT WE'VE CREATED WILL EXCEED ALL YOUR EXPECTATIONS.

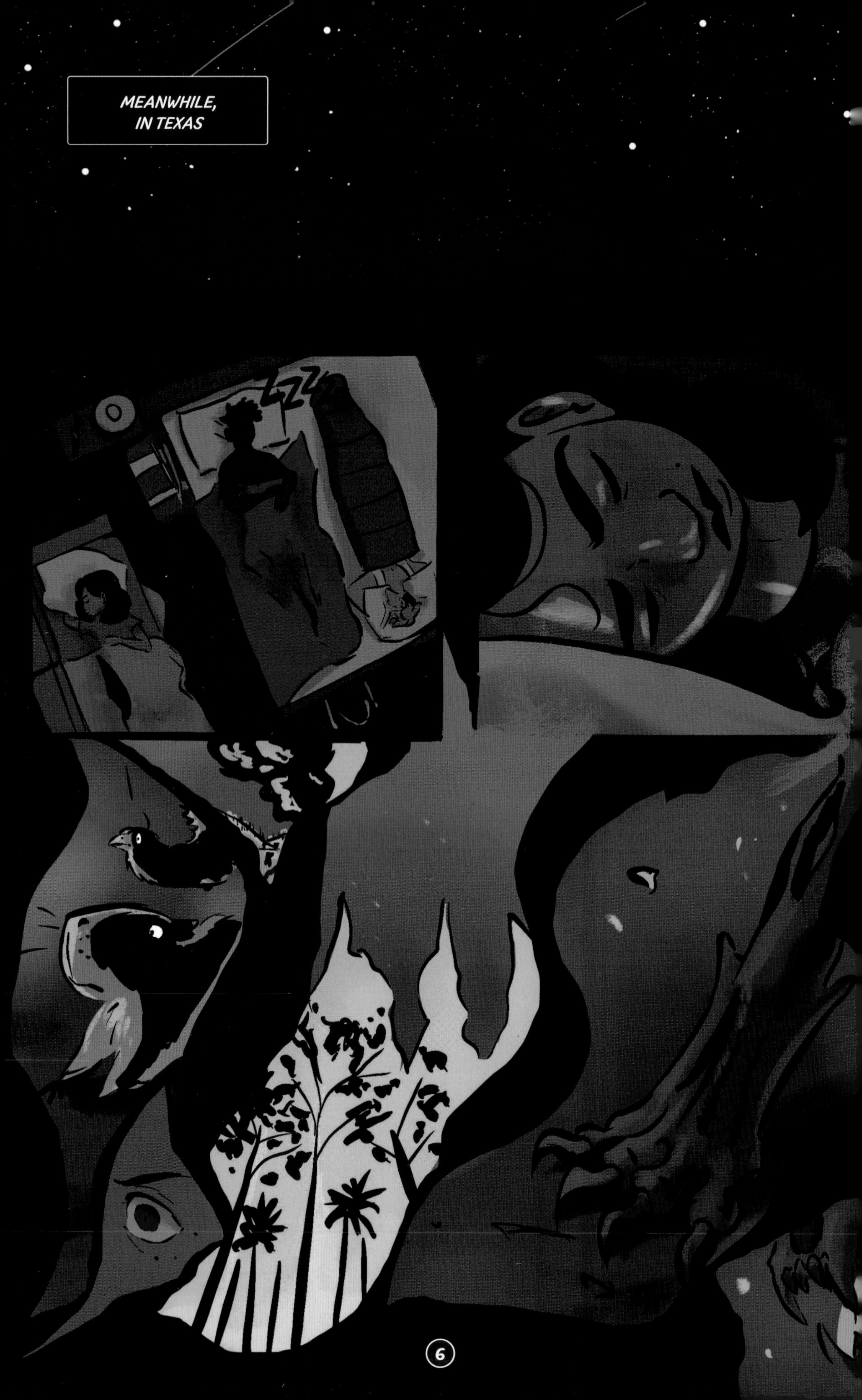
MEANWHILE,
IN TEXAS
ZZZ

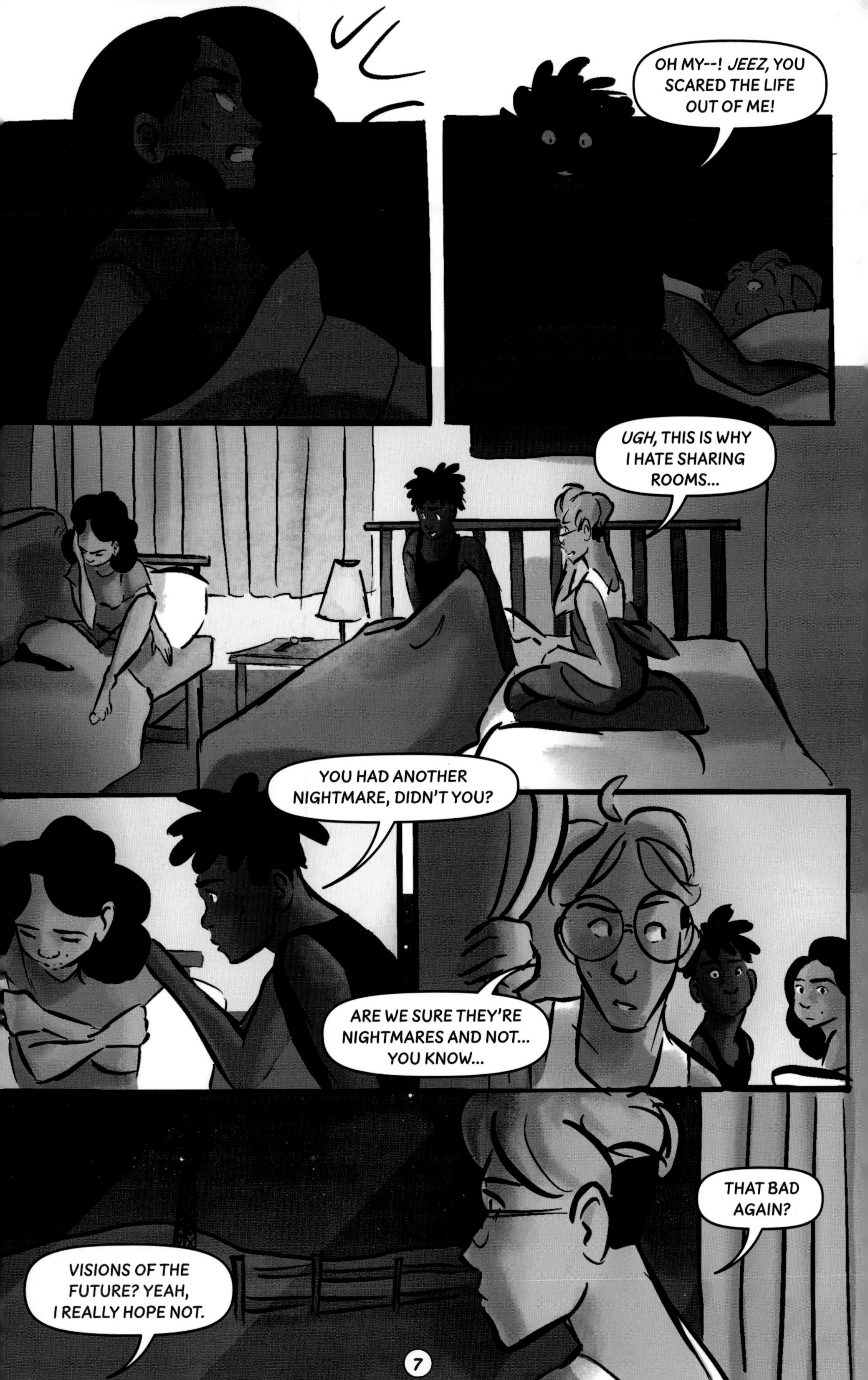
OH MY--! *JEEZ,* YOU SCARED THE LIFE OUT OF ME!
UGH, THIS IS WHY I HATE SHARING ROOMS...
YOU HAD ANOTHER NIGHTMARE, DIDN'T YOU?
ARE WE SURE THEY'RE NIGHTMARES AND NOT... YOU KNOW...
THAT BAD AGAIN?
VISIONS OF THE FUTURE? YEAH, I REALLY HOPE NOT.

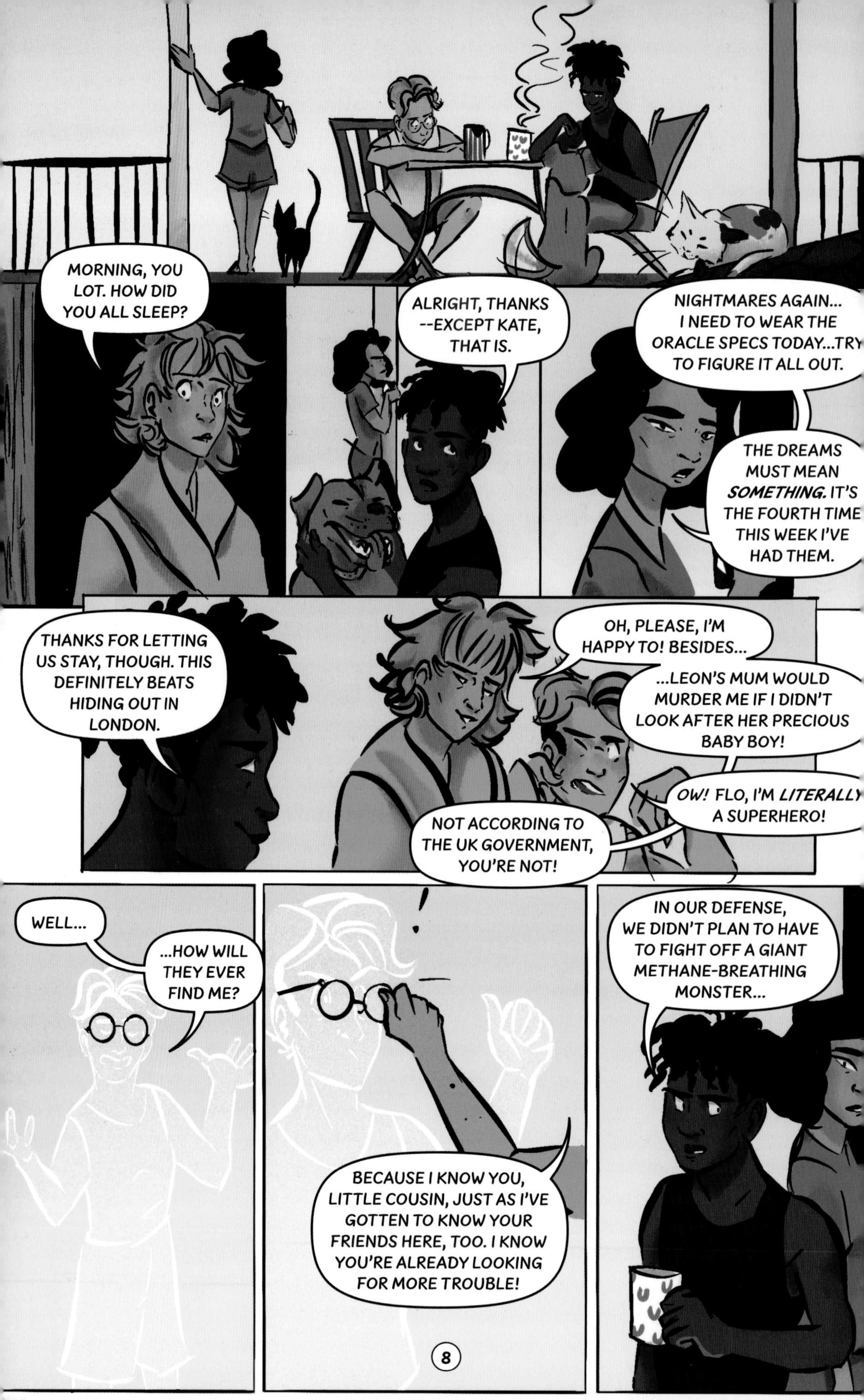
MORNING, YOU LOT. HOW DID YOU ALL SLEEP?
ALRIGHT, THANKS --EXCEPT KATE, THAT IS.
NIGHTMARES AGAIN... I NEED TO WEAR THE ORACLE SPECS TODAY...TRY TO FIGURE IT ALL OUT.
THE DREAMS MUST MEAN *SOMETHING.* IT'S THE FOURTH TIME THIS WEEK I'VE HAD THEM.
THANKS FOR LETTING US STAY, THOUGH. THIS DEFINITELY BEATS HIDING OUT IN LONDON.
OH, PLEASE, I'M HAPPY TO! BESIDES...
...LEON'S MUM WOULD MURDER ME IF I DIDN'T LOOK AFTER HER PRECIOUS BABY BOY!
OW! FLO, I'M *LITERALLY* A SUPERHERO!
NOT ACCORDING TO THE UK GOVERNMENT, YOU'RE NOT!
WELL...
...HOW WILL THEY EVER FIND ME?
!
BECAUSE I KNOW YOU, LITTLE COUSIN, JUST AS I'VE GOTTEN TO KNOW YOUR FRIENDS HERE, TOO. I KNOW YOU'RE ALREADY LOOKING FOR MORE TROUBLE!
IN OUR DEFENSE, WE DIDN'T PLAN TO HAVE TO FIGHT OFF A GIANT METHANE-BREATHING MONSTER...

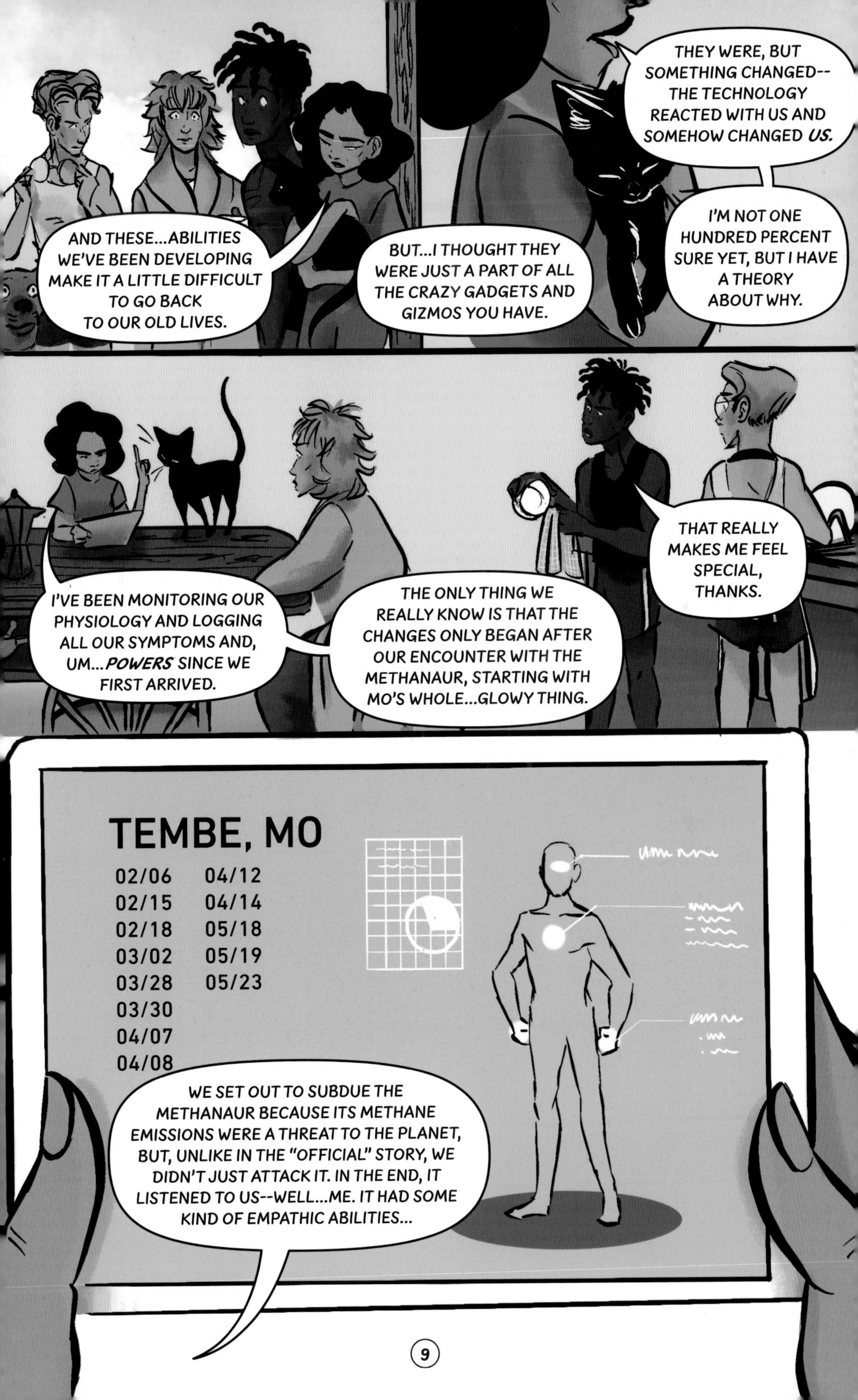
AND THESE...ABILITIES WE'VE BEEN DEVELOPING MAKE IT A LITTLE DIFFICULT TO GO BACK TO OUR OLD LIVES.
BUT...I THOUGHT THEY WERE JUST A PART OF ALL THE CRAZY GADGETS AND GIZMOS YOU HAVE.
THEY WERE, BUT SOMETHING CHANGED--THE TECHNOLOGY REACTED WITH US AND SOMEHOW CHANGED *US.*
I'M NOT ONE HUNDRED PERCENT SURE YET, BUT I HAVE A THEORY ABOUT WHY.
I'VE BEEN MONITORING OUR PHYSIOLOGY AND LOGGING ALL OUR SYMPTOMS AND, UM...*POWERS* SINCE WE FIRST ARRIVED.
THE ONLY THING WE REALLY KNOW IS THAT THE CHANGES ONLY BEGAN AFTER OUR ENCOUNTER WITH THE METHANAUR, STARTING WITH MO'S WHOLE...GLOWY THING.
THAT REALLY MAKES ME FEEL SPECIAL, THANKS.
TEMBE, MO
02/06
02/15
02/18
03/02
03/28
03/30
04/07
04/08
04/12
04/14
05/18
05/19
05/23
WE SET OUT TO SUBDUE THE METHANAUR BECAUSE ITS METHANE EMISSIONS WERE A THREAT TO THE PLANET, BUT, UNLIKE IN THE "OFFICIAL" STORY, WE DIDN'T JUST ATTACK IT. IN THE END, IT LISTENED TO US--WELL...ME. IT HAD SOME KIND OF EMPATHIC ABILITIES...

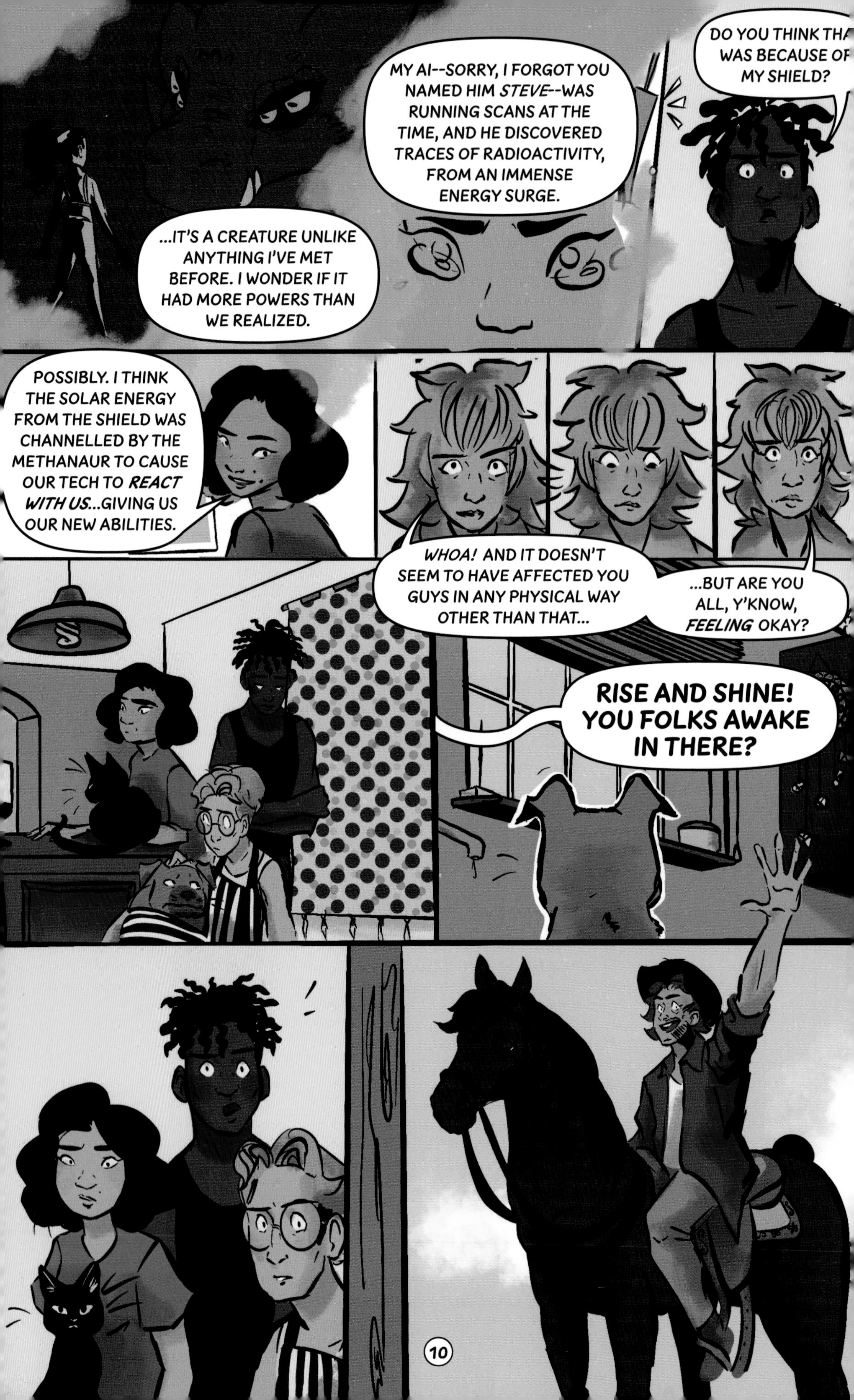
MY AI--SORRY, I FORGOT YOU NAMED HIM *STEVE*--WAS RUNNING SCANS AT THE TIME, AND HE DISCOVERED TRACES OF RADIOACTIVITY, FROM AN IMMENSE ENERGY SURGE.
...IT'S A CREATURE UNLIKE ANYTHING I'VE MET BEFORE. I WONDER IF IT HAD MORE POWERS THAN WE REALIZED.
DO YOU THINK THAT WAS BECAUSE OF MY SHIELD?
POSSIBLY. I THINK THE SOLAR ENERGY FROM THE SHIELD WAS CHANNELLED BY THE METHANAUR TO CAUSE OUR TECH TO *REACT WITH US*...GIVING US OUR NEW ABILITIES.
WHOA! AND IT DOESN'T SEEM TO HAVE AFFECTED YOU GUYS IN ANY PHYSICAL WAY OTHER THAN THAT...
...BUT ARE YOU ALL, Y'KNOW, *FEELING* OKAY?
RISE AND SHINE! YOU FOLKS AWAKE IN THERE?

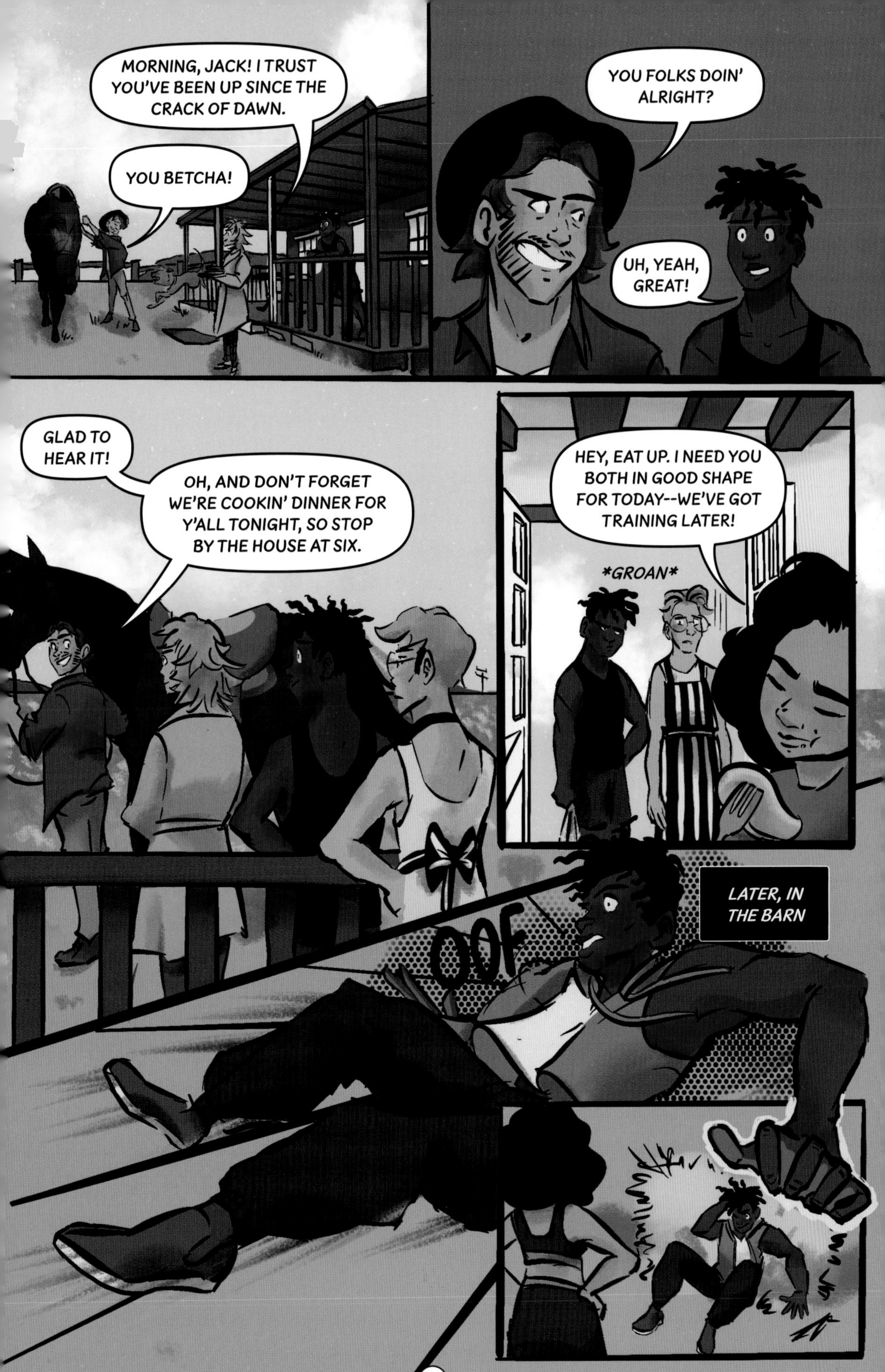
MORNING, JACK! I TRUST YOU'VE BEEN UP SINCE THE CRACK OF DAWN.
YOU BETCHA!
YOU FOLKS DOIN' ALRIGHT?
UH, YEAH, GREAT!
GLAD TO HEAR IT!
OH, AND DON'T FORGET WE'RE COOKIN' DINNER FOR Y'ALL TONIGHT, SO STOP BY THE HOUSE AT SIX.
HEY, EAT UP. I NEED YOU BOTH IN GOOD SHAPE FOR TODAY--WE'VE GOT TRAINING LATER!
GROAN
LATER, IN THE BARN
OOF

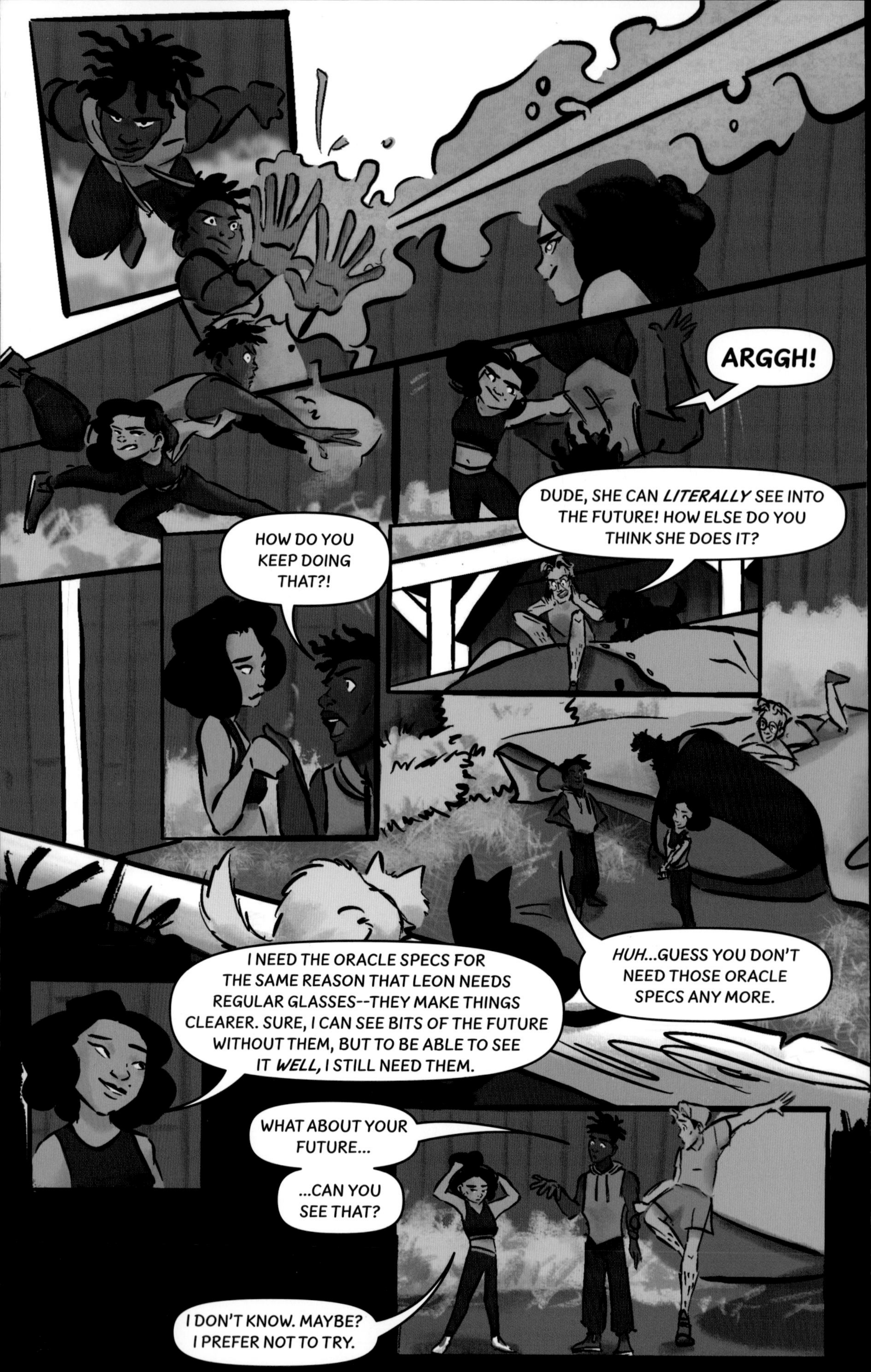
ARGGH!
HOW DO YOU KEEP DOING THAT?!
DUDE, SHE CAN *LITERALLY* SEE INTO THE FUTURE! HOW ELSE DO YOU THINK SHE DOES IT?
HUH...GUESS YOU DON'T NEED THOSE ORACLE SPECS ANY MORE.
I NEED THE ORACLE SPECS FOR THE SAME REASON THAT LEON NEEDS REGULAR GLASSES--THEY MAKE THINGS CLEARER. SURE, I CAN SEE BITS OF THE FUTURE WITHOUT THEM, BUT TO BE ABLE TO SEE IT ***WELL,*** I STILL NEED THEM.
WHAT ABOUT YOUR FUTURE...
...CAN YOU SEE THAT?
I DON'T KNOW. MAYBE? I PREFER NOT TO TRY.

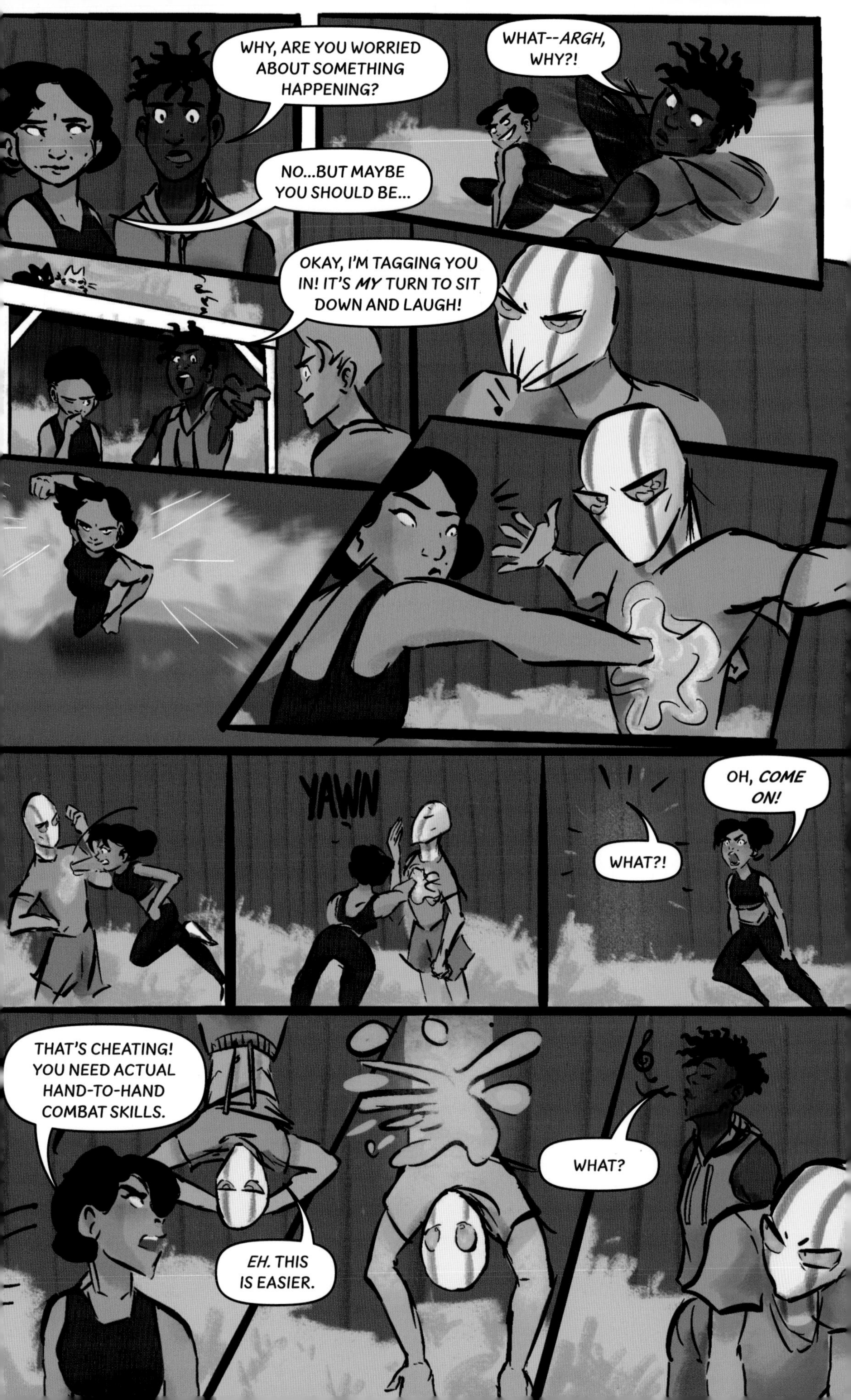
WHY, ARE YOU WORRIED ABOUT SOMETHING HAPPENING?
NO...BUT MAYBE YOU SHOULD BE...
WHAT--*ARGH*, WHY?!
OKAY, I'M TAGGING YOU IN! IT'S *MY* TURN TO SIT DOWN AND LAUGH!
YAWN
WHAT?!
OH, *COME ON!*
THAT'S CHEATING! YOU NEED ACTUAL HAND-TO-HAND COMBAT SKILLS.
EH. THIS IS EASIER.
WHAT?

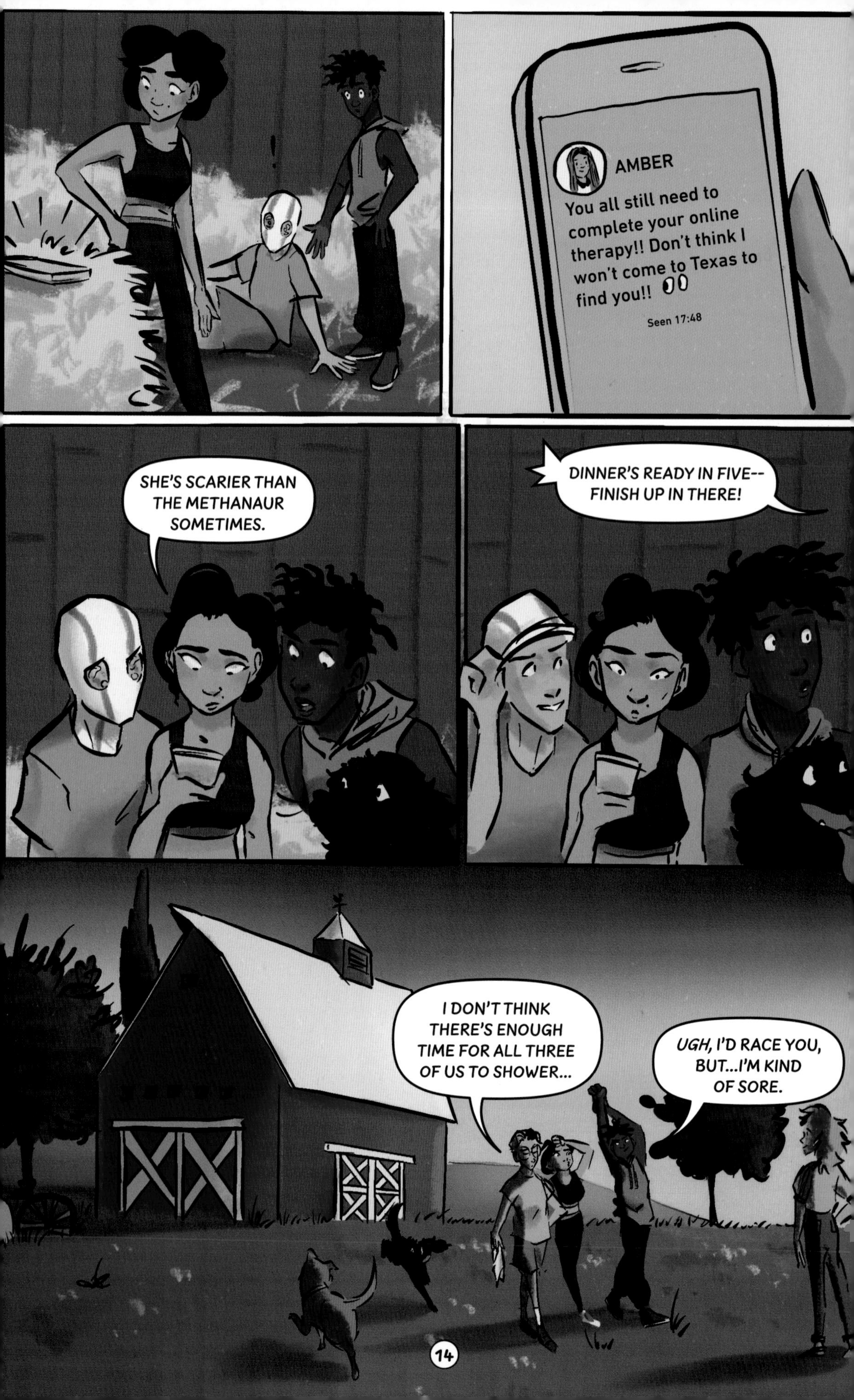
AMBER
You all still need to complete your online therapy!! Don't think I won't come to Texas to find you!!
Seen 17:48
SHE'S SCARIER THAN THE METHANAUR SOMETIMES.
DINNER'S READY IN FIVE-- FINISH UP IN THERE!
I DON'T THINK THERE'S ENOUGH TIME FOR ALL THREE OF US TO SHOWER...
UGH, I'D RACE YOU, BUT...I'M KIND OF SORE.

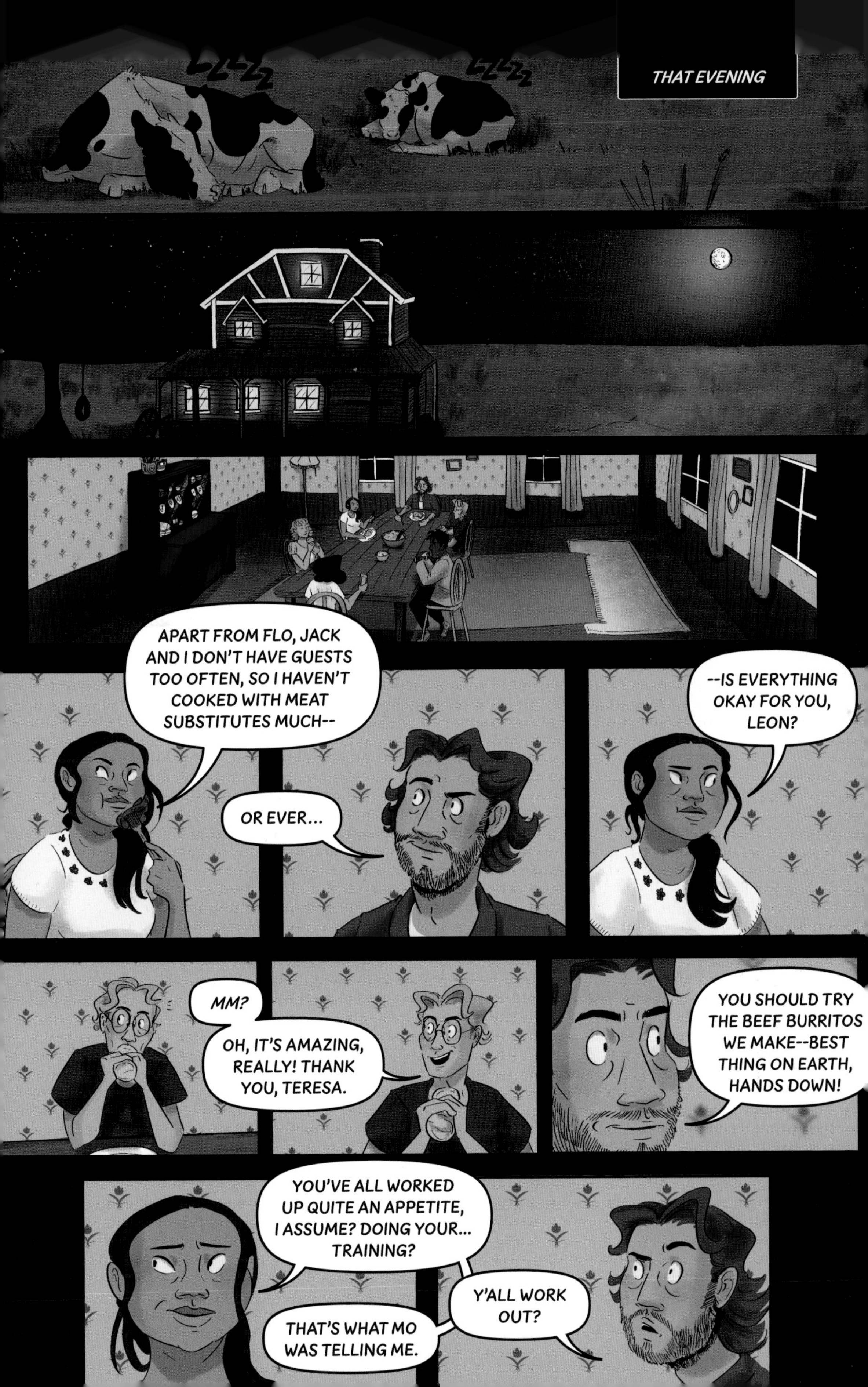
THAT EVENING
ZZZZ
ZZZZ
APART FROM FLO, JACK AND I DON'T HAVE GUESTS TOO OFTEN, SO I HAVEN'T COOKED WITH MEAT SUBSTITUTES MUCH--
OR EVER...
--IS EVERYTHING OKAY FOR YOU, LEON?
MM?
OH, IT'S AMAZING, REALLY! THANK YOU, TERESA.
YOU SHOULD TRY THE BEEF BURRITOS WE MAKE--BEST THING ON EARTH, HANDS DOWN!
YOU'VE ALL WORKED UP QUITE AN APPETITE, I ASSUME? DOING YOUR... TRAINING?
THAT'S WHAT MO WAS TELLING ME.
Y'ALL WORK OUT?

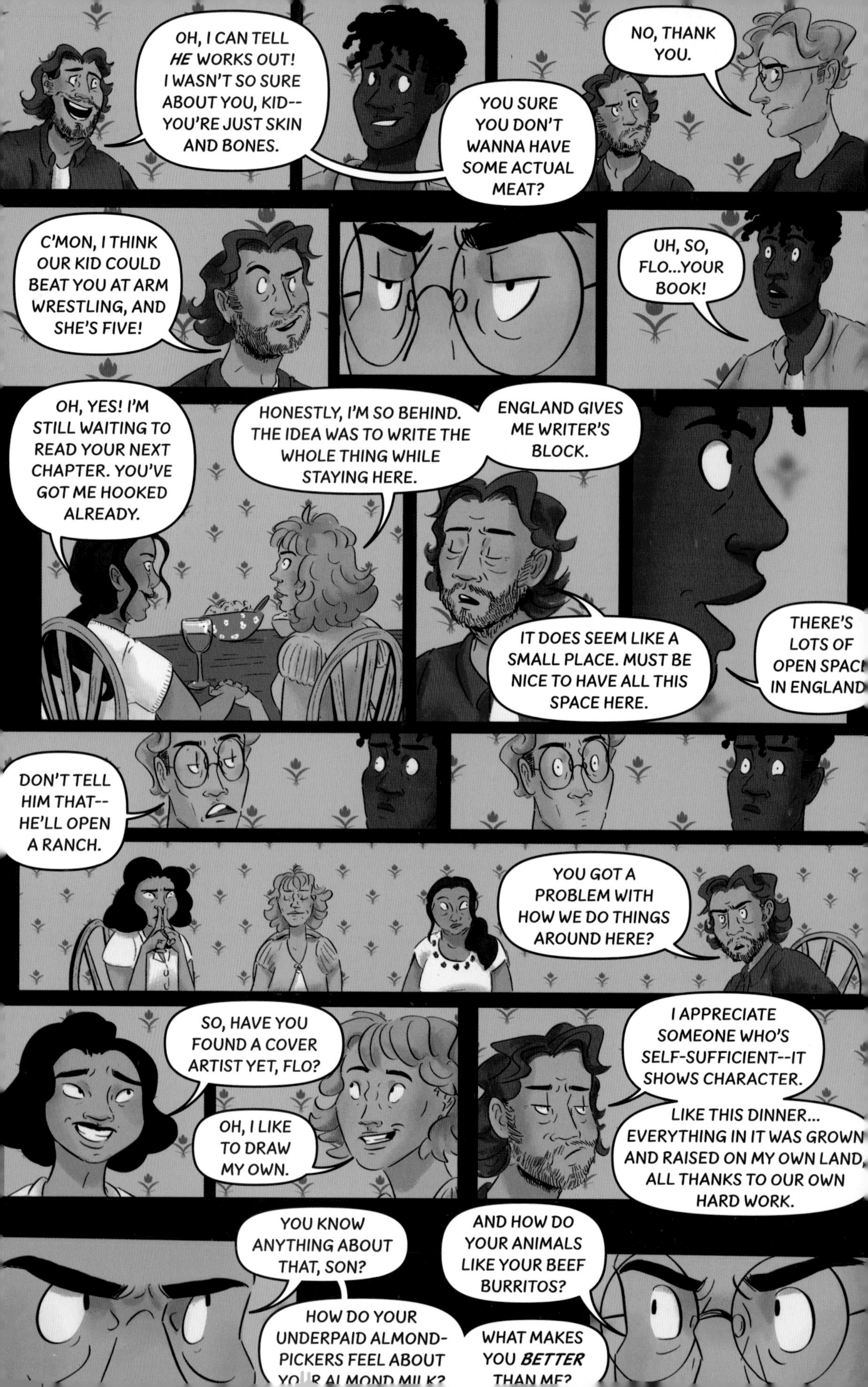
OH, I CAN TELL *HE* WORKS OUT! I WASN'T SO SURE ABOUT YOU, KID-- YOU'RE JUST SKIN AND BONES.
YOU SURE YOU DON'T WANNA HAVE SOME ACTUAL MEAT?
NO, THANK YOU.
C'MON, I THINK OUR KID COULD BEAT YOU AT ARM WRESTLING, AND SHE'S FIVE!
UH, SO, FLO...YOUR BOOK!
OH, YES! I'M STILL WAITING TO READ YOUR NEXT CHAPTER. YOU'VE GOT ME HOOKED ALREADY.
HONESTLY, I'M SO BEHIND. THE IDEA WAS TO WRITE THE WHOLE THING WHILE STAYING HERE.
ENGLAND GIVES ME WRITER'S BLOCK.
IT DOES SEEM LIKE A SMALL PLACE. MUST BE NICE TO HAVE ALL THIS SPACE HERE.
THERE'S LOTS OF OPEN SPAC IN ENGLAND
DON'T TELL HIM THAT-- HE'LL OPEN A RANCH.
YOU GOT A PROBLEM WITH HOW WE DO THINGS AROUND HERE?
SO, HAVE YOU FOUND A COVER ARTIST YET, FLO?
OH, I LIKE TO DRAW MY OWN.
I APPRECIATE SOMEONE WHO'S SELF-SUFFICIENT--IT SHOWS CHARACTER.
LIKE THIS DINNER... EVERYTHING IN IT WAS GROWN AND RAISED ON MY OWN LAND, ALL THANKS TO OUR OWN HARD WORK.
YOU KNOW ANYTHING ABOUT THAT, SON?
HOW DO YOUR UNDERPAID ALMOND-PICKERS FEEL ABOUT
AND HOW DO YOUR ANIMALS LIKE YOUR BEEF BURRITOS?
WHAT MAKES YOU *BETTER*

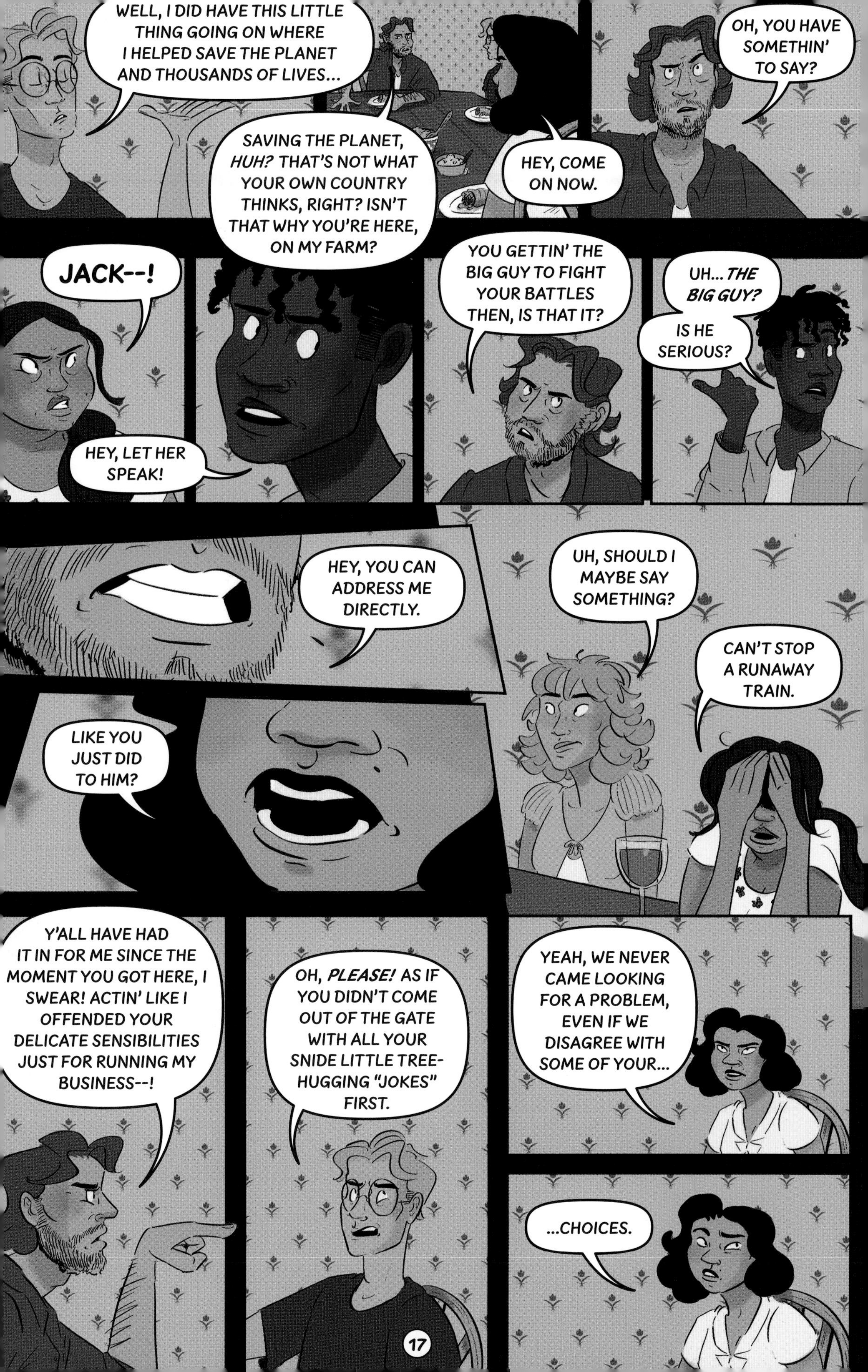
WELL, I DID HAVE THIS LITTLE THING GOING ON WHERE I HELPED SAVE THE PLANET AND THOUSANDS OF LIVES...
SAVING THE PLANET, *HUH?* THAT'S NOT WHAT YOUR OWN COUNTRY THINKS, RIGHT? ISN'T THAT WHY YOU'RE HERE, ON MY FARM?
HEY, COME ON NOW.
OH, YOU HAVE SOMETHIN' TO SAY?
JACK--!
HEY, LET HER SPEAK!
YOU GETTIN' THE BIG GUY TO FIGHT YOUR BATTLES THEN, IS THAT IT?
UH... *THE BIG GUY?*
IS HE SERIOUS?
HEY, YOU CAN ADDRESS ME DIRECTLY.
LIKE YOU JUST DID TO HIM?
UH, SHOULD I MAYBE SAY SOMETHING?
CAN'T STOP A RUNAWAY TRAIN.
Y'ALL HAVE HAD IT IN FOR ME SINCE THE MOMENT YOU GOT HERE, I SWEAR! ACTIN' LIKE I OFFENDED YOUR DELICATE SENSIBILITIES JUST FOR RUNNING MY BUSINESS--!
OH, *PLEASE!* AS IF YOU DIDN'T COME OUT OF THE GATE WITH ALL YOUR SNIDE LITTLE TREE-HUGGING "JOKES" FIRST.
YEAH, WE NEVER CAME LOOKING FOR A PROBLEM, EVEN IF WE DISAGREE WITH SOME OF YOUR...
...CHOICES.

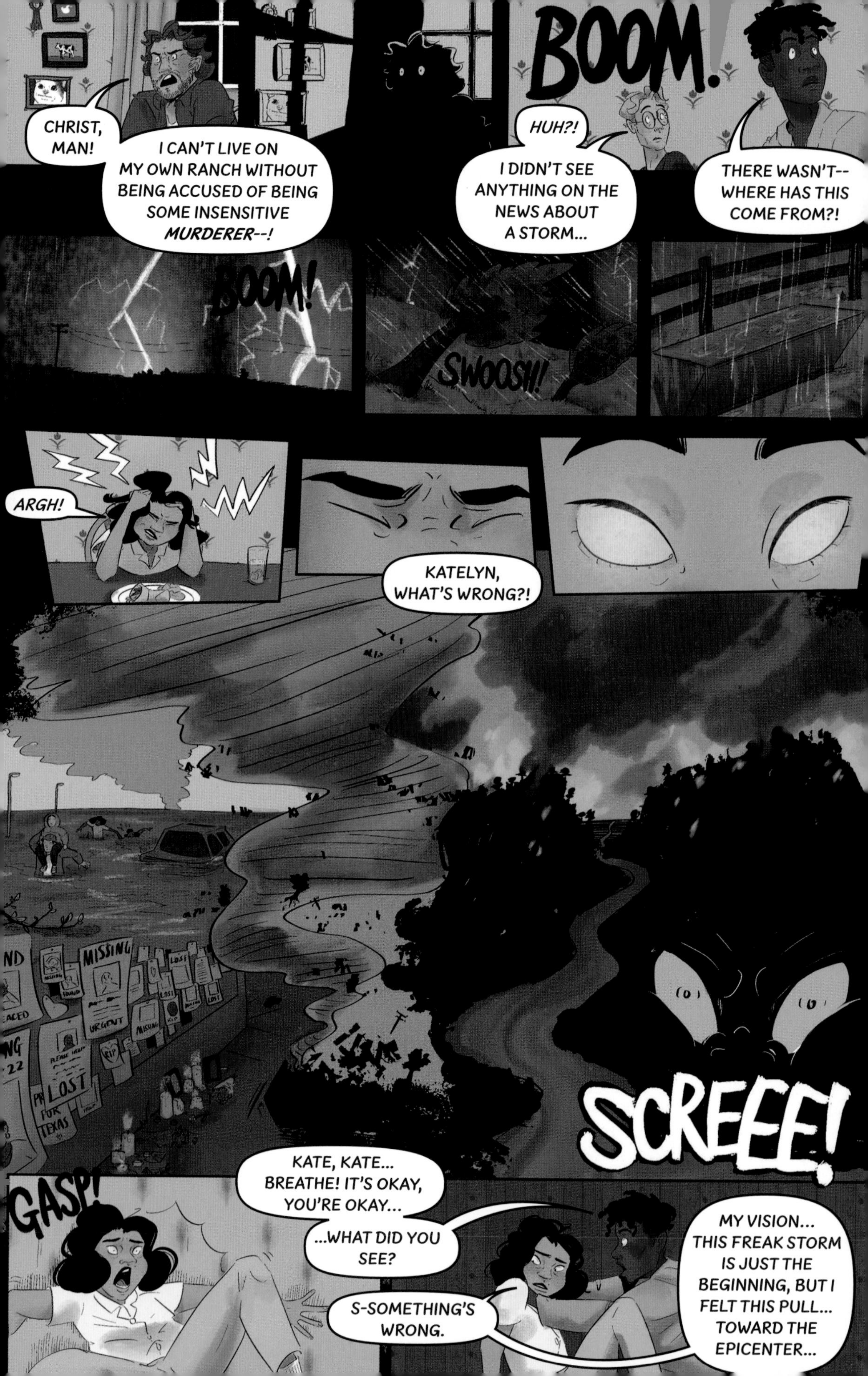
CHRIST, MAN!
I CAN'T LIVE ON MY OWN RANCH WITHOUT BEING ACCUSED OF BEING SOME INSENSITIVE *MURDERER*--!
BOOM!
HUH?!
I DIDN'T SEE ANYTHING ON THE NEWS ABOUT A STORM...
THERE WASN'T-- WHERE HAS THIS COME FROM?!
BOOM!
SWOOSH!
ARGH!
KATELYN, WHAT'S WRONG?!
MISSING
URGENT
LOST
SCREEE!
GASP!
KATE, KATE... BREATHE! IT'S OKAY, YOU'RE OKAY...
...WHAT DID YOU SEE?
S-SOMETHING'S WRONG.
MY VISION... THIS FREAK STORM IS JUST THE BEGINNING, BUT I FELT THIS PULL... TOWARD THE EPICENTER...

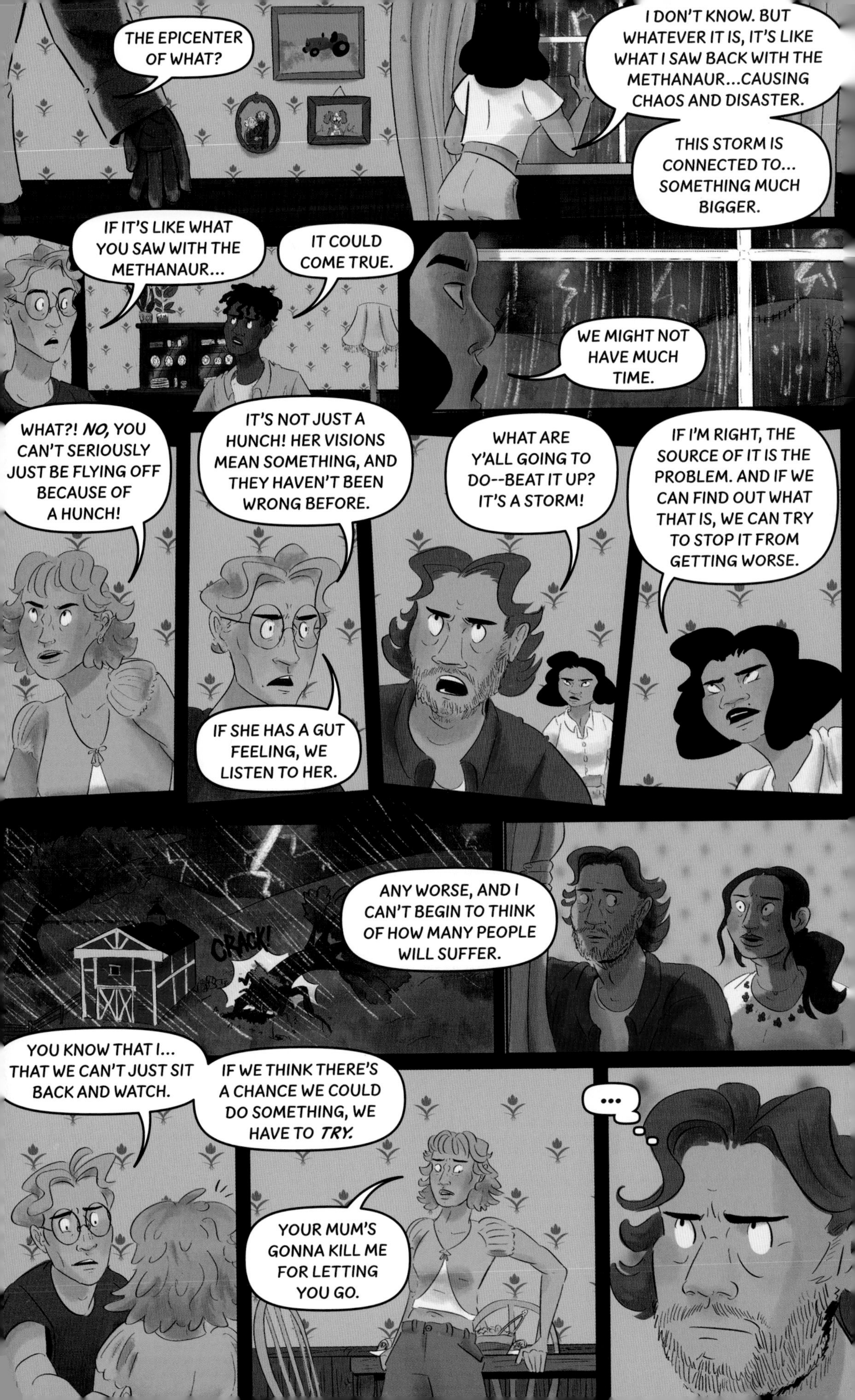
THE EPICENTER OF WHAT?
I DON'T KNOW. BUT WHATEVER IT IS, IT'S LIKE WHAT I SAW BACK WITH THE METHANAUR...CAUSING CHAOS AND DISASTER.
THIS STORM IS CONNECTED TO... SOMETHING MUCH BIGGER.
IF IT'S LIKE WHAT YOU SAW WITH THE METHANAUR...
IT COULD COME TRUE.
WE MIGHT NOT HAVE MUCH TIME.
WHAT?! NO, YOU CAN'T SERIOUSLY JUST BE FLYING OFF BECAUSE OF A HUNCH!
IT'S NOT JUST A HUNCH! HER VISIONS MEAN SOMETHING, AND THEY HAVEN'T BEEN WRONG BEFORE.
IF SHE HAS A GUT FEELING, WE LISTEN TO HER.
WHAT ARE Y'ALL GOING TO DO--BEAT IT UP? IT'S A STORM!
IF I'M RIGHT, THE SOURCE OF IT IS THE PROBLEM. AND IF WE CAN FIND OUT WHAT THAT IS, WE CAN TRY TO STOP IT FROM GETTING WORSE.
CRACK!
ANY WORSE, AND I CAN'T BEGIN TO THINK OF HOW MANY PEOPLE WILL SUFFER.
YOU KNOW THAT I... THAT WE CAN'T JUST SIT BACK AND WATCH.
IF WE THINK THERE'S A CHANCE WE COULD DO SOMETHING, WE HAVE TO TRY.
YOUR MUM'S GONNA KILL ME FOR LETTING YOU GO.
...

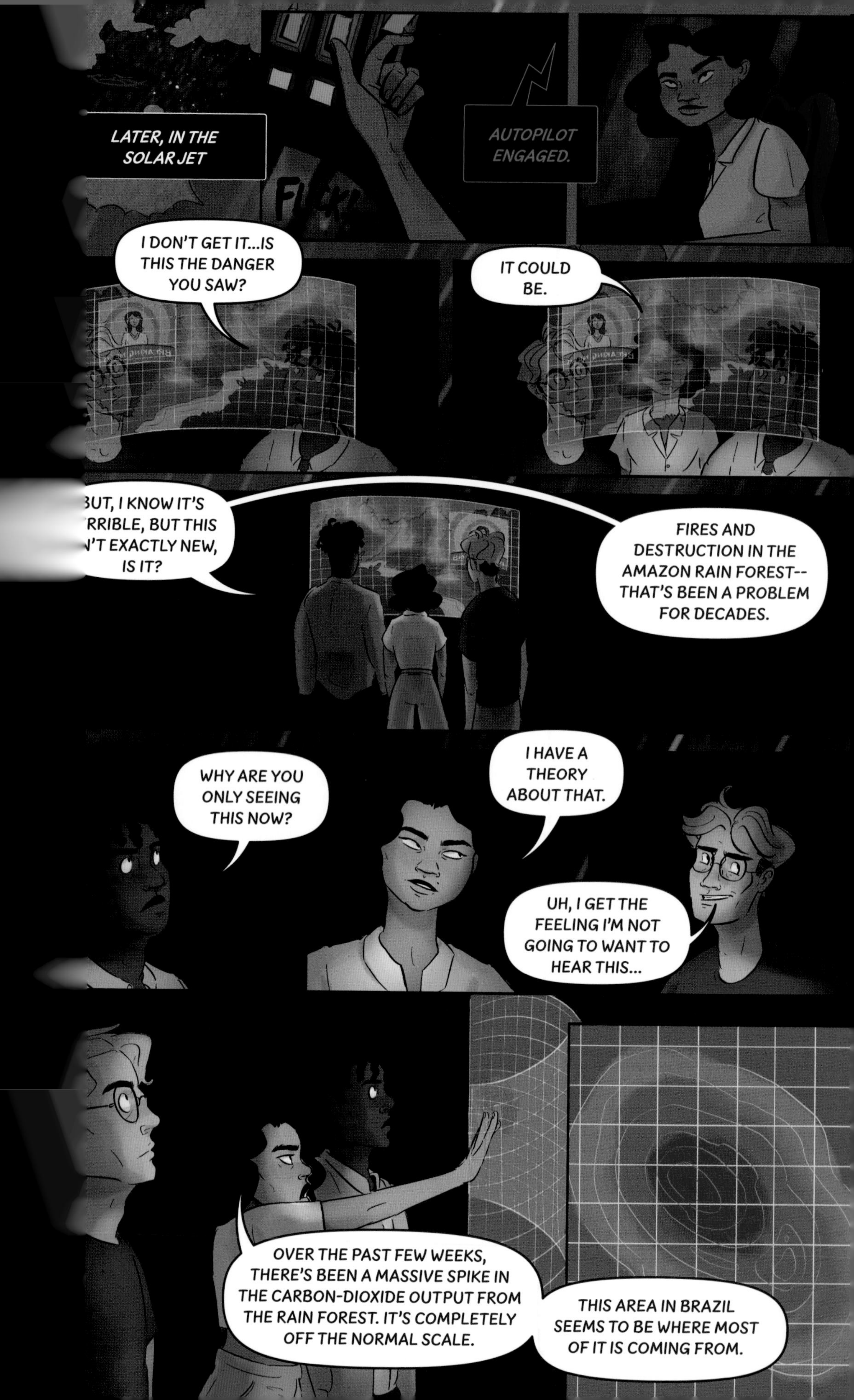
LATER, IN THE SOLAR JET
AUTOPILOT ENGAGED.
I DON'T GET IT...IS THIS THE DANGER YOU SAW?
IT COULD BE.
UT, I KNOW IT'S RRIBLE, BUT THIS 'T EXACTLY NEW, IS IT?
FIRES AND DESTRUCTION IN THE AMAZON RAIN FOREST-- THAT'S BEEN A PROBLEM FOR DECADES.
WHY ARE YOU ONLY SEEING THIS NOW?
I HAVE A THEORY ABOUT THAT.
UH, I GET THE FEELING I'M NOT GOING TO WANT TO HEAR THIS...
OVER THE PAST FEW WEEKS, THERE'S BEEN A MASSIVE SPIKE IN THE CARBON-DIOXIDE OUTPUT FROM THE RAIN FOREST. IT'S COMPLETELY OFF THE NORMAL SCALE.
THIS AREA IN BRAZIL SEEMS TO BE WHERE MOST OF IT IS COMING FROM.

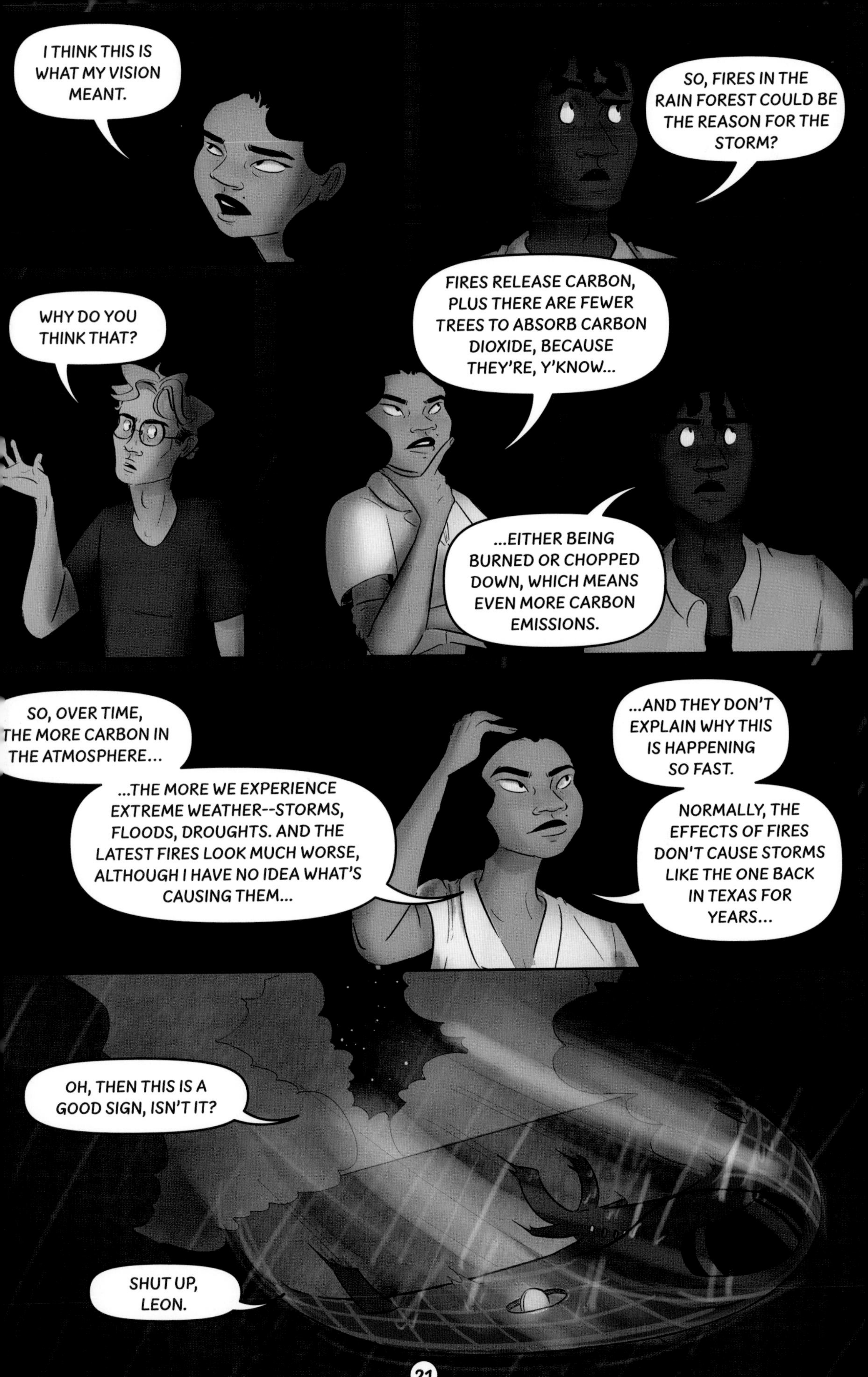
I THINK THIS IS WHAT MY VISION MEANT.
SO, FIRES IN THE RAIN FOREST COULD BE THE REASON FOR THE STORM?
WHY DO YOU THINK THAT?
FIRES RELEASE CARBON, PLUS THERE ARE FEWER TREES TO ABSORB CARBON DIOXIDE, BECAUSE THEY'RE, Y'KNOW...
...EITHER BEING BURNED OR CHOPPED DOWN, WHICH MEANS EVEN MORE CARBON EMISSIONS.
SO, OVER TIME, THE MORE CARBON IN THE ATMOSPHERE...
...THE MORE WE EXPERIENCE EXTREME WEATHER--STORMS, FLOODS, DROUGHTS. AND THE LATEST FIRES LOOK MUCH WORSE, ALTHOUGH I HAVE NO IDEA WHAT'S CAUSING THEM...
...AND THEY DON'T EXPLAIN WHY THIS IS HAPPENING SO FAST.
NORMALLY, THE EFFECTS OF FIRES DON'T CAUSE STORMS LIKE THE ONE BACK IN TEXAS FOR YEARS...
OH, THEN THIS IS A GOOD SIGN, ISN'T IT?
SHUT UP, LEON.

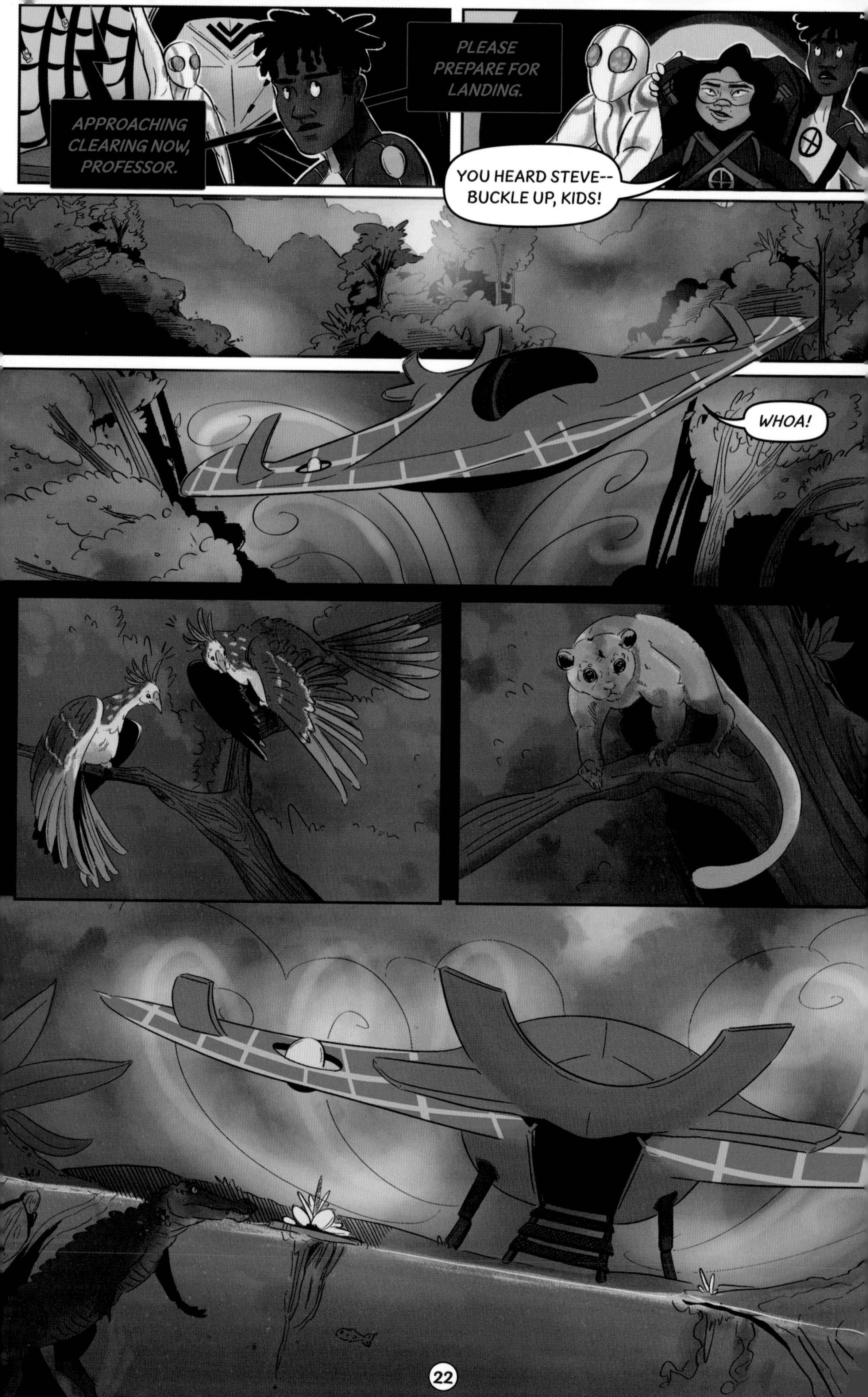
APPROACHING CLEARING NOW, PROFESSOR.
PLEASE PREPARE FOR LANDING.
YOU HEARD STEVE-- BUCKLE UP, KIDS!
WHOA!

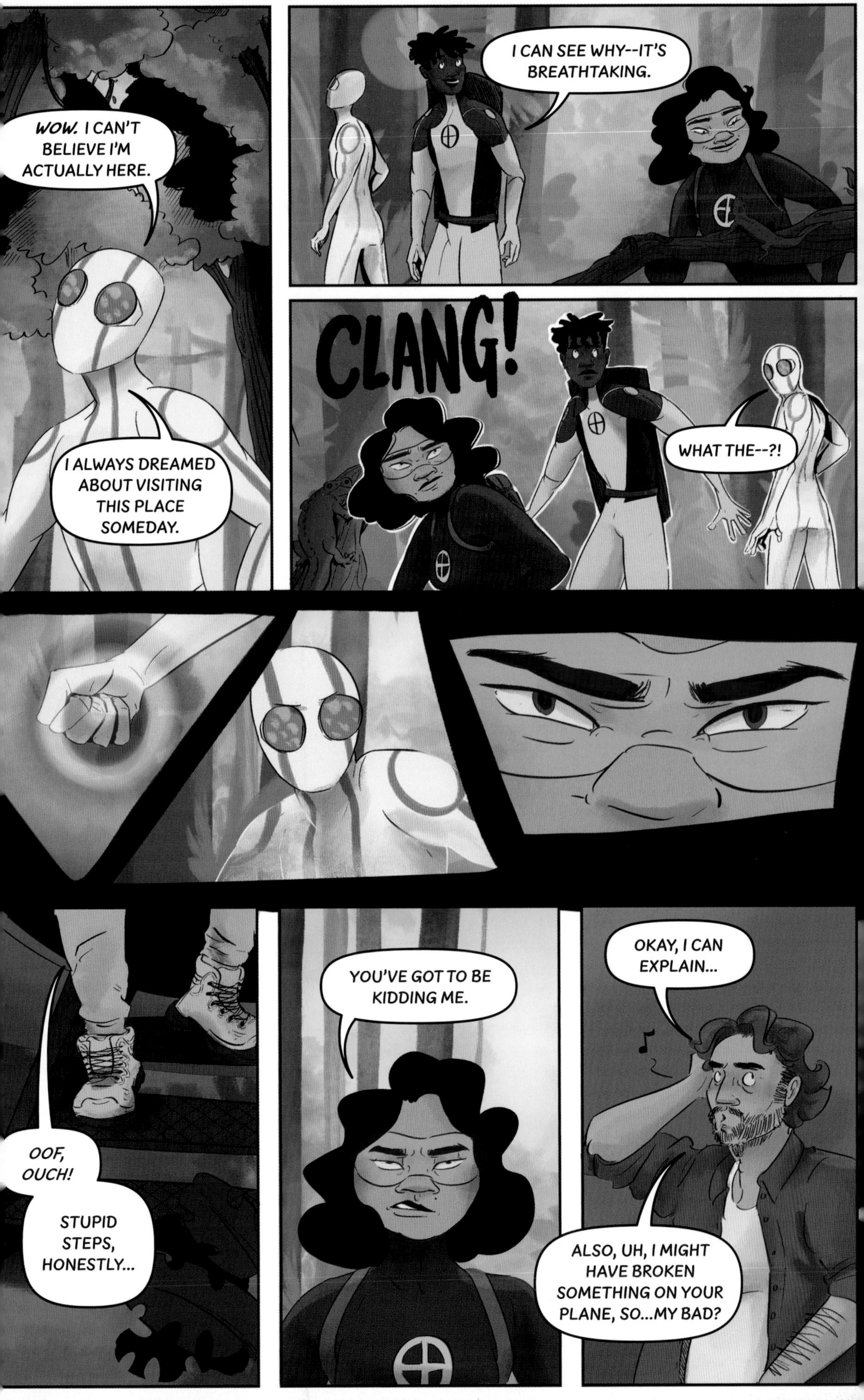

WOW. I CAN'T BELIEVE I'M ACTUALLY HERE.
I ALWAYS DREAMED ABOUT VISITING THIS PLACE SOMEDAY.
I CAN SEE WHY--IT'S BREATHTAKING.
CLANG!
WHAT THE--?!
OOF, OUCH!
STUPID STEPS, HONESTLY...
YOU'VE GOT TO BE KIDDING ME.
OKAY, I CAN EXPLAIN...
ALSO, UH, I MIGHT HAVE BROKEN SOMETHING ON YOUR PLANE, SO...MY BAD?

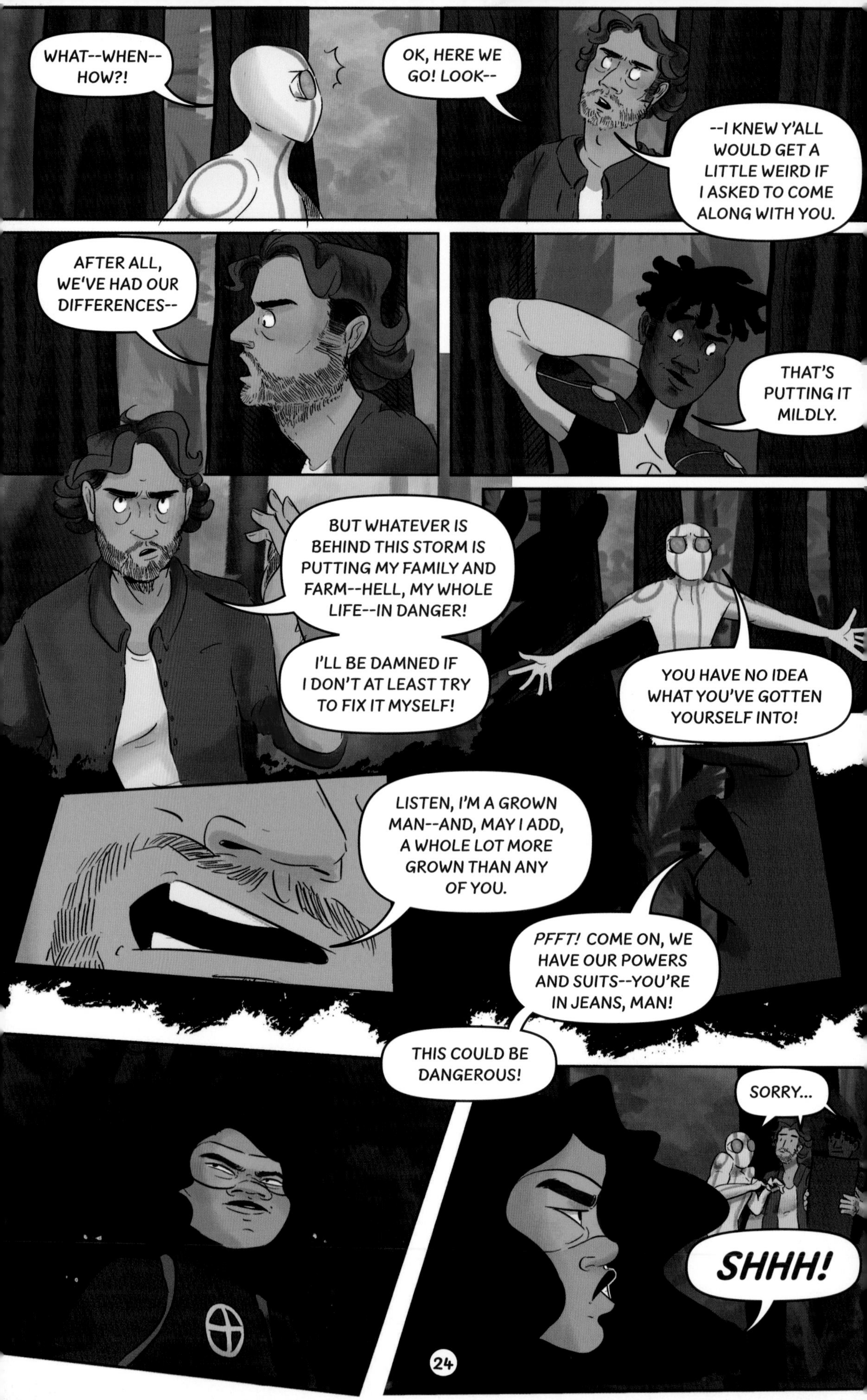
WHAT--WHEN--
HOW?!
OK, HERE WE GO! LOOK--
--I KNEW Y'ALL WOULD GET A LITTLE WEIRD IF I ASKED TO COME ALONG WITH YOU.
AFTER ALL, WE'VE HAD OUR DIFFERENCES--
THAT'S PUTTING IT MILDLY.
BUT WHATEVER IS BEHIND THIS STORM IS PUTTING MY FAMILY AND FARM--HELL, MY WHOLE LIFE--IN DANGER!
I'LL BE DAMNED IF I DON'T AT LEAST TRY TO FIX IT MYSELF!
YOU HAVE NO IDEA WHAT YOU'VE GOTTEN YOURSELF INTO!
LISTEN, I'M A GROWN MAN--AND, MAY I ADD, A WHOLE LOT MORE GROWN THAN ANY OF YOU.
PFFT! COME ON, WE HAVE OUR POWERS AND SUITS--YOU'RE IN JEANS, MAN!
THIS COULD BE DANGEROUS!
SORRY...
SHHH!

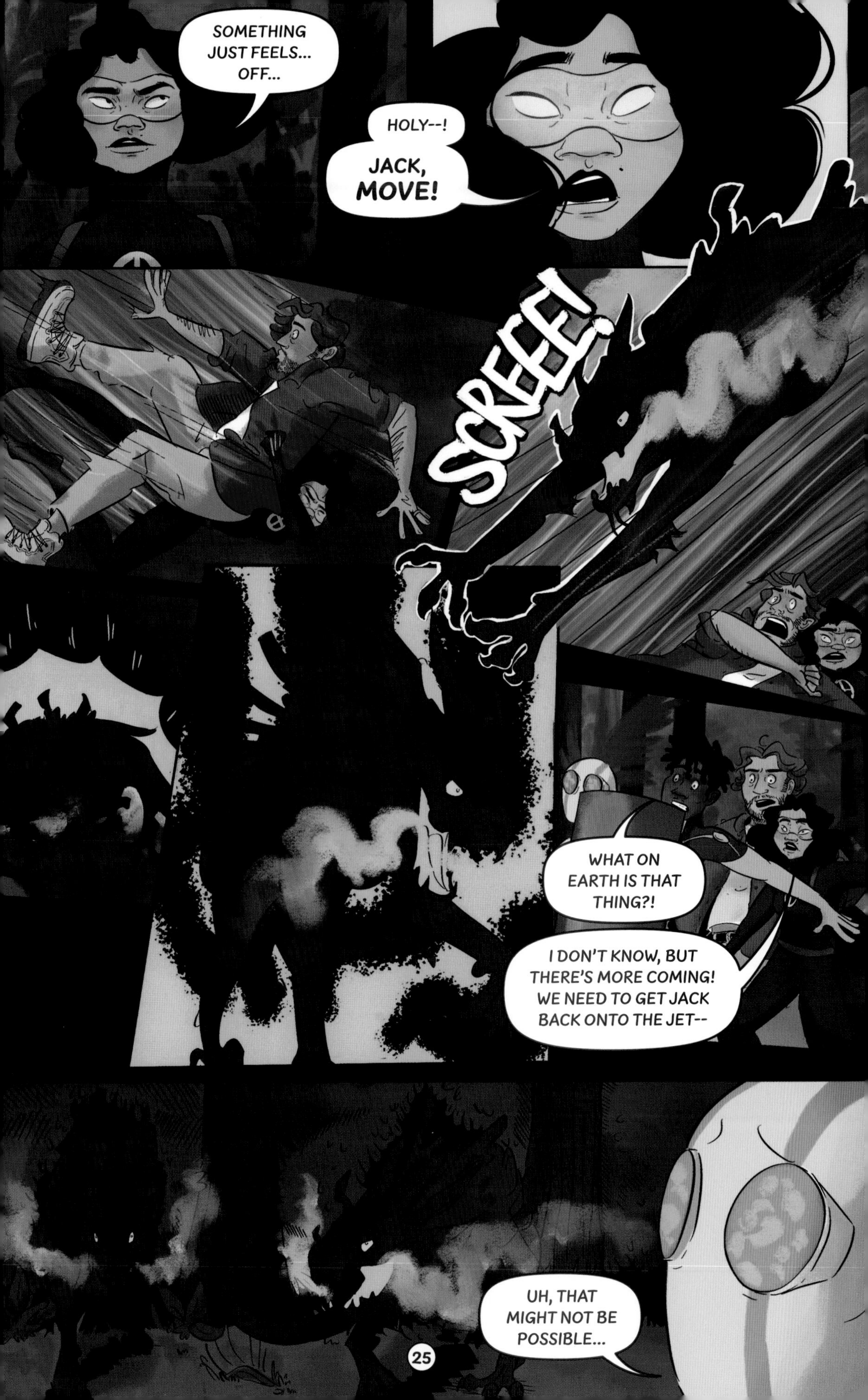
SOMETHING JUST FEELS... OFF...
HOLY--!
JACK, MOVE!
SCREEE!
WHAT ON EARTH IS THAT THING?!
I DON'T KNOW, BUT THERE'S MORE COMING! WE NEED TO GET JACK BACK ONTO THE JET--
UH, THAT MIGHT NOT BE POSSIBLE...

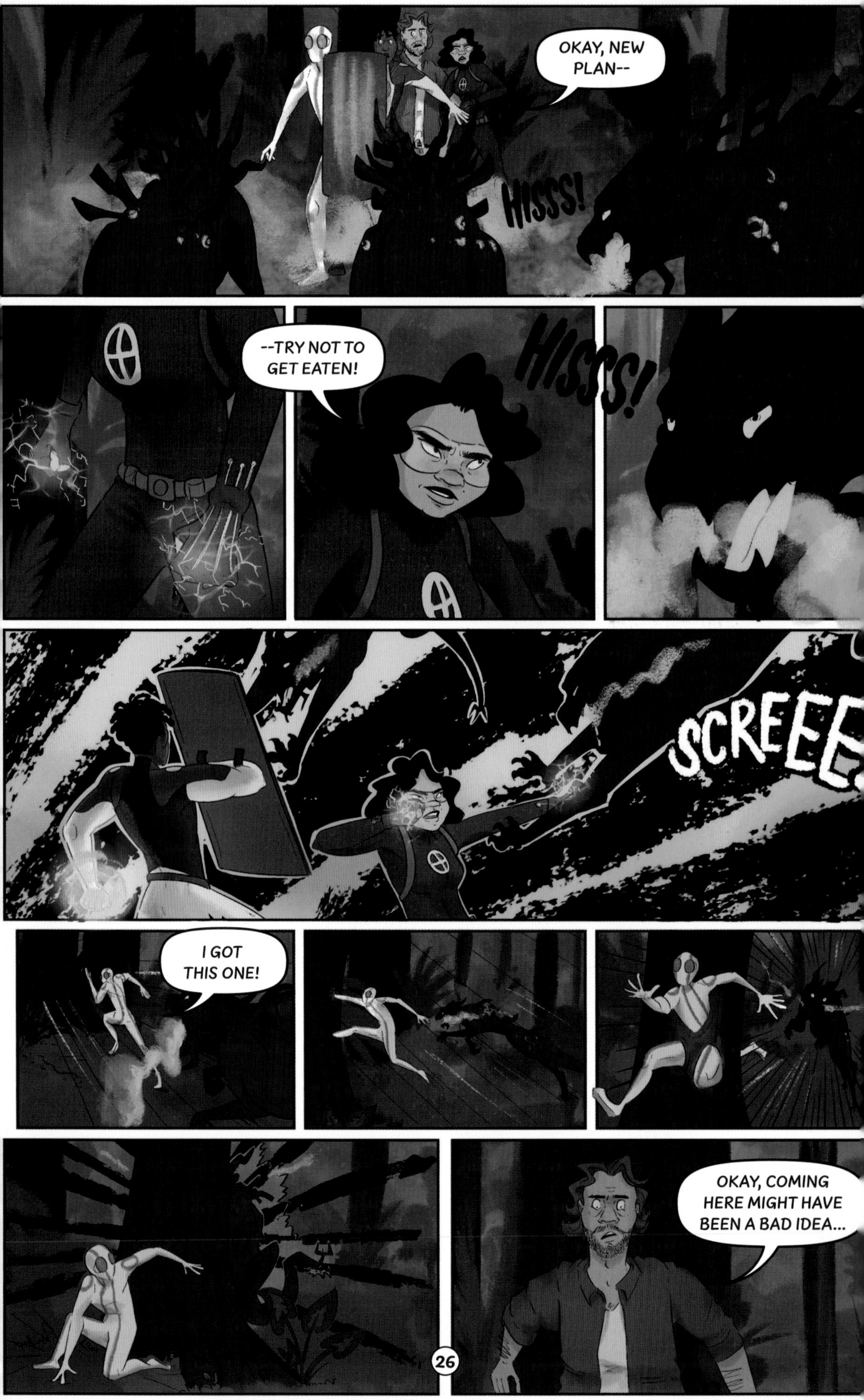
OKAY, NEW PLAN--
HISSS!
--TRY NOT TO GET EATEN!
HISSS!
SCREEE
I GOT THIS ONE!
OKAY, COMING HERE MIGHT HAVE BEEN A BAD IDEA...

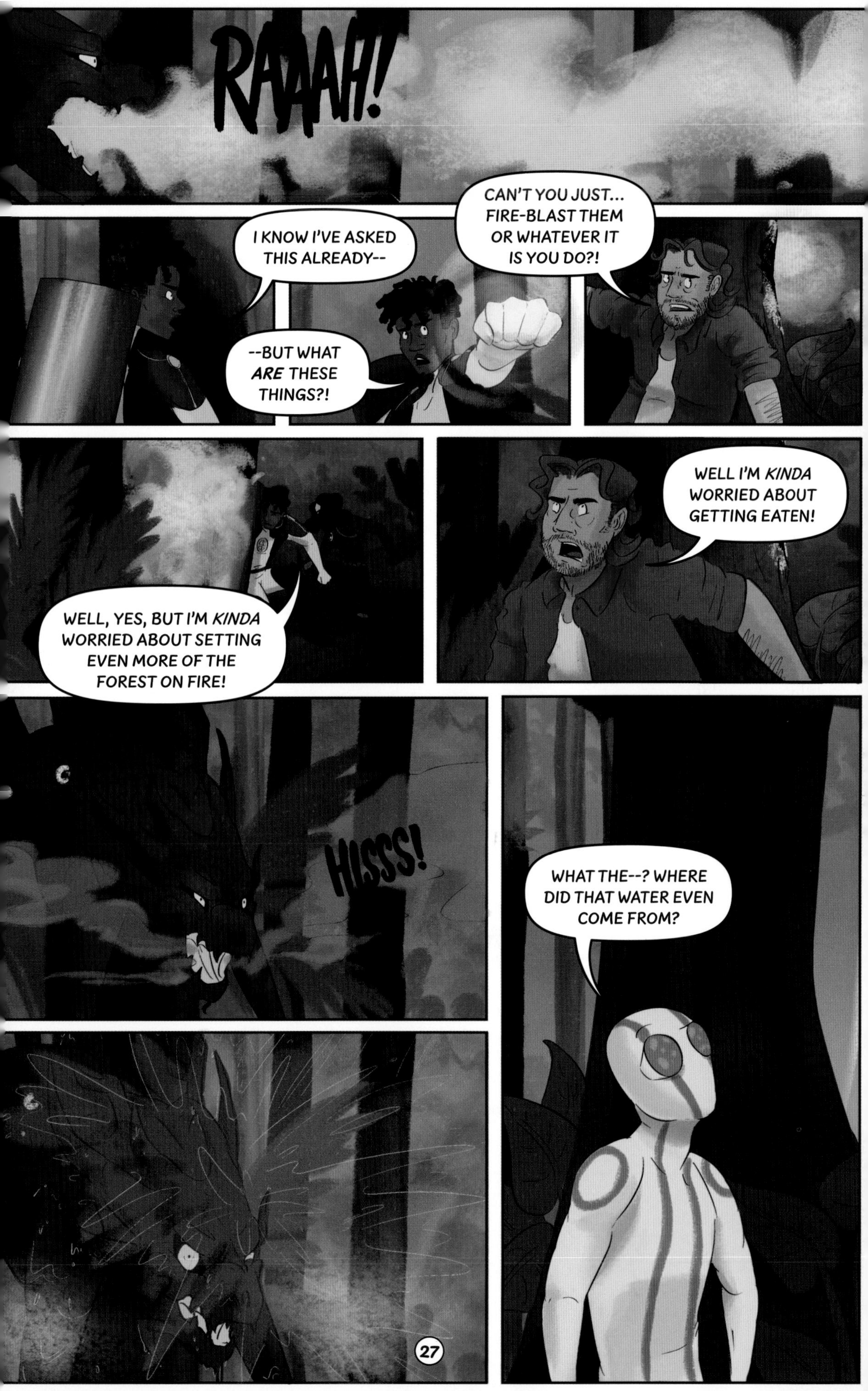
RAAAH!
I KNOW I'VE ASKED THIS ALREADY--
--BUT WHAT *ARE* THESE THINGS?!
CAN'T YOU JUST... FIRE-BLAST THEM OR WHATEVER IT IS YOU DO?!
WELL, YES, BUT I'M *KINDA* WORRIED ABOUT SETTING EVEN MORE OF THE FOREST ON FIRE!
WELL I'M *KINDA* WORRIED ABOUT GETTING EATEN!
HISSS!
WHAT THE--? WHERE DID THAT WATER EVEN COME FROM?

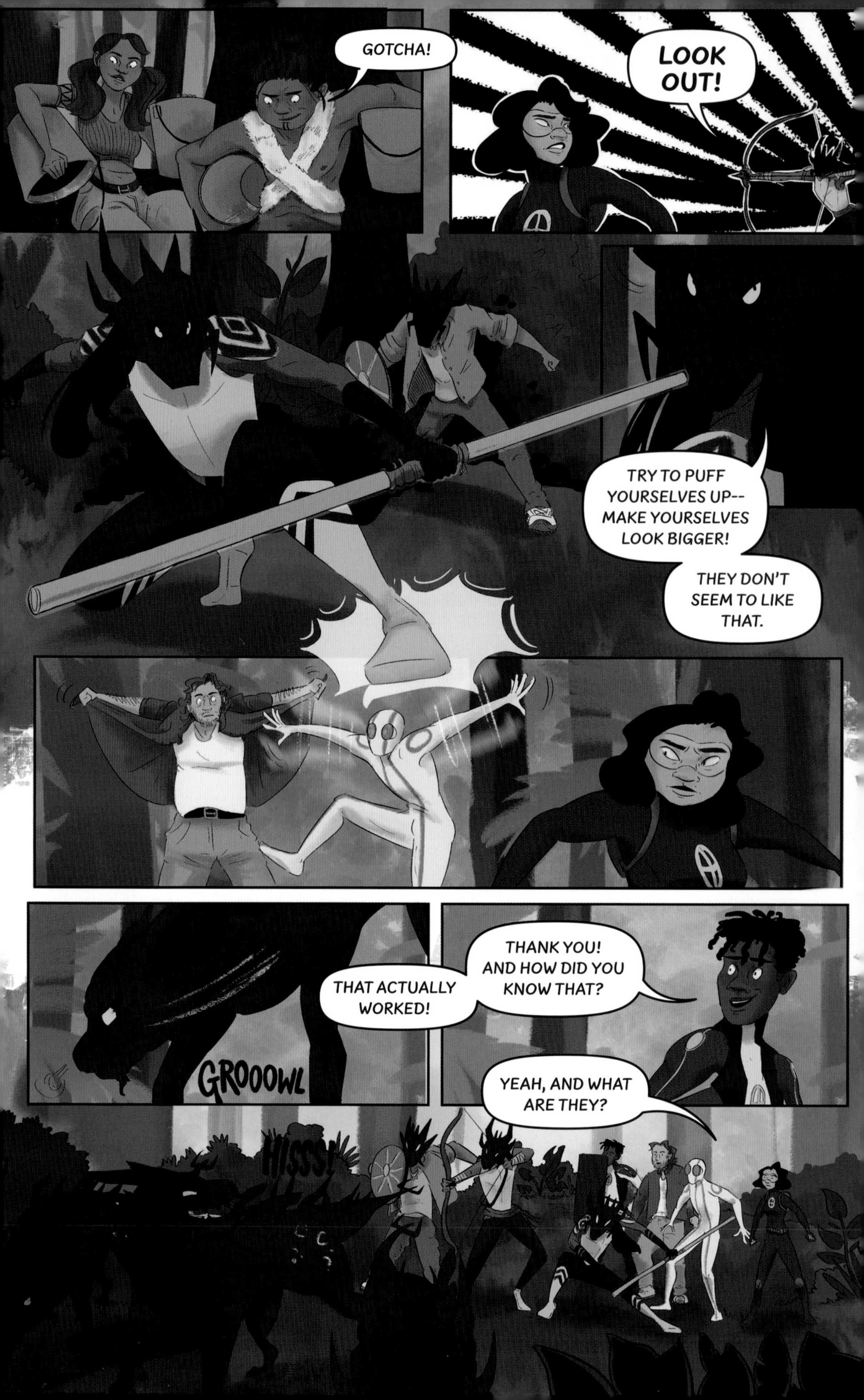
GOTCHA!
LOOK OUT!
TRY TO PUFF YOURSELVES UP-- MAKE YOURSELVES LOOK BIGGER!
THEY DON'T SEEM TO LIKE THAT.
GROOOWL
THAT ACTUALLY WORKED!
THANK YOU! AND HOW DID YOU KNOW THAT?
YEAH, AND WHAT ARE THEY?
HISSS!

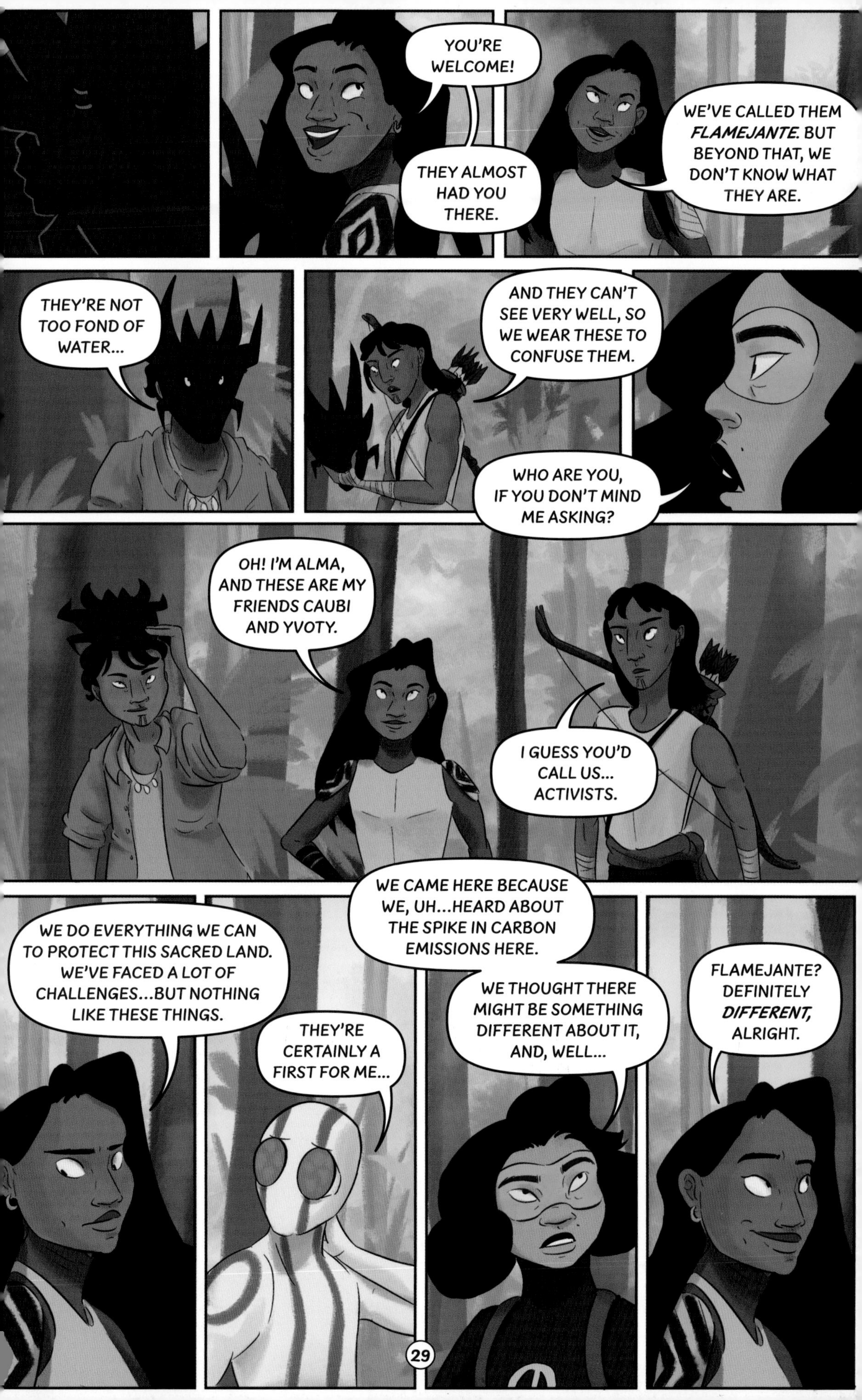
YOU'RE WELCOME!
THEY ALMOST HAD YOU THERE.
WE'VE CALLED THEM *FLAMEJANTE*. BUT BEYOND THAT, WE DON'T KNOW WHAT THEY ARE.
THEY'RE NOT TOO FOND OF WATER...
AND THEY CAN'T SEE VERY WELL, SO WE WEAR THESE TO CONFUSE THEM.
WHO ARE YOU, IF YOU DON'T MIND ME ASKING?
OH! I'M ALMA, AND THESE ARE MY FRIENDS CAUBI AND YVOTY.
I GUESS YOU'D CALL US... ACTIVISTS.
WE DO EVERYTHING WE CAN TO PROTECT THIS SACRED LAND. WE'VE FACED A LOT OF CHALLENGES...BUT NOTHING LIKE THESE THINGS.
THEY'RE CERTAINLY A FIRST FOR ME...
WE CAME HERE BECAUSE WE, UH...HEARD ABOUT THE SPIKE IN CARBON EMISSIONS HERE.
WE THOUGHT THERE MIGHT BE SOMETHING DIFFERENT ABOUT IT, AND, WELL...
FLAMEJANTE? DEFINITELY *DIFFERENT,* ALRIGHT.

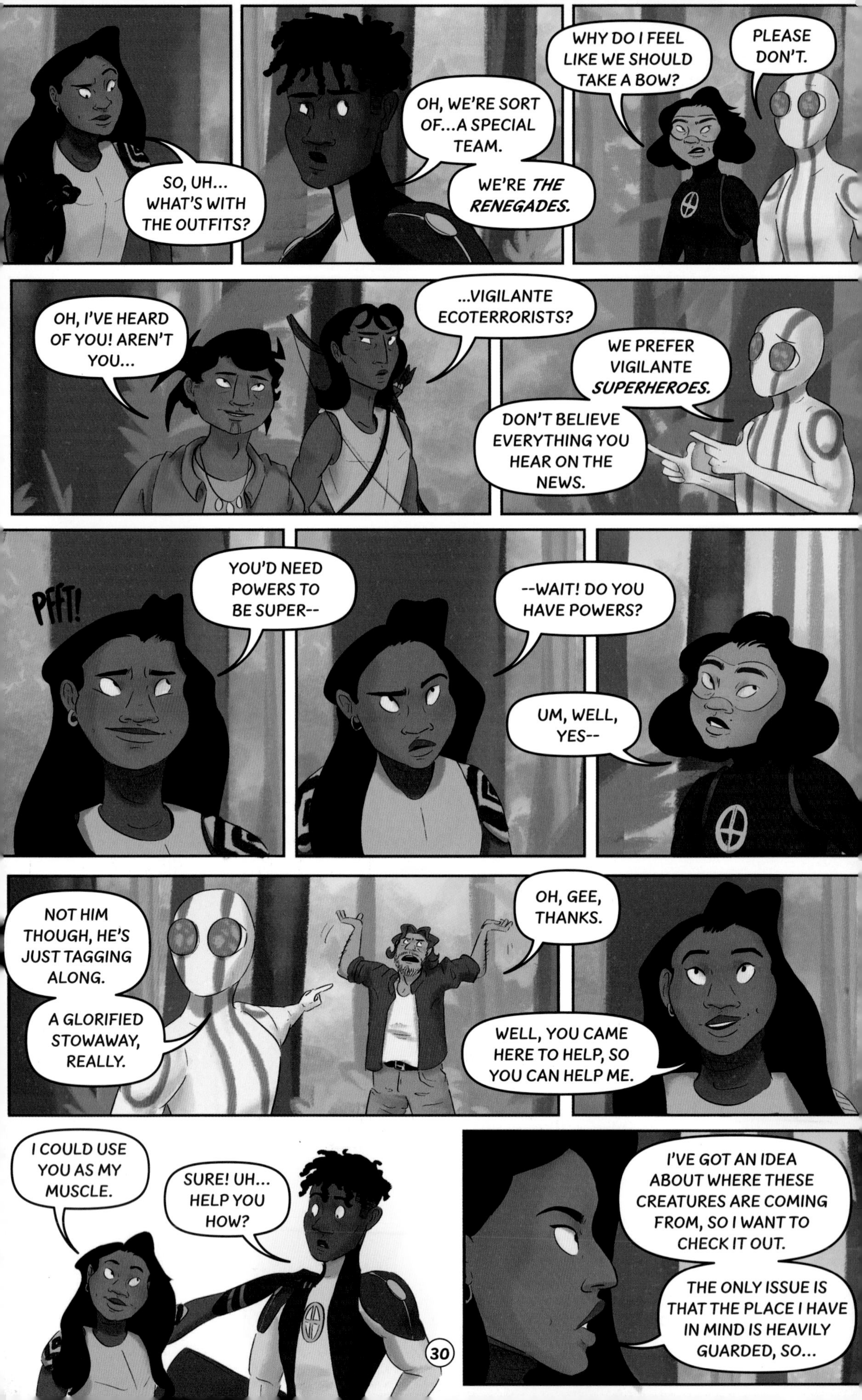
SO, UH... WHAT'S WITH THE OUTFITS?
OH, WE'RE SORT OF...A SPECIAL TEAM.
WE'RE *THE RENEGADES.*
WHY DO I FEEL LIKE WE SHOULD TAKE A BOW?
PLEASE DON'T.
OH, I'VE HEARD OF YOU! AREN'T YOU...
...VIGILANTE ECOTERRORISTS?
WE PREFER VIGILANTE *SUPERHEROES.*
DON'T BELIEVE EVERYTHING YOU HEAR ON THE NEWS.
PFFT!
YOU'D NEED POWERS TO BE SUPER--
--WAIT! DO YOU HAVE POWERS?
UM, WELL, YES--
NOT HIM THOUGH, HE'S JUST TAGGING ALONG.
A GLORIFIED STOWAWAY, REALLY.
OH, GEE, THANKS.
WELL, YOU CAME HERE TO HELP, SO YOU CAN HELP ME.
I COULD USE YOU AS MY MUSCLE.
SURE! UH... HELP YOU HOW?
I'VE GOT AN IDEA ABOUT WHERE THESE CREATURES ARE COMING FROM, SO I WANT TO CHECK IT OUT.
THE ONLY ISSUE IS THAT THE PLACE I HAVE IN MIND IS HEAVILY GUARDED, SO...

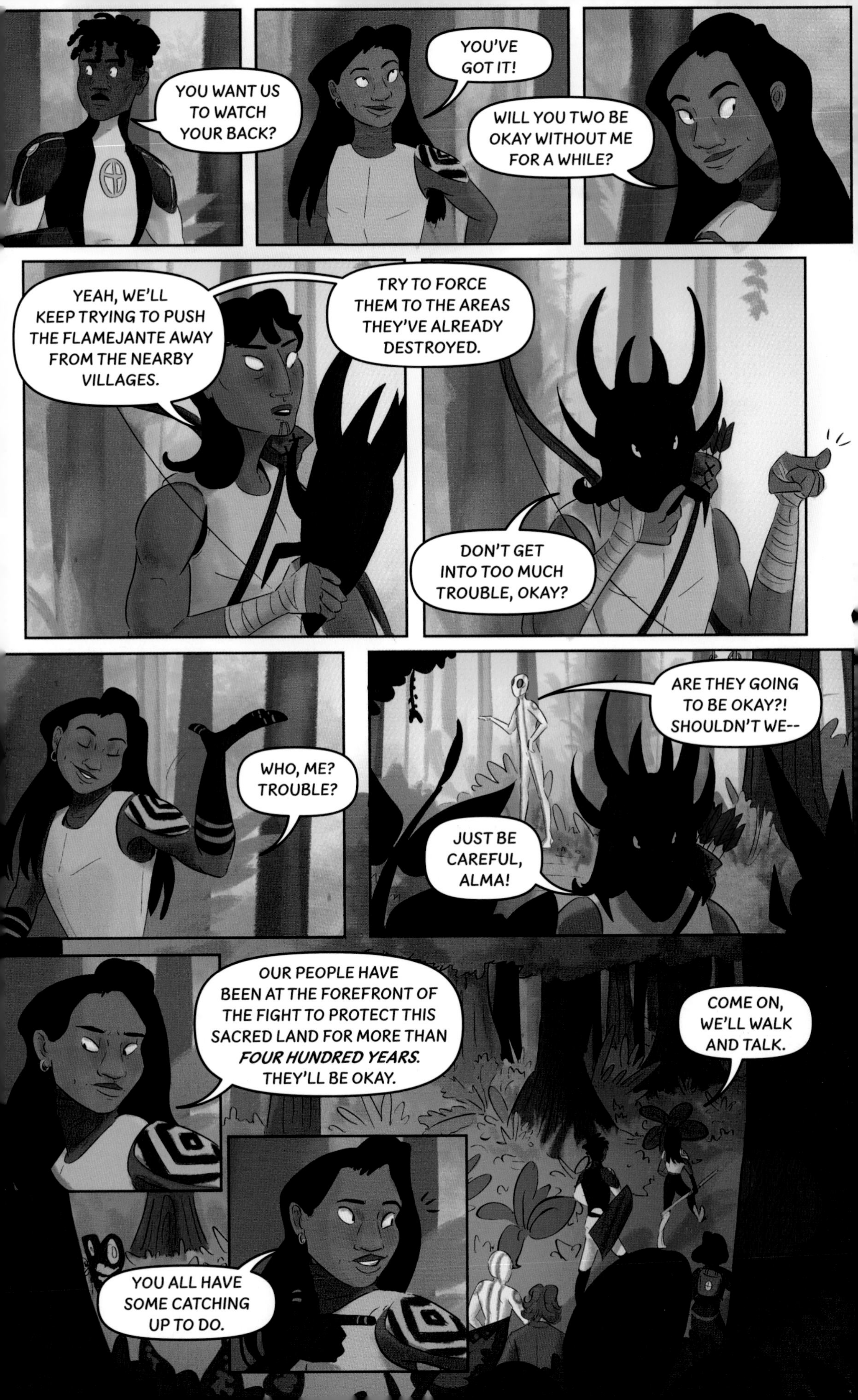
YOU WANT US TO WATCH YOUR BACK?
YOU'VE GOT IT!
WILL YOU TWO BE OKAY WITHOUT ME FOR A WHILE?
YEAH, WE'LL KEEP TRYING TO PUSH THE FLAMEJANTE AWAY FROM THE NEARBY VILLAGES.
TRY TO FORCE THEM TO THE AREAS THEY'VE ALREADY DESTROYED.
DON'T GET INTO TOO MUCH TROUBLE, OKAY?
WHO, ME? TROUBLE?
ARE THEY GOING TO BE OKAY?! SHOULDN'T WE--
JUST BE CAREFUL, ALMA!
OUR PEOPLE HAVE BEEN AT THE FOREFRONT OF THE FIGHT TO PROTECT THIS SACRED LAND FOR MORE THAN *FOUR HUNDRED YEARS.* THEY'LL BE OKAY.
COME ON, WE'LL WALK AND TALK.
YOU ALL HAVE SOME CATCHING UP TO DO.

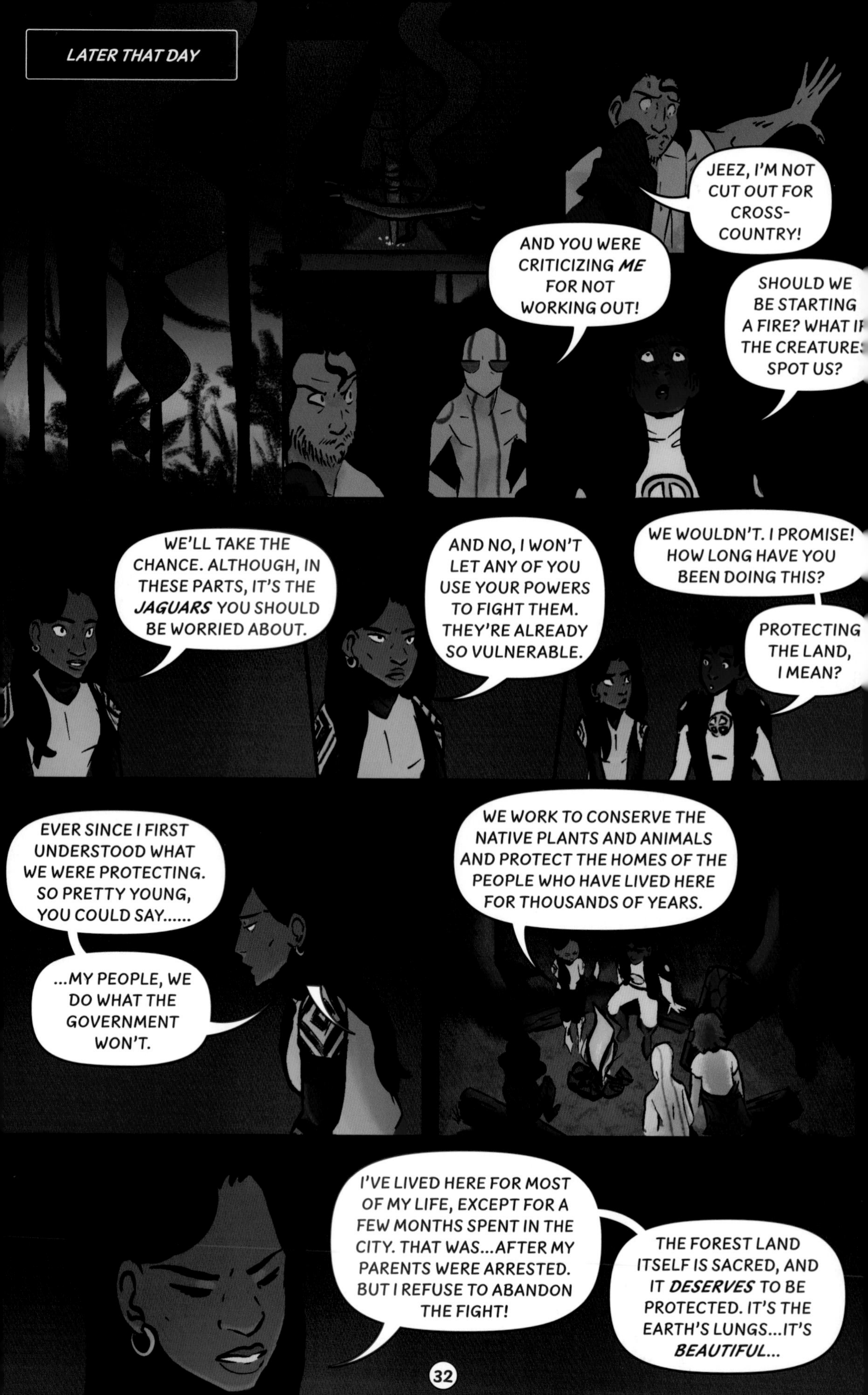
LATER THAT DAY
JEEZ, I'M NOT CUT OUT FOR CROSS-COUNTRY!
AND YOU WERE CRITICIZING *ME* FOR NOT WORKING OUT!
SHOULD WE BE STARTING A FIRE? WHAT IF THE CREATURES SPOT US?
WE'LL TAKE THE CHANCE. ALTHOUGH, IN THESE PARTS, IT'S THE *JAGUARS* YOU SHOULD BE WORRIED ABOUT.
AND NO, I WON'T LET ANY OF YOU USE YOUR POWERS TO FIGHT THEM. THEY'RE ALREADY SO VULNERABLE.
WE WOULDN'T. I PROMISE! HOW LONG HAVE YOU BEEN DOING THIS?
PROTECTING THE LAND, I MEAN?
EVER SINCE I FIRST UNDERSTOOD WHAT WE WERE PROTECTING. SO PRETTY YOUNG, YOU COULD SAY......
...MY PEOPLE, WE DO WHAT THE GOVERNMENT WON'T.
WE WORK TO CONSERVE THE NATIVE PLANTS AND ANIMALS AND PROTECT THE HOMES OF THE PEOPLE WHO HAVE LIVED HERE FOR THOUSANDS OF YEARS.
I'VE LIVED HERE FOR MOST OF MY LIFE, EXCEPT FOR A FEW MONTHS SPENT IN THE CITY. THAT WAS...AFTER MY PARENTS WERE ARRESTED. BUT I REFUSE TO ABANDON THE FIGHT!
THE FOREST LAND ITSELF IS SACRED, AND IT *DESERVES* TO BE PROTECTED. IT'S THE EARTH'S LUNGS...IT'S *BEAUTIFUL*...

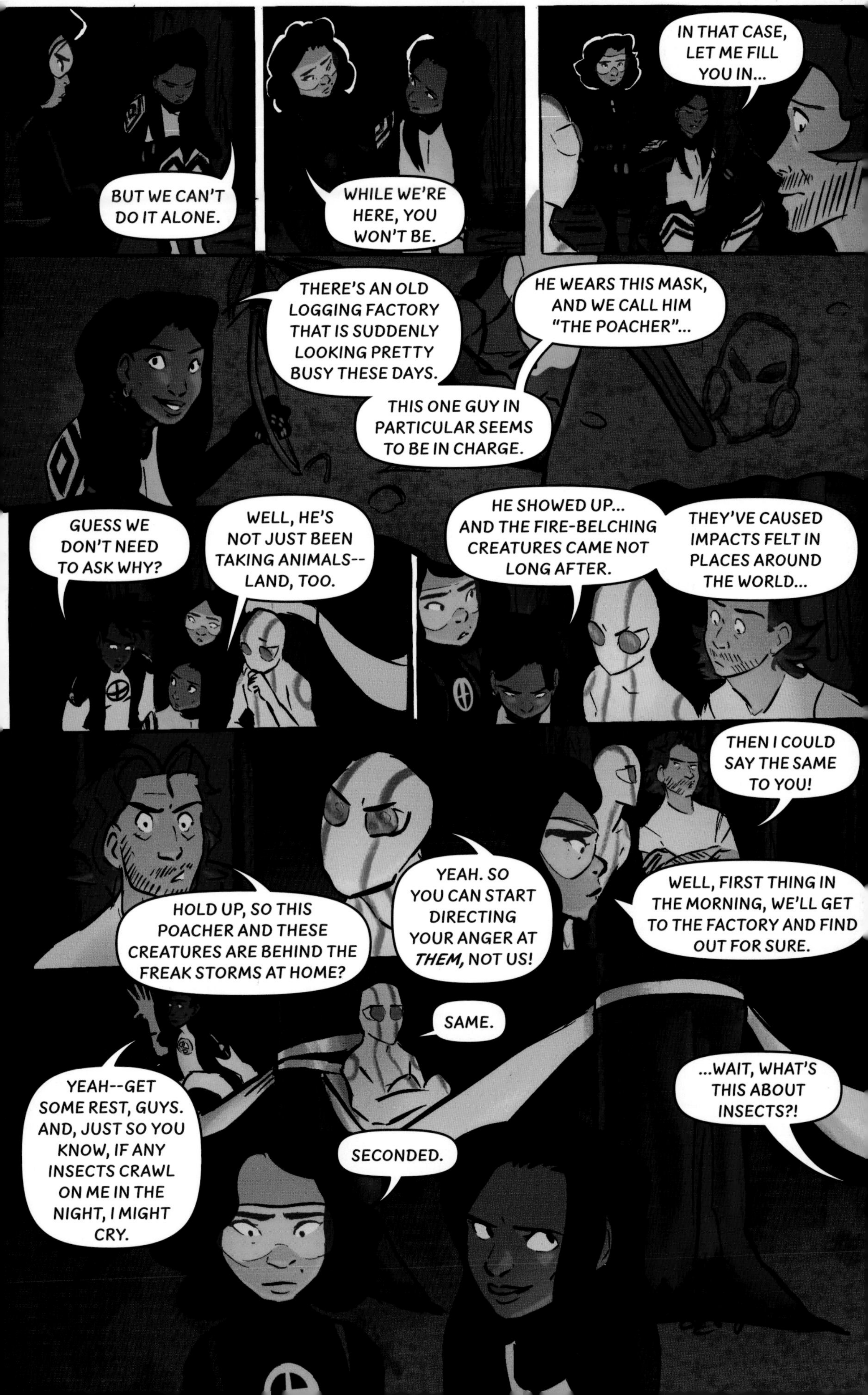
BUT WE CAN'T DO IT ALONE.
WHILE WE'RE HERE, YOU WON'T BE.
IN THAT CASE, LET ME FILL YOU IN...
THERE'S AN OLD LOGGING FACTORY THAT IS SUDDENLY LOOKING PRETTY BUSY THESE DAYS.
THIS ONE GUY IN PARTICULAR SEEMS TO BE IN CHARGE.
HE WEARS THIS MASK, AND WE CALL HIM "THE POACHER"...
GUESS WE DON'T NEED TO ASK WHY?
WELL, HE'S NOT JUST BEEN TAKING ANIMALS-- LAND, TOO.
HE SHOWED UP... AND THE FIRE-BELCHING CREATURES CAME NOT LONG AFTER.
THEY'VE CAUSED IMPACTS FELT IN PLACES AROUND THE WORLD...
HOLD UP, SO THIS POACHER AND THESE CREATURES ARE BEHIND THE FREAK STORMS AT HOME?
YEAH. SO YOU CAN START DIRECTING YOUR ANGER AT *THEM,* NOT US!
THEN I COULD SAY THE SAME TO YOU!
WELL, FIRST THING IN THE MORNING, WE'LL GET TO THE FACTORY AND FIND OUT FOR SURE.
SAME.
YEAH--GET SOME REST, GUYS. AND, JUST SO YOU KNOW, IF ANY INSECTS CRAWL ON ME IN THE NIGHT, I MIGHT CRY.
SECONDED.
...WAIT, WHAT'S THIS ABOUT INSECTS?!

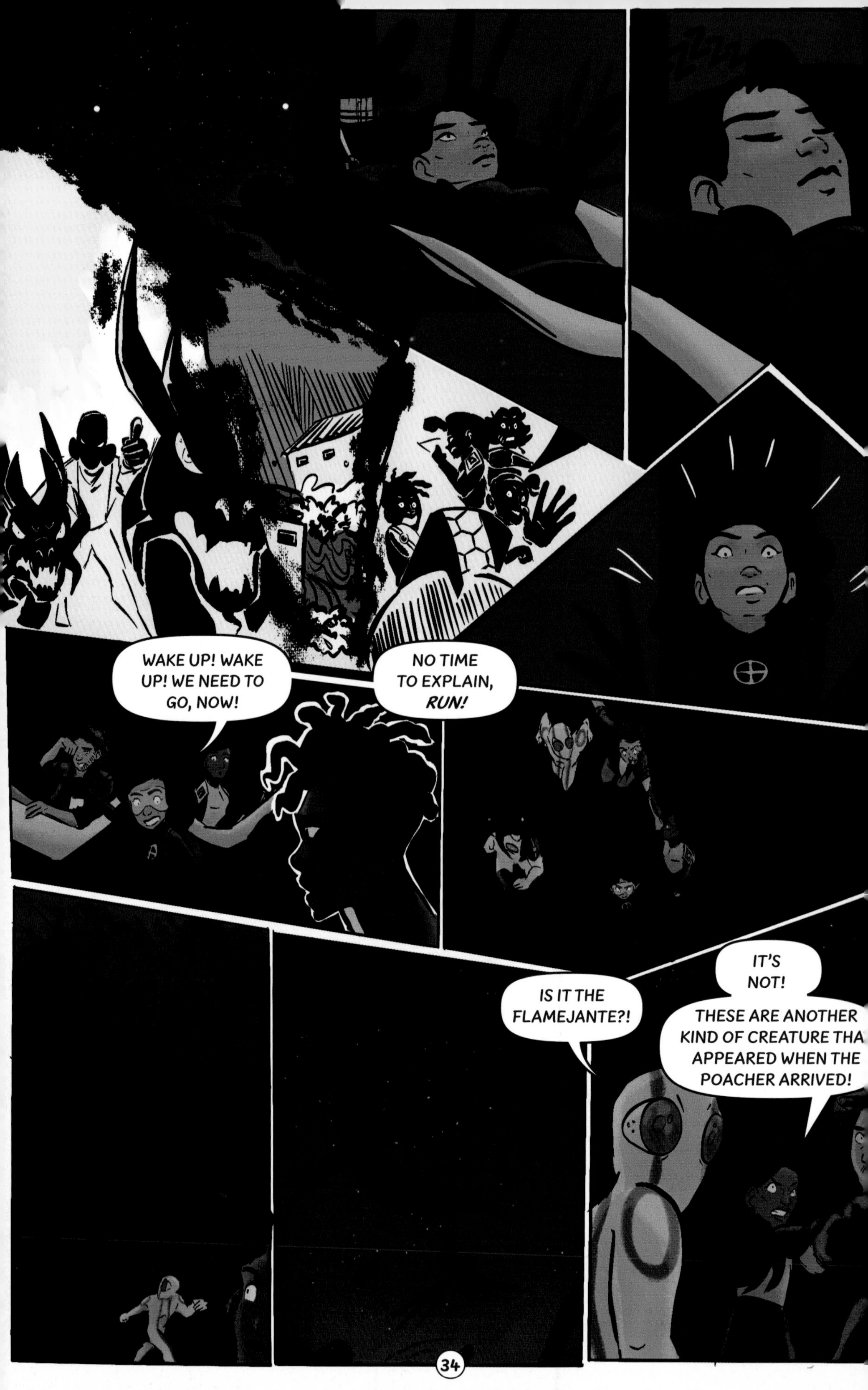
WAKE UP! WAKE UP! WE NEED TO GO, NOW!
NO TIME TO EXPLAIN, *RUN!*
IS IT THE FLAMEJANTE?!
IT'S NOT!
THESE ARE ANOTHER KIND OF CREATURE THA APPEARED WHEN THE POACHER ARRIVED!

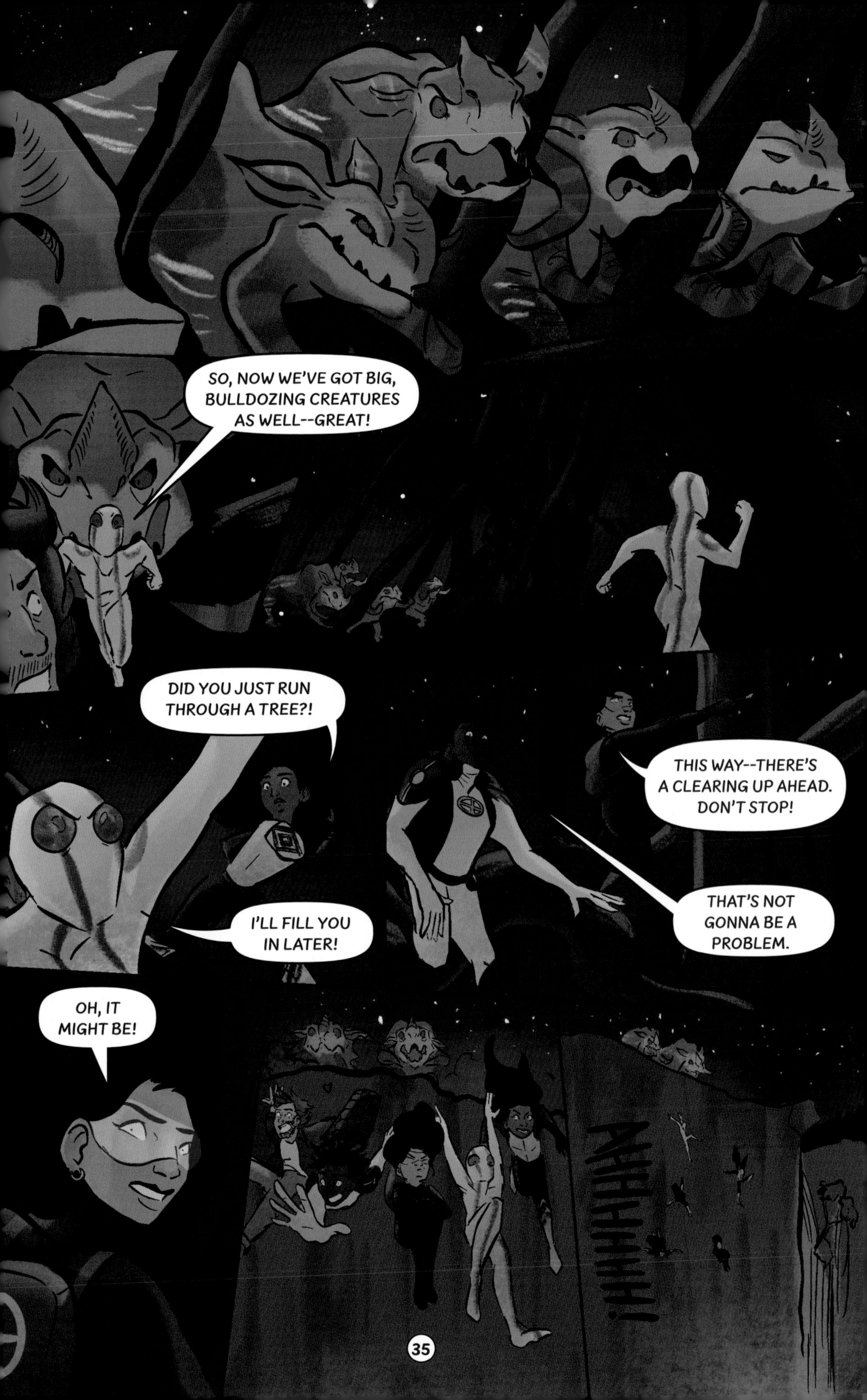
SO, NOW WE'VE GOT BIG, BULLDOZING CREATURES AS WELL--GREAT!
DID YOU JUST RUN THROUGH A TREE?!
I'LL FILL YOU IN LATER!
THIS WAY--THERE'S A CLEARING UP AHEAD. DON'T STOP!
THAT'S NOT GONNA BE A PROBLEM.
OH, IT MIGHT BE!
AHHHHHH!

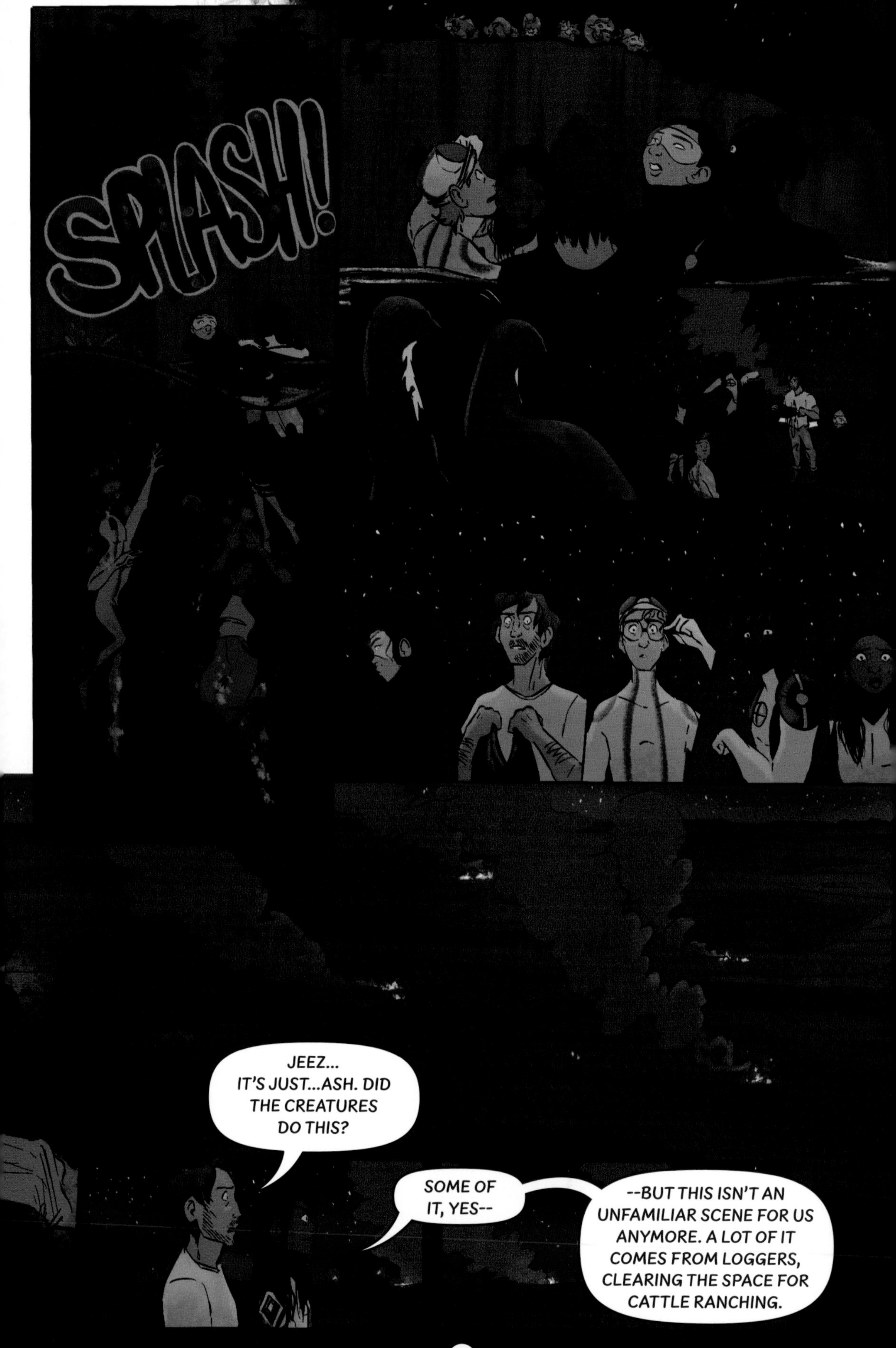
SPLASH!
JEEZ... IT'S JUST...ASH. DID THE CREATURES DO THIS?
SOME OF IT, YES--
--BUT THIS ISN'T AN UNFAMILIAR SCENE FOR US ANYMORE. A LOT OF IT COMES FROM LOGGERS, CLEARING THE SPACE FOR CATTLE RANCHING.

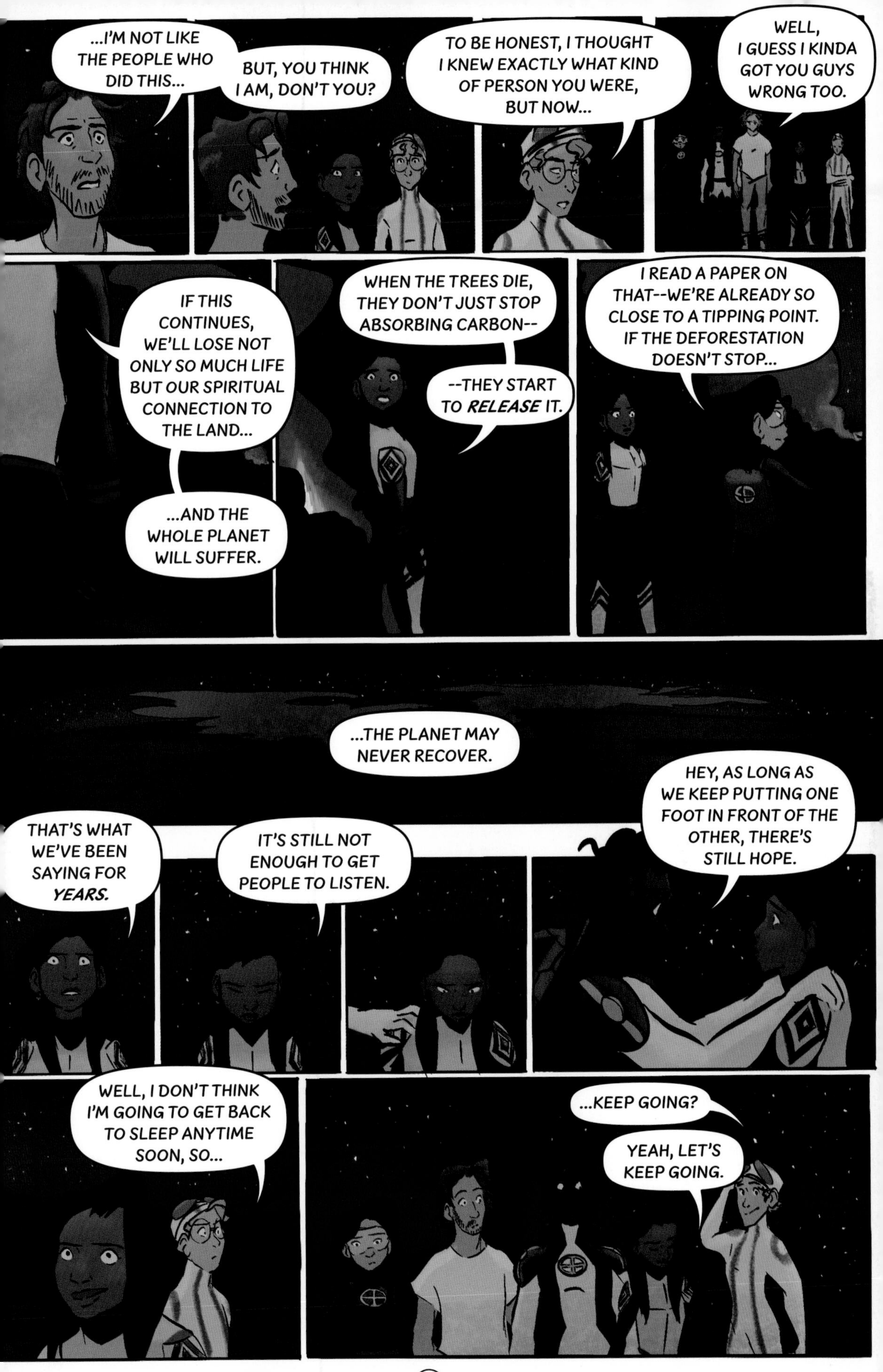
...I'M NOT LIKE THE PEOPLE WHO DID THIS...
BUT, YOU THINK I AM, DON'T YOU?
TO BE HONEST, I THOUGHT I KNEW EXACTLY WHAT KIND OF PERSON YOU WERE, BUT NOW...
WELL, I GUESS I KINDA GOT YOU GUYS WRONG TOO.
IF THIS CONTINUES, WE'LL LOSE NOT ONLY SO MUCH LIFE BUT OUR SPIRITUAL CONNECTION TO THE LAND...
...AND THE WHOLE PLANET WILL SUFFER.
WHEN THE TREES DIE, THEY DON'T JUST STOP ABSORBING CARBON--
--THEY START TO *RELEASE* IT.
I READ A PAPER ON THAT--WE'RE ALREADY SO CLOSE TO A TIPPING POINT. IF THE DEFORESTATION DOESN'T STOP...
...THE PLANET MAY NEVER RECOVER.
THAT'S WHAT WE'VE BEEN SAYING FOR *YEARS.*
IT'S STILL NOT ENOUGH TO GET PEOPLE TO LISTEN.
HEY, AS LONG AS WE KEEP PUTTING ONE FOOT IN FRONT OF THE OTHER, THERE'S STILL HOPE.
WELL, I DON'T THINK I'M GOING TO GET BACK TO SLEEP ANYTIME SOON, SO...
...KEEP GOING?
YEAH, LET'S KEEP GOING.

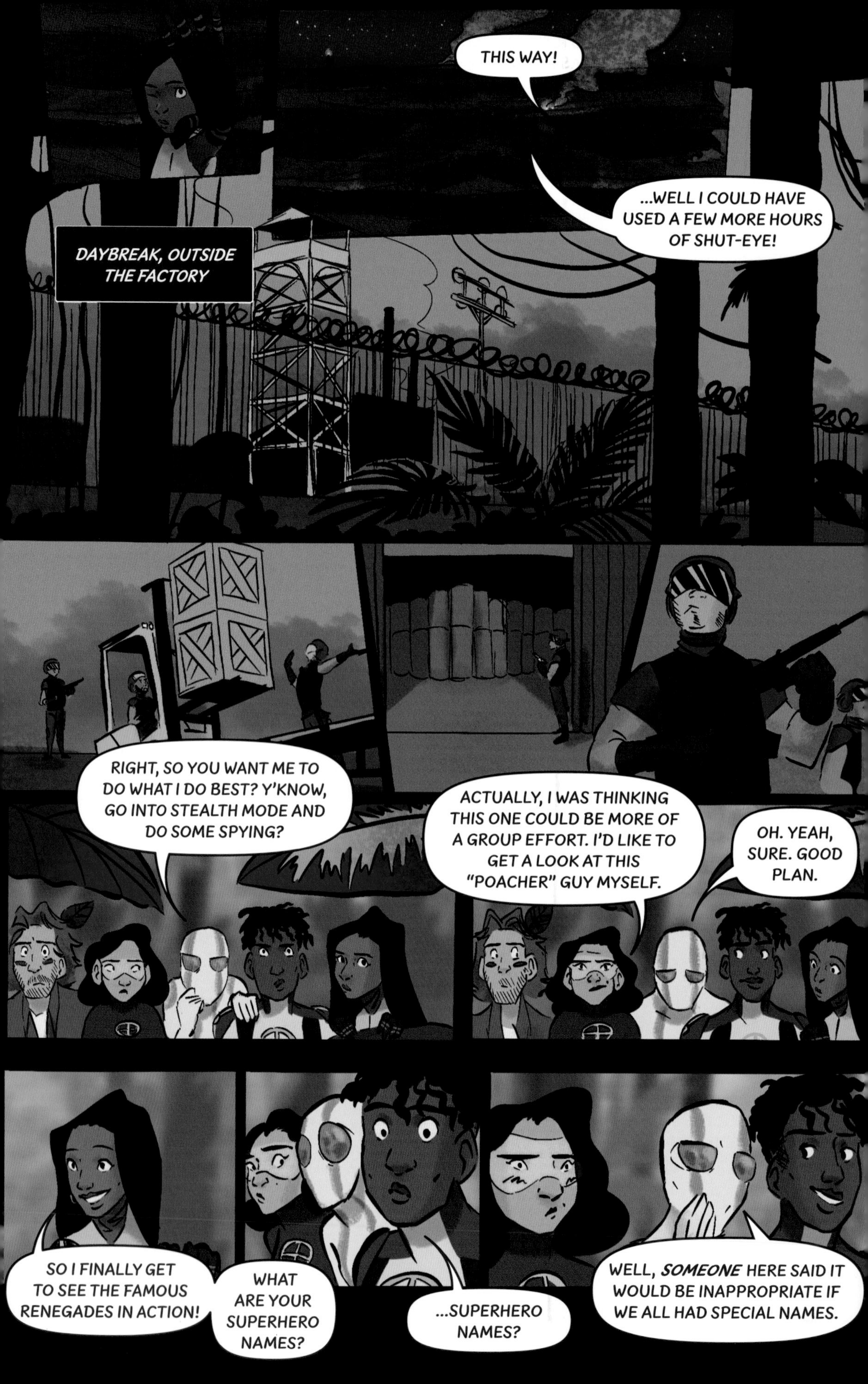
THIS WAY!
...WELL I COULD HAVE USED A FEW MORE HOURS OF SHUT-EYE!
DAYBREAK, OUTSIDE THE FACTORY
RIGHT, SO YOU WANT ME TO DO WHAT I DO BEST? Y'KNOW, GO INTO STEALTH MODE AND DO SOME SPYING?
ACTUALLY, I WAS THINKING THIS ONE COULD BE MORE OF A GROUP EFFORT. I'D LIKE TO GET A LOOK AT THIS "POACHER" GUY MYSELF.
OH. YEAH, SURE. GOOD PLAN.
SO I FINALLY GET TO SEE THE FAMOUS RENEGADES IN ACTION!
WHAT ARE YOUR SUPERHERO NAMES?
...SUPERHERO NAMES?
WELL, *SOMEONE* HERE SAID IT WOULD BE INAPPROPRIATE IF WE ALL HAD SPECIAL NAMES.

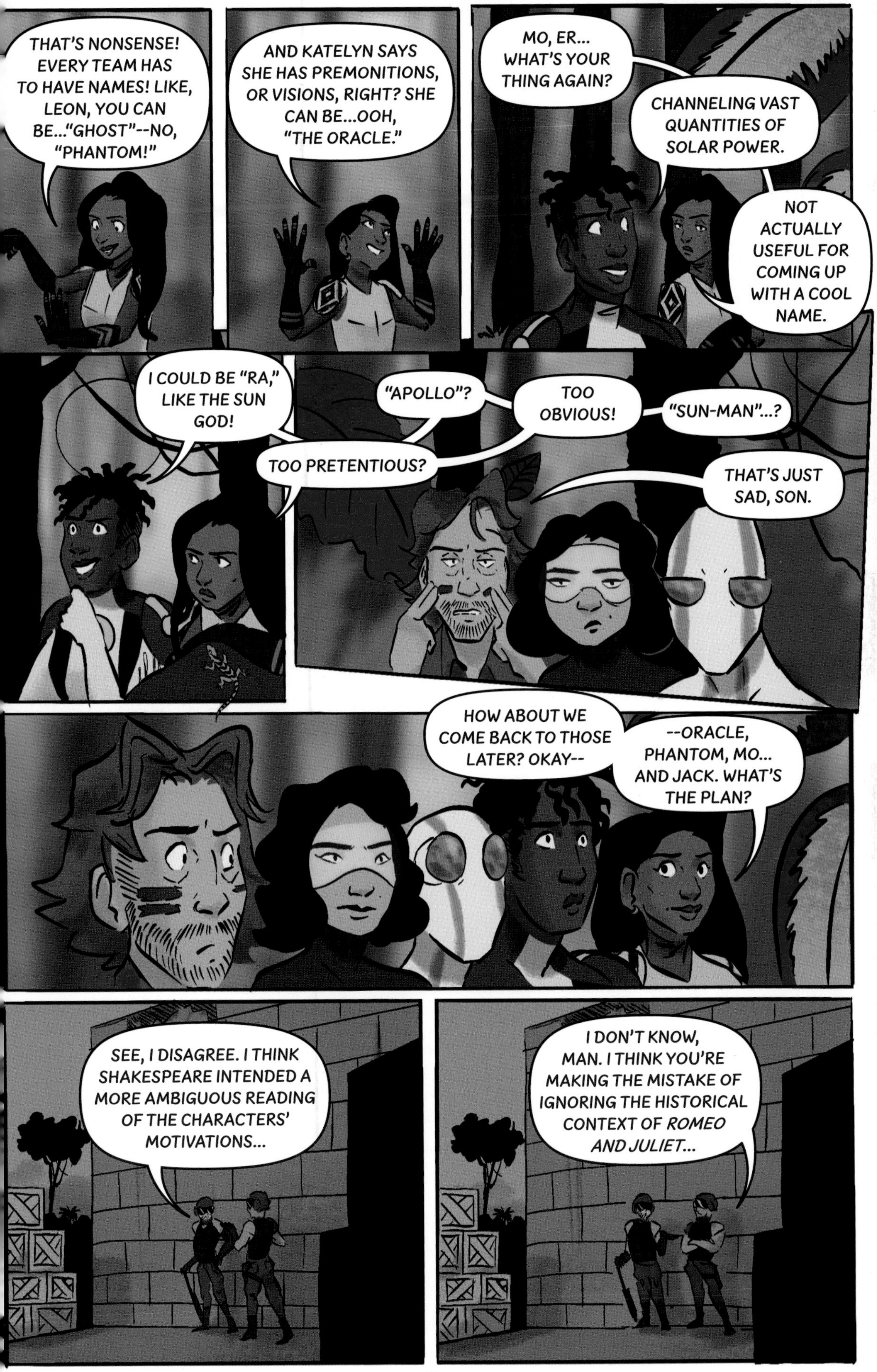
THAT'S NONSENSE! EVERY TEAM HAS TO HAVE NAMES! LIKE, LEON, YOU CAN BE..."GHOST"--NO, "PHANTOM!"
AND KATELYN SAYS SHE HAS PREMONITIONS, OR VISIONS, RIGHT? SHE CAN BE...OOH, "THE ORACLE."
MO, ER... WHAT'S YOUR THING AGAIN?
CHANNELING VAST QUANTITIES OF SOLAR POWER.
NOT ACTUALLY USEFUL FOR COMING UP WITH A COOL NAME.
I COULD BE "RA," LIKE THE SUN GOD!
TOO PRETENTIOUS?
"APOLLO"?
TOO OBVIOUS!
"SUN-MAN"...?
THAT'S JUST SAD, SON.
HOW ABOUT WE COME BACK TO THOSE LATER? OKAY--
--ORACLE, PHANTOM, MO... AND JACK. WHAT'S THE PLAN?
SEE, I DISAGREE. I THINK SHAKESPEARE INTENDED A MORE AMBIGUOUS READING OF THE CHARACTERS' MOTIVATIONS...
I DON'T KNOW, MAN. I THINK YOU'RE MAKING THE MISTAKE OF IGNORING THE HISTORICAL CONTEXT OF *ROMEO AND JULIET*...

WHAT THE--

I TOLD YOU TO STRAP THOSE CRATES DOWN!

DO YOU EVER LISTEN TO ME?

OKAY, GUARDS DISTRACTED!

ALSO, I MIGHT HAVE RUINED A FRIENDSHIP, BUT IT'S ALL IN THE NAME OF SUPERHEROISM, SO HEY. PHANTOM *ONE*, POACHER ZIP.

RIGHT. DO YOUR THING, SUN-BOY!

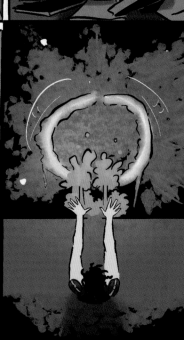

NICE WORK, MO!

GREAT. SO AM I WITH SHAGGY AND SCOOBY HERE OR WITH YOU?

NOW I THINK WE SHOULD SPLIT OFF INTO GROUPS AND LOOK AROUND. I NEED TO SEE WHAT THEY'VE GOT GOING ON HERE.

MAYBE THEY HAVE A COMPUTER ROOM OR LAB--SOMETHING I CAN BREAK INTO!

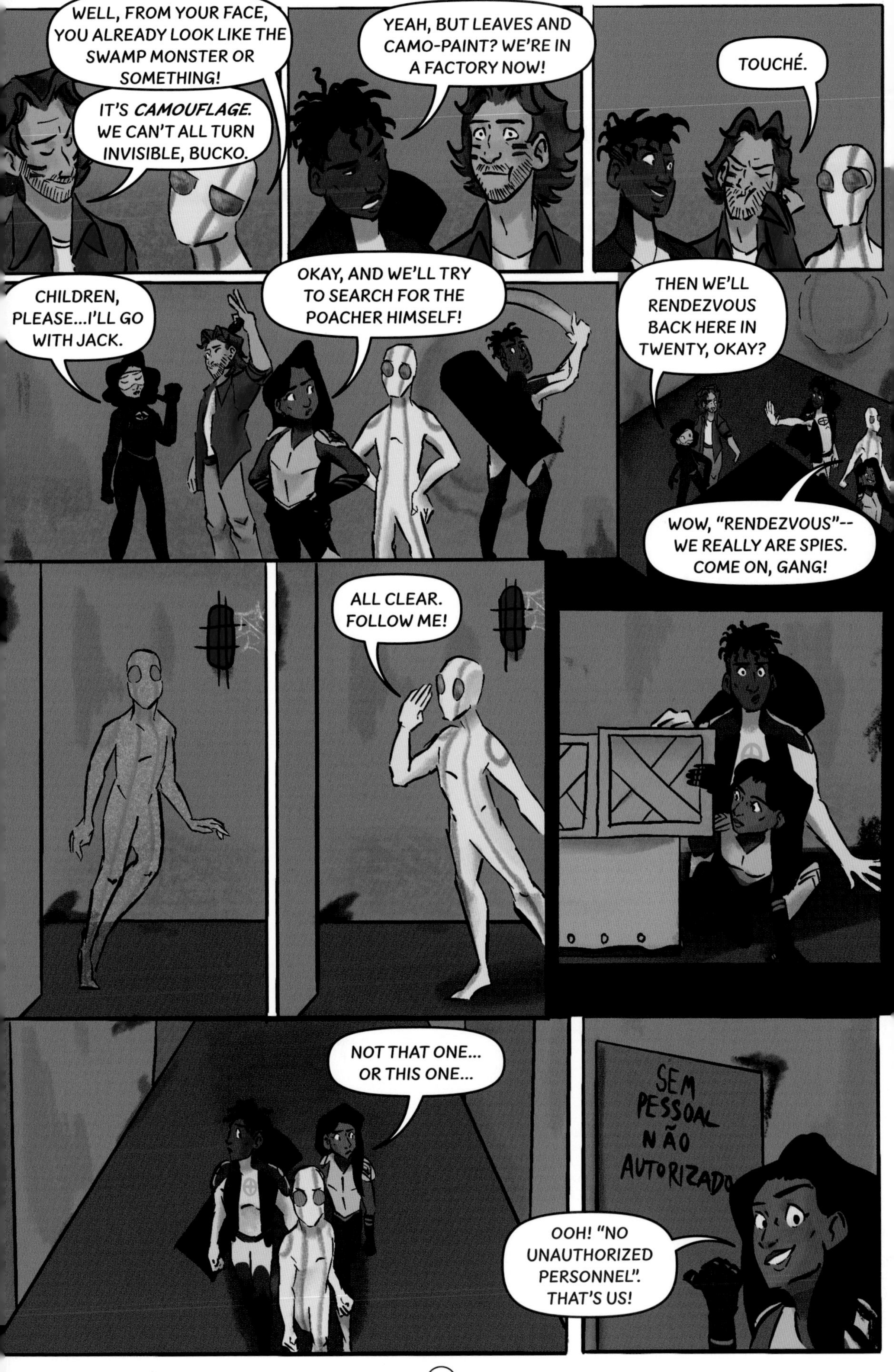
WELL, FROM YOUR FACE, YOU ALREADY LOOK LIKE THE SWAMP MONSTER OR SOMETHING!
IT'S *CAMOUFLAGE*. WE CAN'T ALL TURN INVISIBLE, BUCKO.
YEAH, BUT LEAVES AND CAMO-PAINT? WE'RE IN A FACTORY NOW!
TOUCHÉ.
CHILDREN, PLEASE...I'LL GO WITH JACK.
OKAY, AND WE'LL TRY TO SEARCH FOR THE POACHER HIMSELF!
THEN WE'LL RENDEZVOUS BACK HERE IN TWENTY, OKAY?
WOW, "RENDEZVOUS"-- WE REALLY ARE SPIES. COME ON, GANG!
ALL CLEAR. FOLLOW ME!
NOT THAT ONE... OR THIS ONE...
SEM PESSOAL NÃO AUTORIZADO
OOH! "NO UNAUTHORIZED PERSONNEL". THAT'S US!

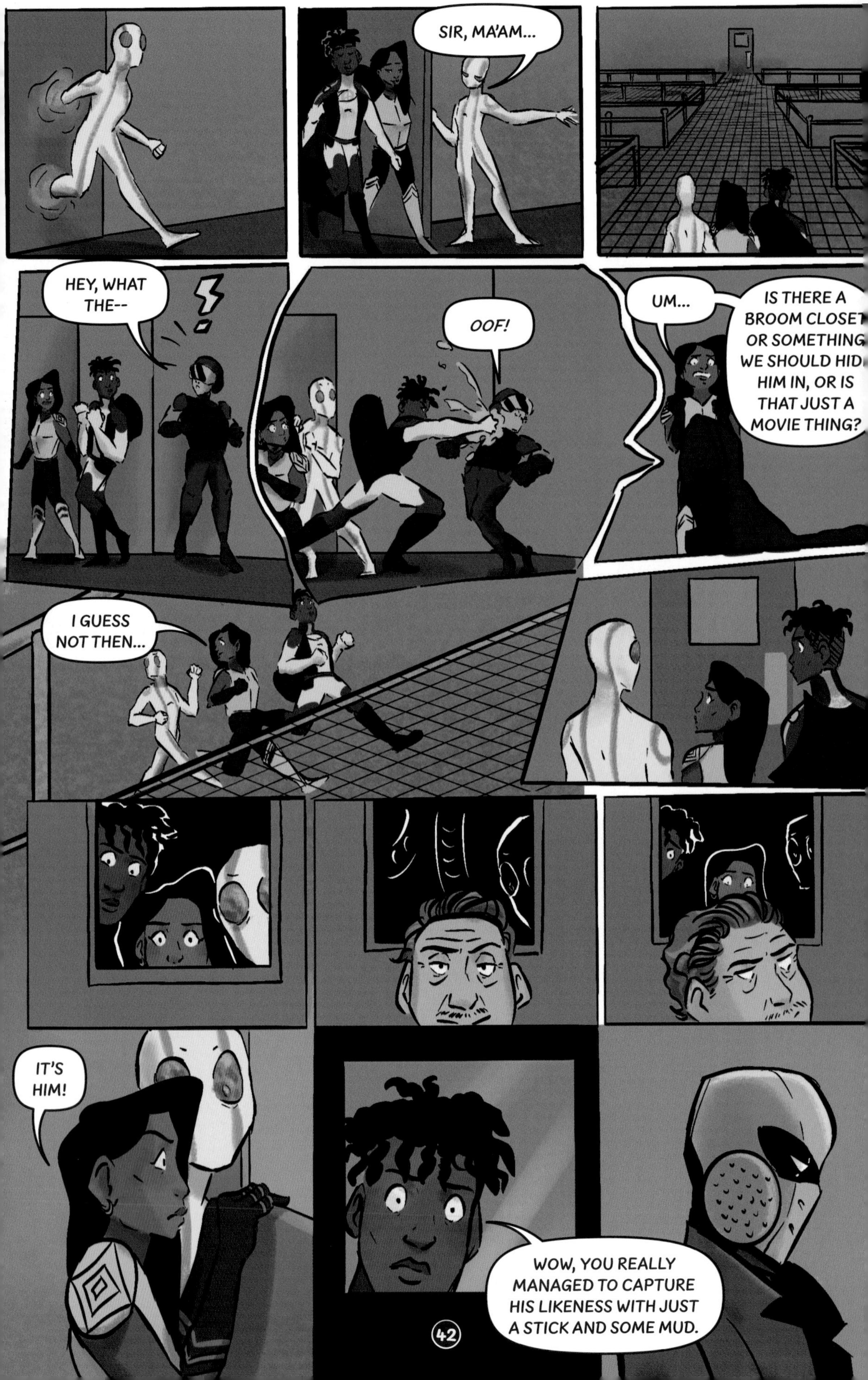
SIR, MA'AM...
HEY, WHAT THE--
OOF!
UM...
IS THERE A BROOM CLOSET OR SOMETHING WE SHOULD HIDE HIM IN, OR IS THAT JUST A MOVIE THING?
I GUESS NOT THEN...
IT'S HIM!
WOW, YOU REALLY MANAGED TO CAPTURE HIS LIKENESS WITH JUST A STICK AND SOME MUD.

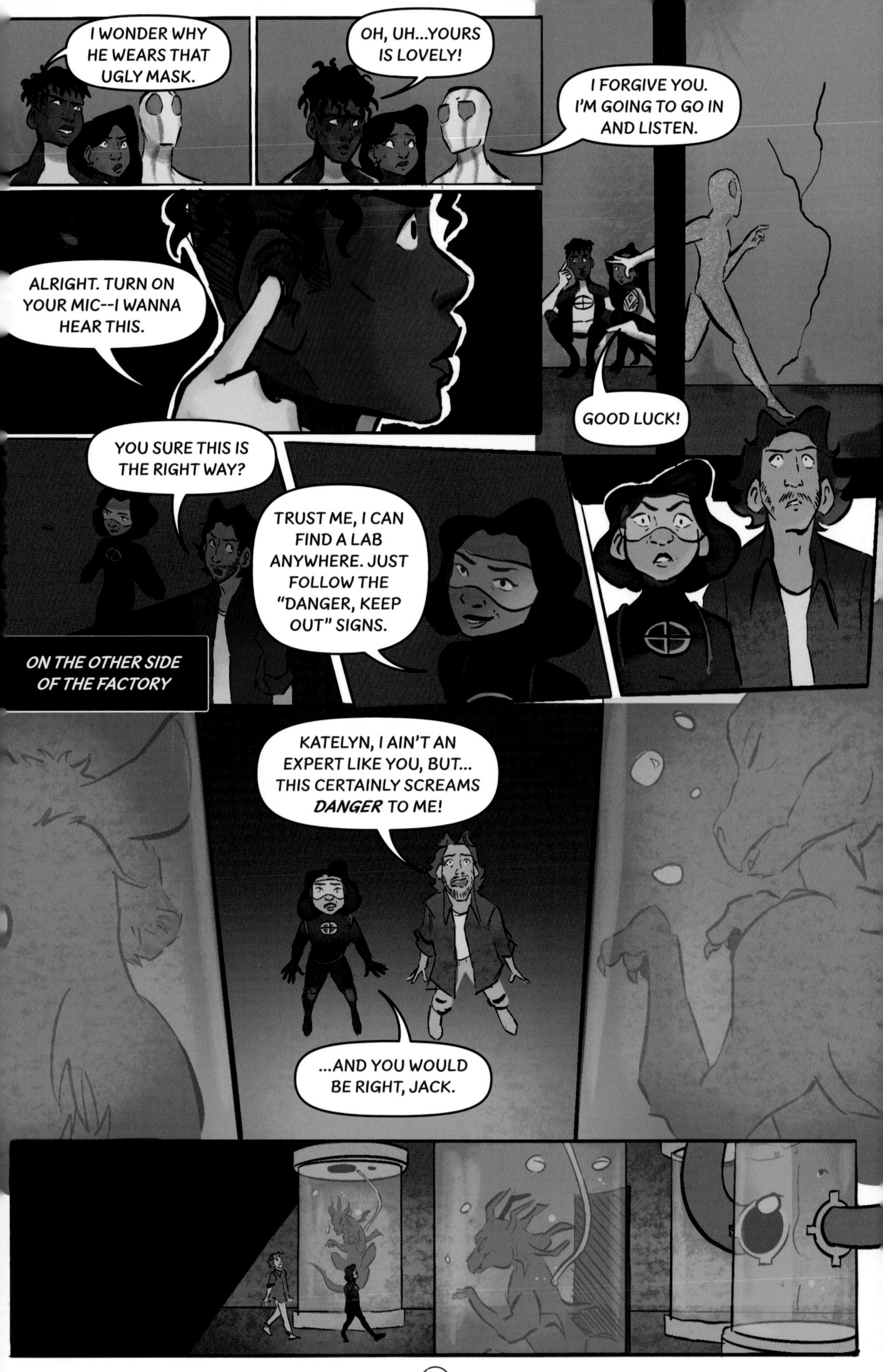
I WONDER WHY HE WEARS THAT UGLY MASK.
OH, UH...YOURS IS LOVELY!
I FORGIVE YOU. I'M GOING TO GO IN AND LISTEN.
ALRIGHT. TURN ON YOUR MIC--I WANNA HEAR THIS.
GOOD LUCK!
ON THE OTHER SIDE OF THE FACTORY
YOU SURE THIS IS THE RIGHT WAY?
TRUST ME, I CAN FIND A LAB ANYWHERE. JUST FOLLOW THE "DANGER, KEEP OUT" SIGNS.
KATELYN, I AIN'T AN EXPERT LIKE YOU, BUT... THIS CERTAINLY SCREAMS *DANGER* TO ME!
...AND YOU WOULD BE RIGHT, JACK.

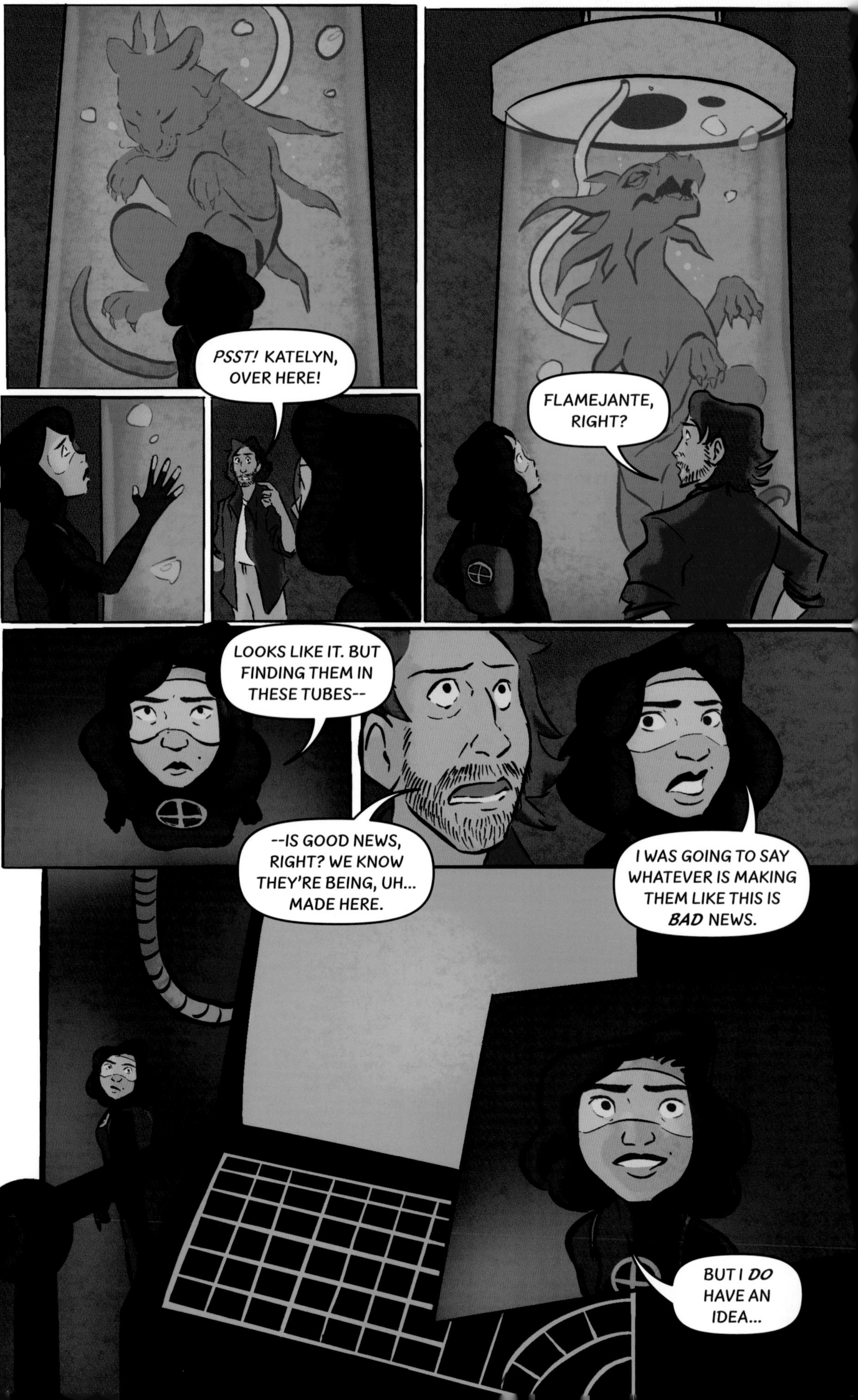
PSST! KATELYN, OVER HERE!
FLAMEJANTE, RIGHT?
LOOKS LIKE IT. BUT FINDING THEM IN THESE TUBES--
--IS GOOD NEWS, RIGHT? WE KNOW THEY'RE BEING, UH... MADE HERE.
I WAS GOING TO SAY WHATEVER IS MAKING THEM LIKE THIS IS BAD NEWS.
BUT I DO HAVE AN IDEA...

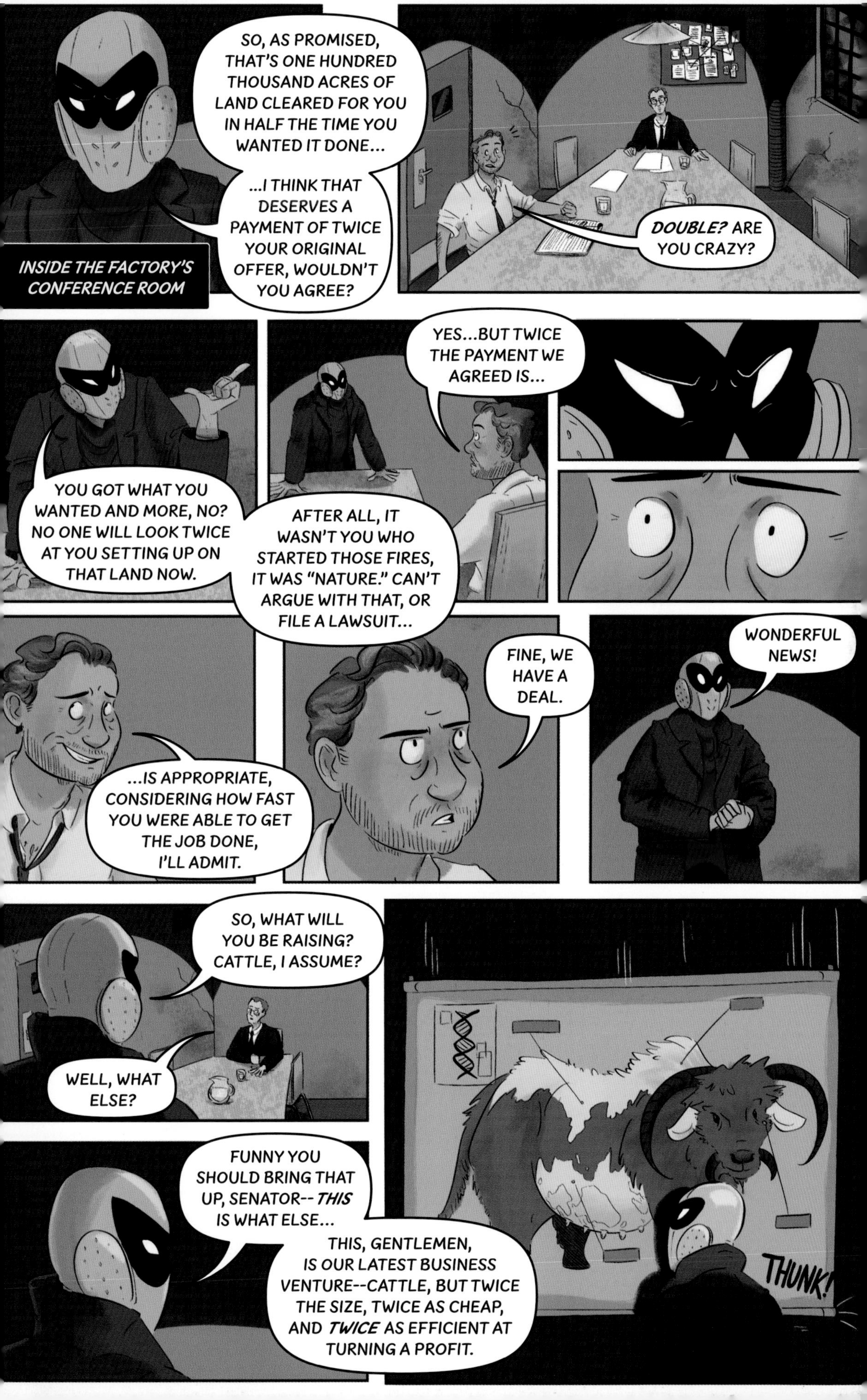
SO, AS PROMISED, THAT'S ONE HUNDRED THOUSAND ACRES OF LAND CLEARED FOR YOU IN HALF THE TIME YOU WANTED IT DONE...
...I THINK THAT DESERVES A PAYMENT OF TWICE YOUR ORIGINAL OFFER, WOULDN'T YOU AGREE?
INSIDE THE FACTORY'S CONFERENCE ROOM
DOUBLE? ARE YOU CRAZY?
YOU GOT WHAT YOU WANTED AND MORE, NO? NO ONE WILL LOOK TWICE AT YOU SETTING UP ON THAT LAND NOW.
YES...BUT TWICE THE PAYMENT WE AGREED IS...
AFTER ALL, IT WASN'T YOU WHO STARTED THOSE FIRES, IT WAS "NATURE." CAN'T ARGUE WITH THAT, OR FILE A LAWSUIT...
...IS APPROPRIATE, CONSIDERING HOW FAST YOU WERE ABLE TO GET THE JOB DONE, I'LL ADMIT.
FINE, WE HAVE A DEAL.
WONDERFUL NEWS!
SO, WHAT WILL YOU BE RAISING? CATTLE, I ASSUME?
WELL, WHAT ELSE?
FUNNY YOU SHOULD BRING THAT UP, SENATOR-- *THIS* IS WHAT ELSE...
THIS, GENTLEMEN, IS OUR LATEST BUSINESS VENTURE--CATTLE, BUT TWICE THE SIZE, TWICE AS CHEAP, AND *TWICE* AS EFFICIENT AT TURNING A PROFIT.
THUNK!

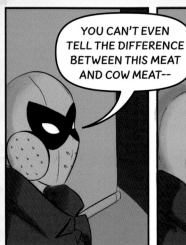

YOU CAN'T EVEN TELL THE DIFFERENCE BETWEEN THIS MEAT AND COW MEAT--

--BELIEVE ME, MY SCIENTISTS MADE SURE OF THAT.

THIS IS DR. MANON CARBONNEAU, MY HEAD SCIENTIST AND ONE OF THE MOST BRILLIANT MINDS I'VE EVER WORKED WITH.

PLEASE...

IF YOU LOOK HERE, GENTLEMEN, YOU'LL SEE THAT WE'VE FABRICATED THIS CREATURE'S GENETIC CODE TO BE BARELY DISTINGUISHABLE FROM THAT OF YOUR AVERAGE COW.

SO, NOW THAT YOU'VE GOT ALL THAT LOVELY NEW ROOM FOR CATTLE...MAY I SUGGEST THESE? AND FOR LOYAL CUSTOMERS LIKE YOU, I'M SURE WE CAN COME TO AN AGREEABLE PRICE.

THAT DOESN'T SOUND GOOD...

IN THE LAB

HOLY COW...THE GENETIC CODE OF THESE THINGS IS REMARKABLE.

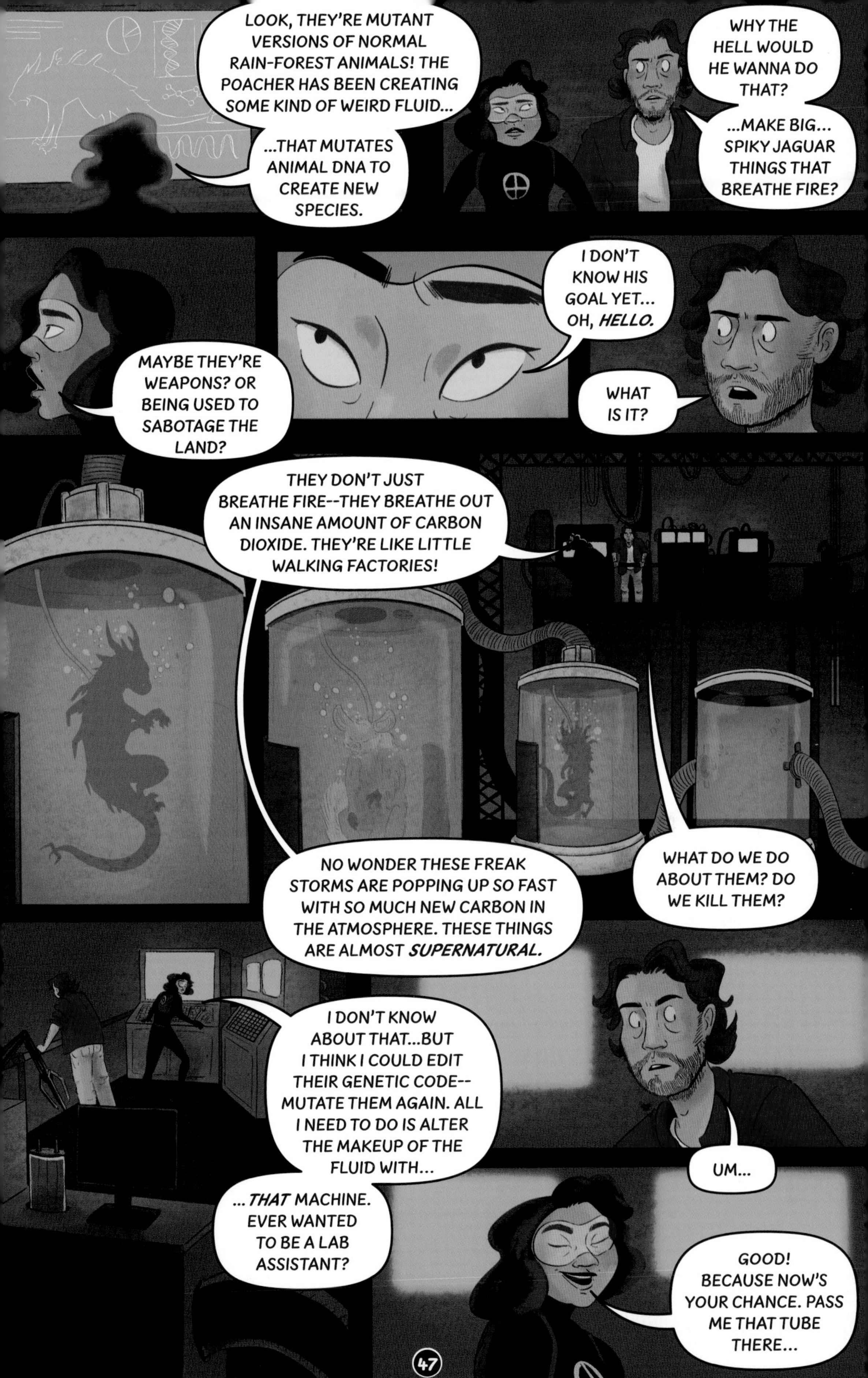

LOOK, THEY'RE MUTANT VERSIONS OF NORMAL RAIN-FOREST ANIMALS! THE POACHER HAS BEEN CREATING SOME KIND OF WEIRD FLUID...
...THAT MUTATES ANIMAL DNA TO CREATE NEW SPECIES.
WHY THE HELL WOULD HE WANNA DO THAT?
...MAKE BIG... SPIKY JAGUAR THINGS THAT BREATHE FIRE?
MAYBE THEY'RE WEAPONS? OR BEING USED TO SABOTAGE THE LAND?
I DON'T KNOW HIS GOAL YET... OH, *HELLO.*
WHAT IS IT?
THEY DON'T JUST BREATHE FIRE--THEY BREATHE OUT AN INSANE AMOUNT OF CARBON DIOXIDE. THEY'RE LIKE LITTLE WALKING FACTORIES!
NO WONDER THESE FREAK STORMS ARE POPPING UP SO FAST WITH SO MUCH NEW CARBON IN THE ATMOSPHERE. THESE THINGS ARE ALMOST ***SUPERNATURAL.***
WHAT DO WE DO ABOUT THEM? DO WE KILL THEM?
I DON'T KNOW ABOUT THAT...BUT I THINK I COULD EDIT THEIR GENETIC CODE--MUTATE THEM AGAIN. ALL I NEED TO DO IS ALTER THE MAKEUP OF THE FLUID WITH...
UM...
...*THAT* MACHINE. EVER WANTED TO BE A LAB ASSISTANT?
GOOD! BECAUSE NOW'S YOUR CHANCE. PASS ME THAT TUBE THERE...

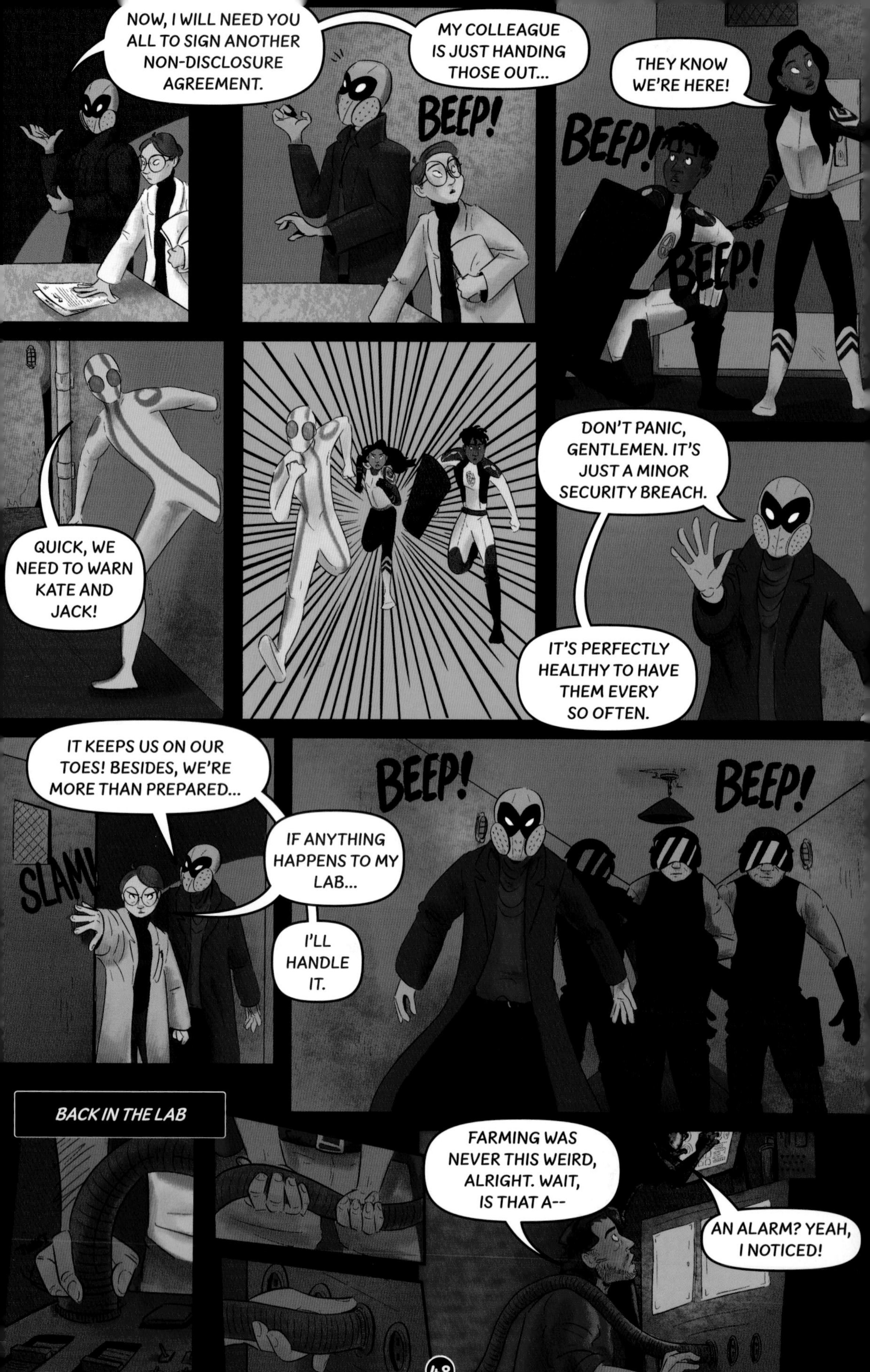
NOW, I WILL NEED YOU ALL TO SIGN ANOTHER NON-DISCLOSURE AGREEMENT.
MY COLLEAGUE IS JUST HANDING THOSE OUT...
BEEP!
THEY KNOW WE'RE HERE!
BEEP!
BEEP!
QUICK, WE NEED TO WARN KATE AND JACK!
DON'T PANIC, GENTLEMEN. IT'S JUST A MINOR SECURITY BREACH.
IT'S PERFECTLY HEALTHY TO HAVE THEM EVERY SO OFTEN.
IT KEEPS US ON OUR TOES! BESIDES, WE'RE MORE THAN PREPARED...
SLAM!
IF ANYTHING HAPPENS TO MY LAB...
I'LL HANDLE IT.
BEEP!
BEEP!
BACK IN THE LAB
FARMING WAS NEVER THIS WEIRD, ALRIGHT. WAIT, IS THAT A--
AN ALARM? YEAH, I NOTICED!

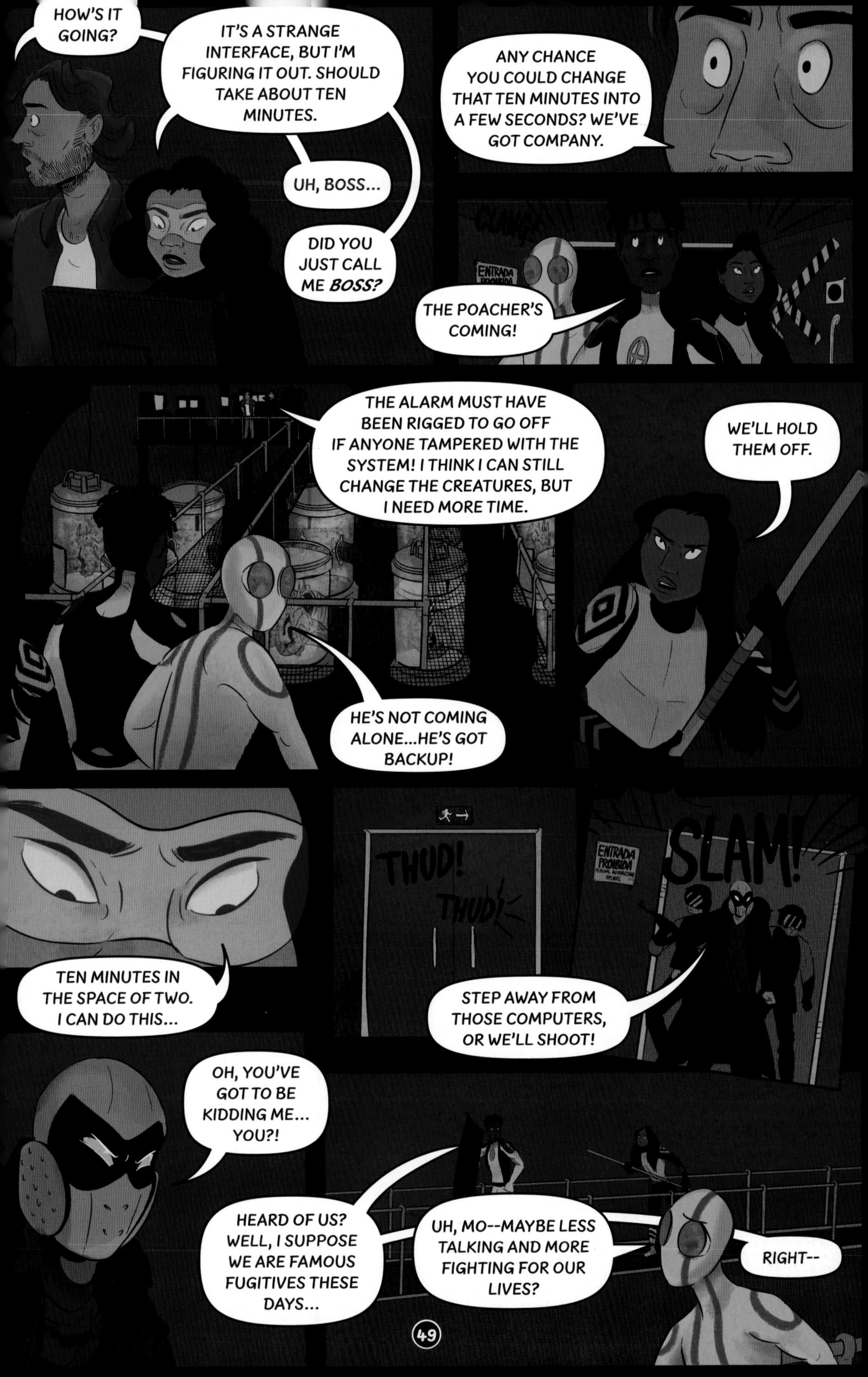
HOW'S IT GOING?
IT'S A STRANGE INTERFACE, BUT I'M FIGURING IT OUT. SHOULD TAKE ABOUT TEN MINUTES.
UH, BOSS...
DID YOU JUST CALL ME *BOSS?*
ANY CHANCE YOU COULD CHANGE THAT TEN MINUTES INTO A FEW SECONDS? WE'VE GOT COMPANY.
ENTRADA PROHIBIDA
THE POACHER'S COMING!
THE ALARM MUST HAVE BEEN RIGGED TO GO OFF IF ANYONE TAMPERED WITH THE SYSTEM! I THINK I CAN STILL CHANGE THE CREATURES, BUT I NEED MORE TIME.
WE'LL HOLD THEM OFF.
HE'S NOT COMING ALONE...HE'S GOT BACKUP!
TEN MINUTES IN THE SPACE OF TWO. I CAN DO THIS...
THUD!
THUD!
ENTRADA PROHIBIDA
SLAM!
STEP AWAY FROM THOSE COMPUTERS, OR WE'LL SHOOT!
OH, YOU'VE GOT TO BE KIDDING ME... YOU?!
HEARD OF US? WELL, I SUPPOSE WE ARE FAMOUS FUGITIVES THESE DAYS...
UH, MO--MAYBE LESS TALKING AND MORE FIGHTING FOR OUR LIVES?
RIGHT--

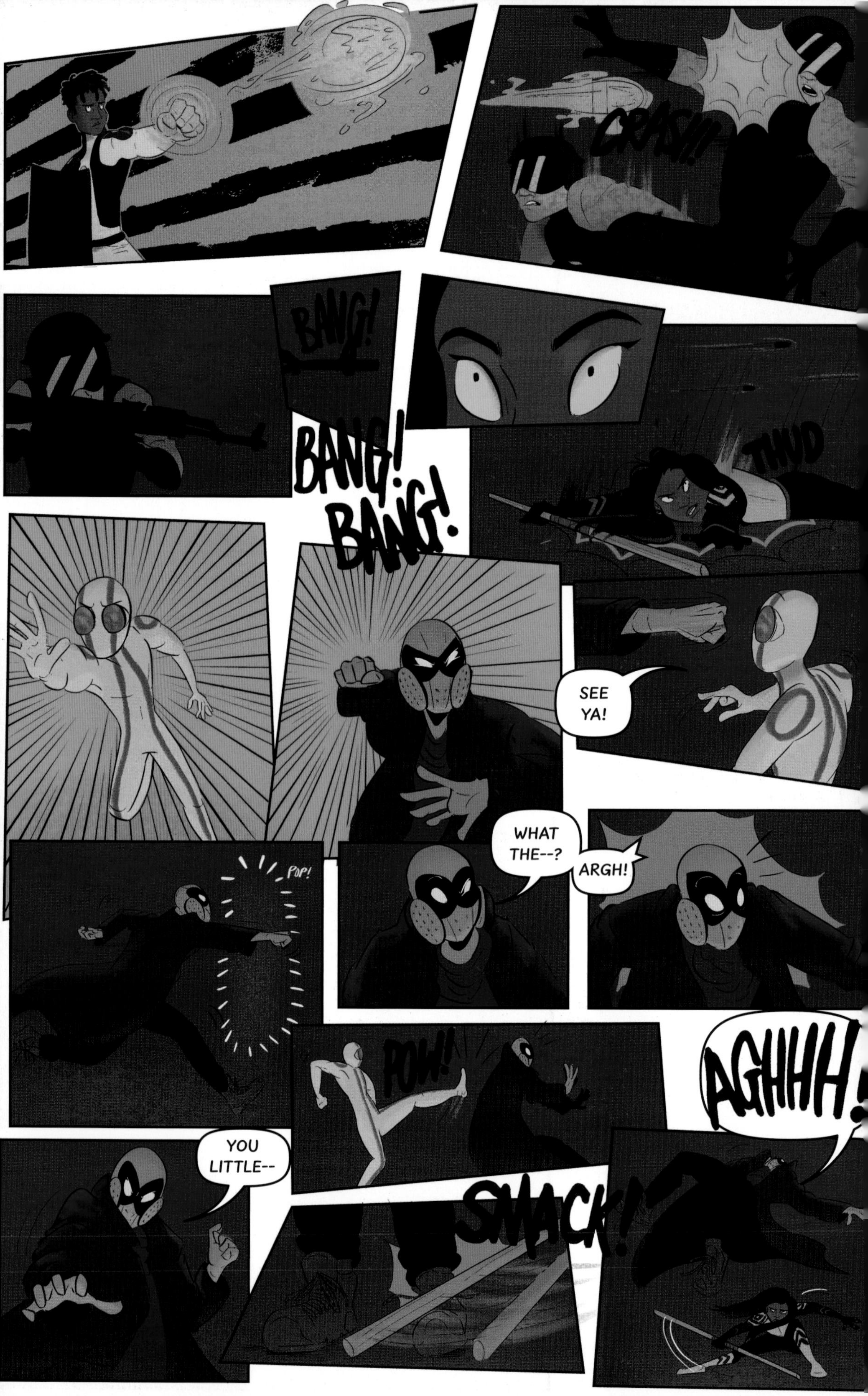
CRASH!!
BANG!
BANG!
BANG!
THUD
SEE YA!
WHAT THE--?
ARGH!
POP!
POW!
AGHHH!
YOU LITTLE--
SMACK!

UGH...

THAT'S IT.

WOOSH!

THWACK!

OFF YOU GO, LITTLE GIRL.

HEY!

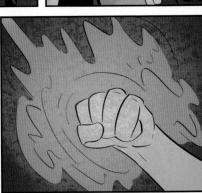

AHHH!

OOF!

GOOD CATCH!

NO PROB-- UH OH.

CLICK

ARGH!

SMACK!

CRASH!

COME ON, COME ON...

HEY, PAL!

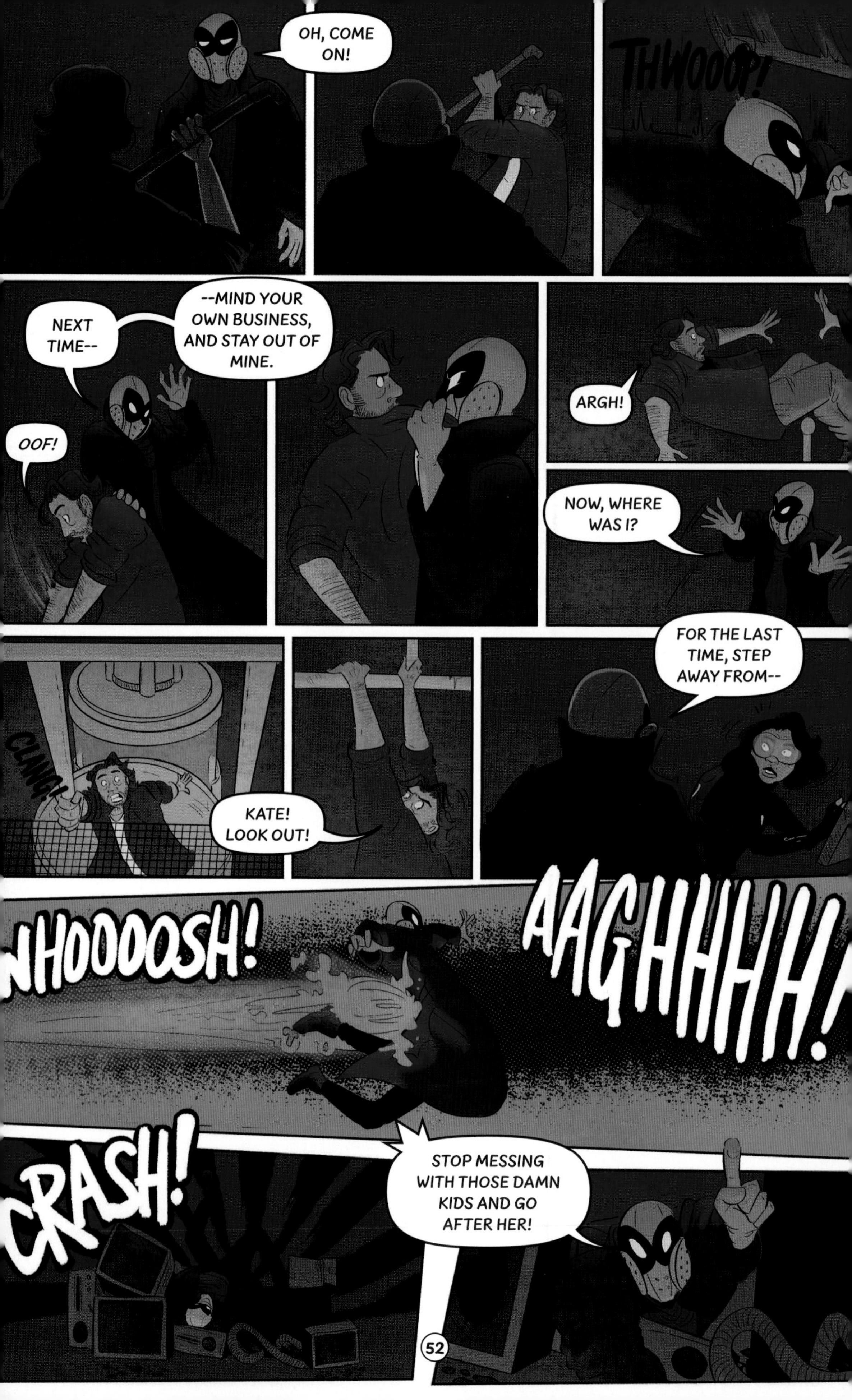
OH, COME ON!
THWOOOP!
NEXT TIME--
--MIND YOUR OWN BUSINESS, AND STAY OUT OF MINE.
OOF!
ARGH!
NOW, WHERE WAS I?
CLANG!
KATE! LOOK OUT!
FOR THE LAST TIME, STEP AWAY FROM--
HOOOOSH!
AAGHHHHH!
CRASH!
STOP MESSING WITH THOSE DAMN KIDS AND GO AFTER HER!

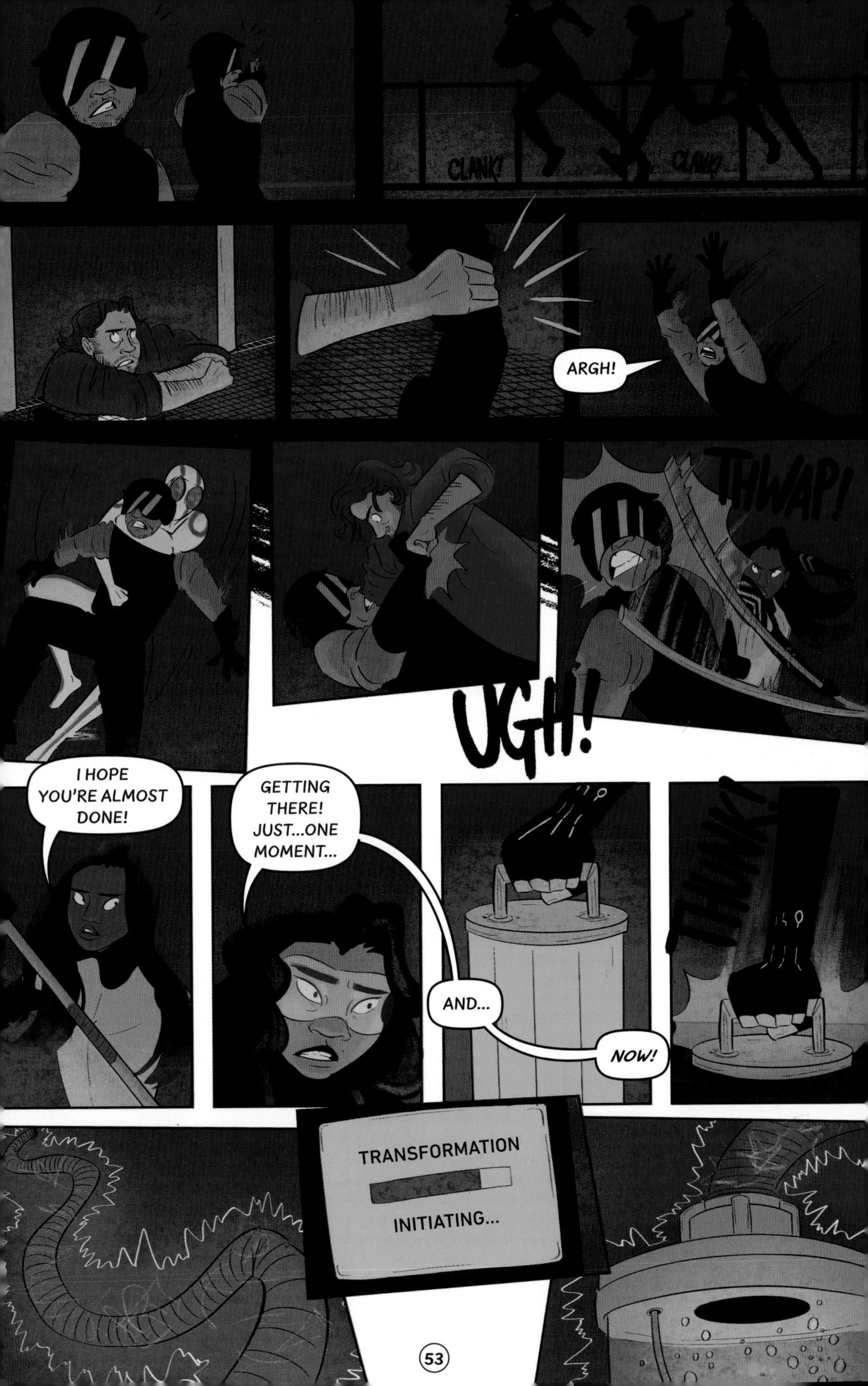
CLANK!
CLANK!
ARGH!
THWAP!
UGH!
I HOPE YOU'RE ALMOST DONE!
GETTING THERE! JUST...ONE MOMENT...
AND...
NOW!
TRANSFORMATION
INITIATING...

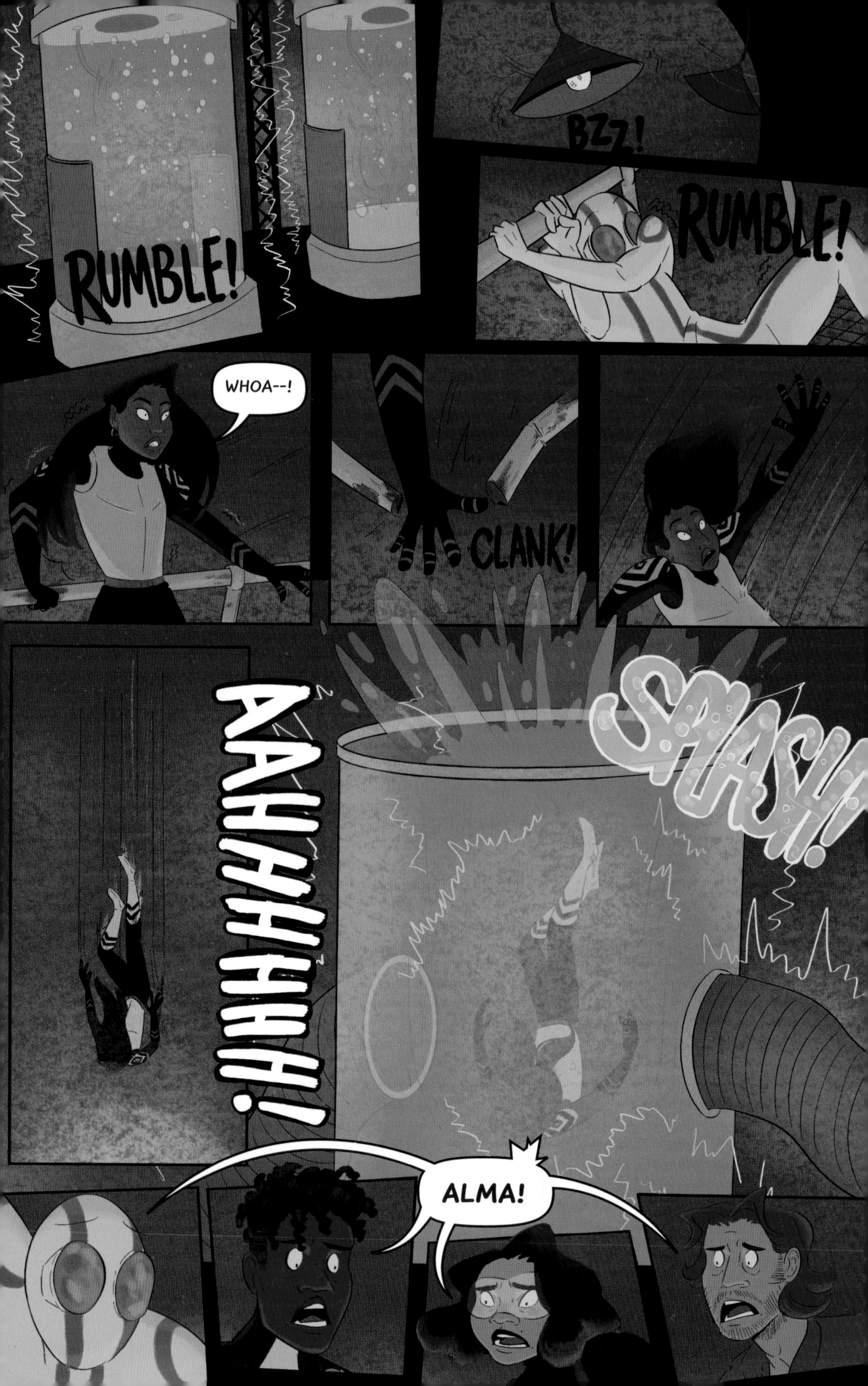
RUMBLE!
BZZ!
RUMBLE!
WHOA--!
CLANK!
AAHHHHHHH!
SPLASH!
ALMA!

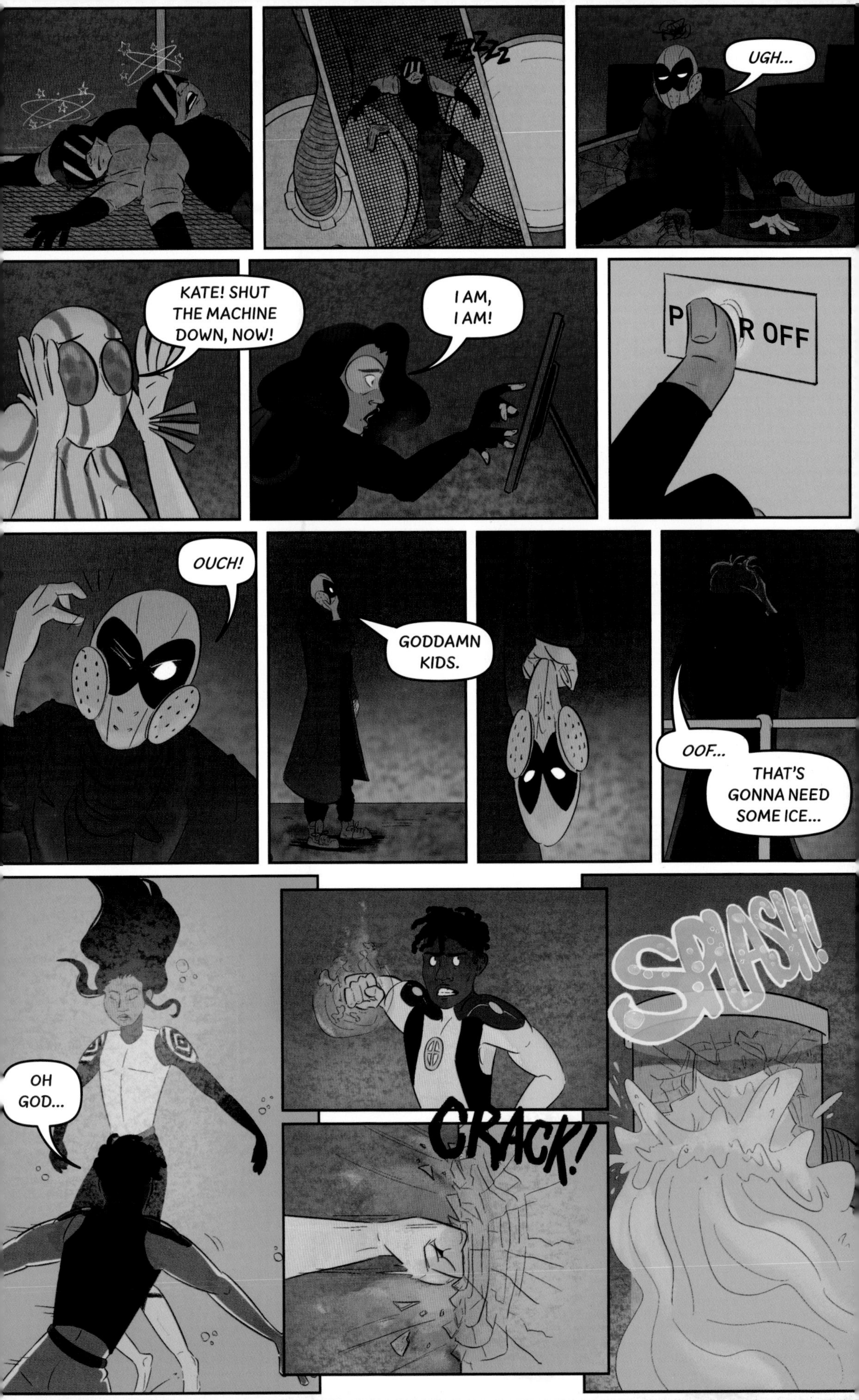
UGH...
KATE! SHUT THE MACHINE DOWN, NOW!
I AM, I AM!
P R OFF
OUCH!
GODDAMN KIDS.
OOF...
THAT'S GONNA NEED SOME ICE...
OH GOD...
CRACK!
SPLASH!

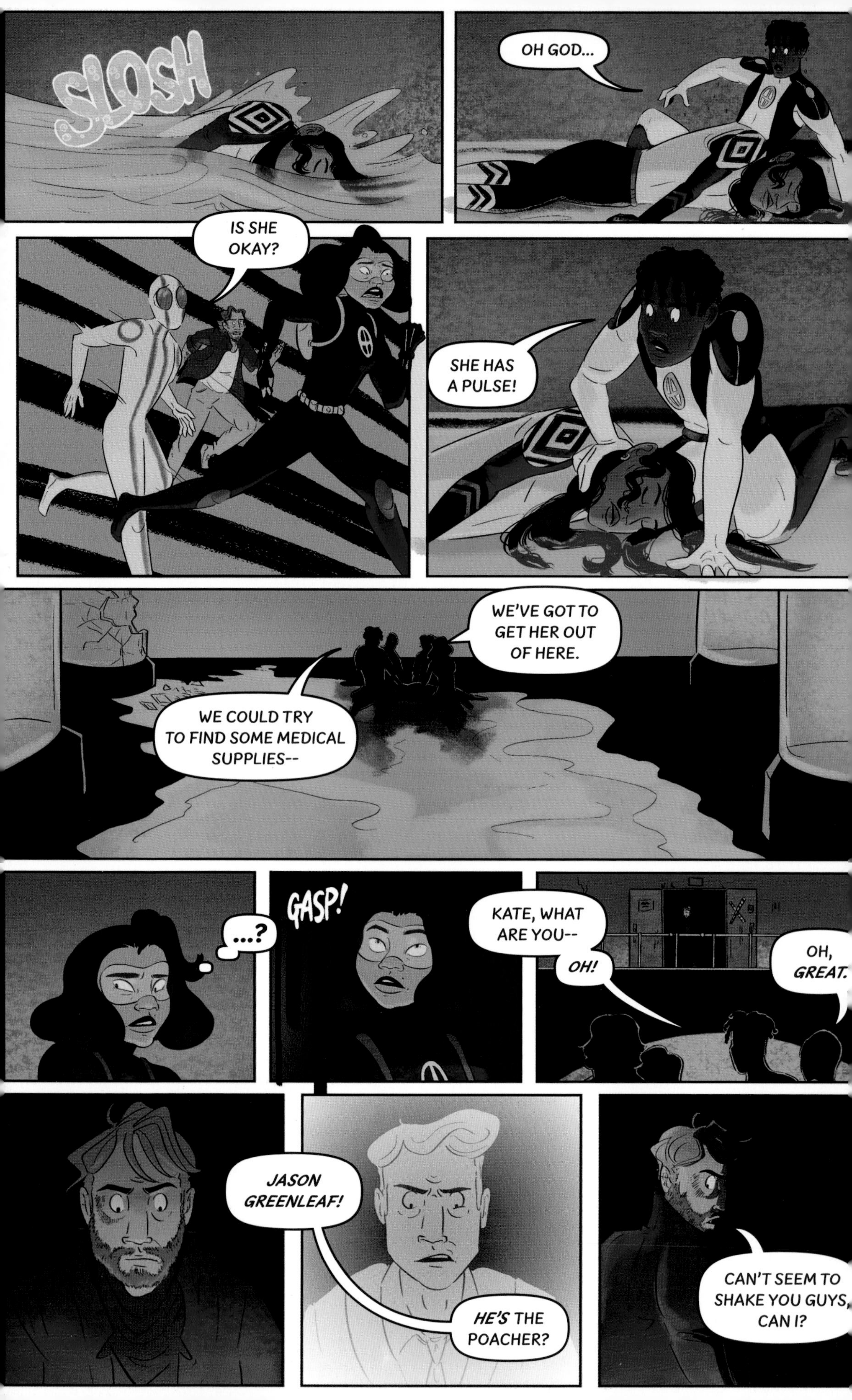
SLOSH
OH GOD...
IS SHE OKAY?
SHE HAS A PULSE!
WE'VE GOT TO GET HER OUT OF HERE.
WE COULD TRY TO FIND SOME MEDICAL SUPPLIES--
...?
GASP!
KATE, WHAT ARE YOU--
OH!
OH, GREAT.
JASON GREENLEAF!
HE'S THE POACHER?
CAN'T SEEM TO SHAKE YOU GUYS, CAN I?

GET HIM! WE CAN'T LET HIM--!

UH, KATE!

WHAT IS IT?!

AH...

PING!

CRACK!

CRASH!

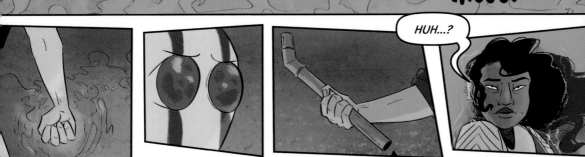

HISSS!

GROOOWL

HISSS!

HUH...?

NO, WAIT! STOP!

LOOK!

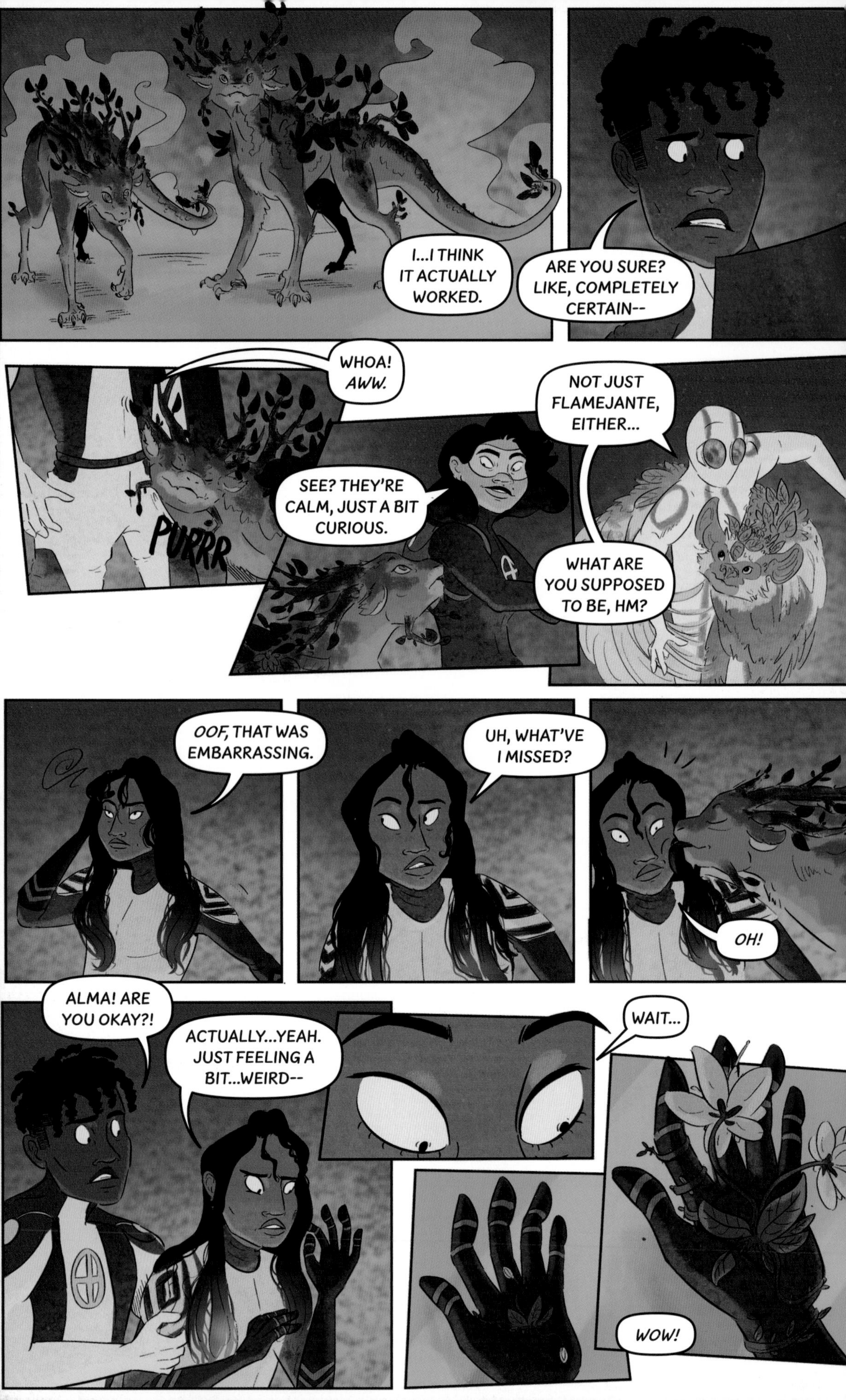
I...I THINK IT ACTUALLY WORKED.
ARE YOU SURE? LIKE, COMPLETELY CERTAIN--
WHOA! AWW.
PURRR
SEE? THEY'RE CALM, JUST A BIT CURIOUS.
NOT JUST FLAMEJANTE, EITHER...
WHAT ARE YOU SUPPOSED TO BE, HM?
OOF, THAT WAS EMBARRASSING.
UH, WHAT'VE I MISSED?
OH!
ALMA! ARE YOU OKAY?!
ACTUALLY...YEAH. JUST FEELING A BIT...WEIRD--
WAIT...
WOW!

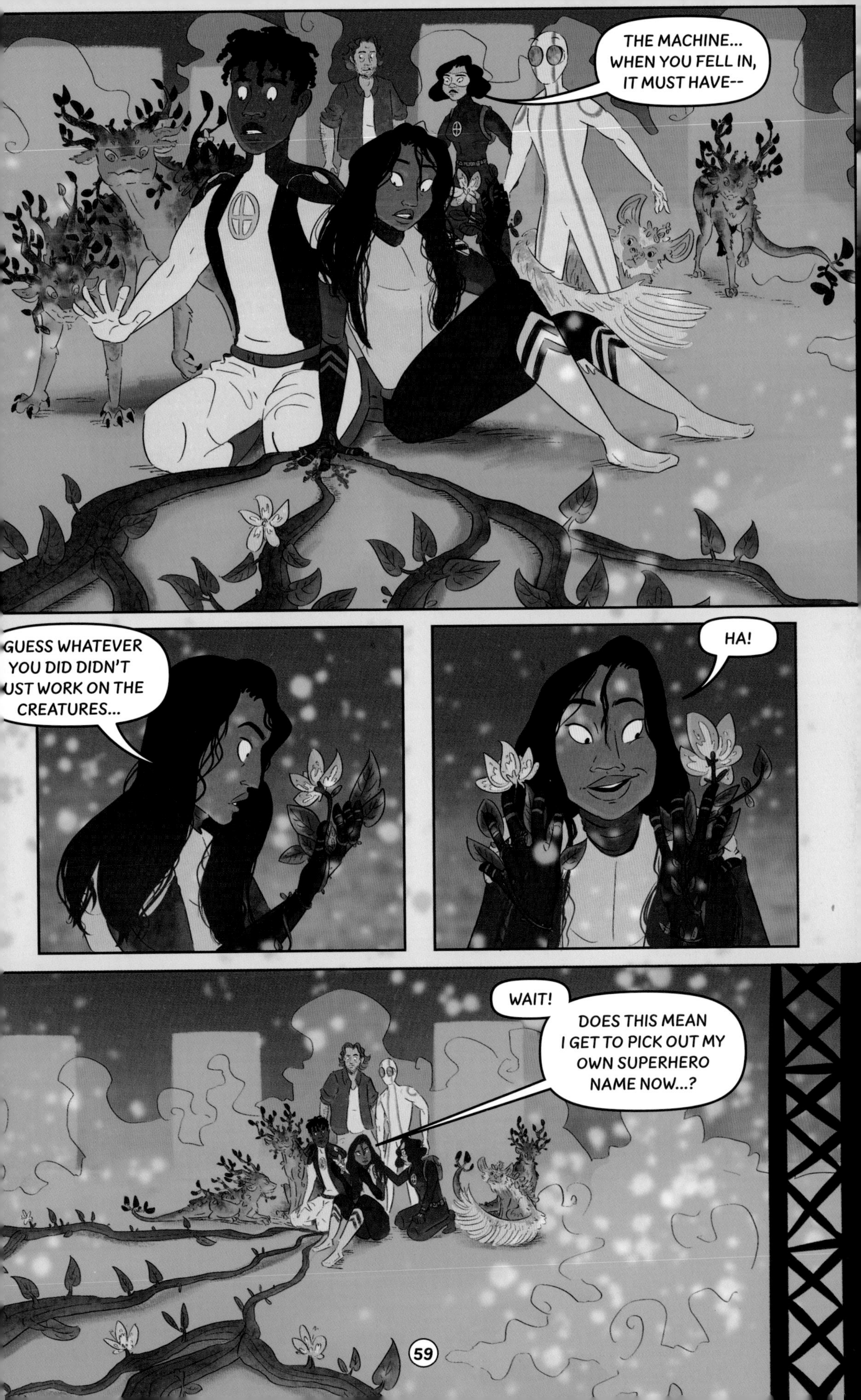
THE MACHINE... WHEN YOU FELL IN, IT MUST HAVE--
GUESS WHATEVER YOU DID DIDN'T UST WORK ON THE CREATURES...
HA!
WAIT!
DOES THIS MEAN I GET TO PICK OUT MY OWN SUPERHERO NAME NOW...?

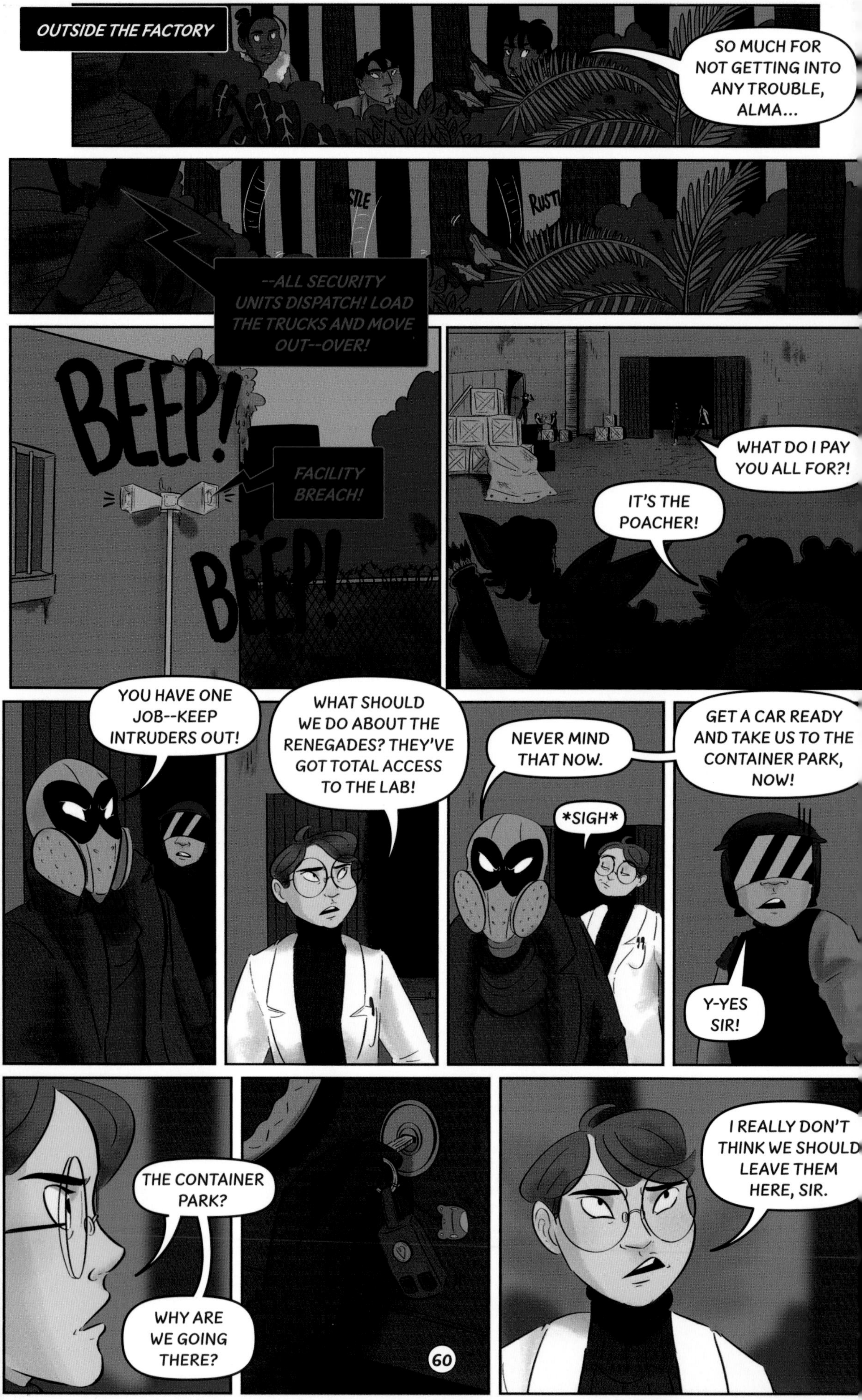

OUTSIDE THE FACTORY
SO MUCH FOR NOT GETTING INTO ANY TROUBLE, ALMA...
--ALL SECURITY UNITS DISPATCH! LOAD THE TRUCKS AND MOVE OUT--OVER!
BEEP!
FACILITY BREACH!
BEEP!
WHAT DO I PAY YOU ALL FOR?!
IT'S THE POACHER!
YOU HAVE ONE JOB--KEEP INTRUDERS OUT!
WHAT SHOULD WE DO ABOUT THE RENEGADES? THEY'VE GOT TOTAL ACCESS TO THE LAB!
NEVER MIND THAT NOW.
GET A CAR READY AND TAKE US TO THE CONTAINER PARK, NOW!
SIGH
Y-YES SIR!
THE CONTAINER PARK?
WHY ARE WE GOING THERE?
I REALLY DON'T THINK WE SHOULD LEAVE THEM HERE, SIR.

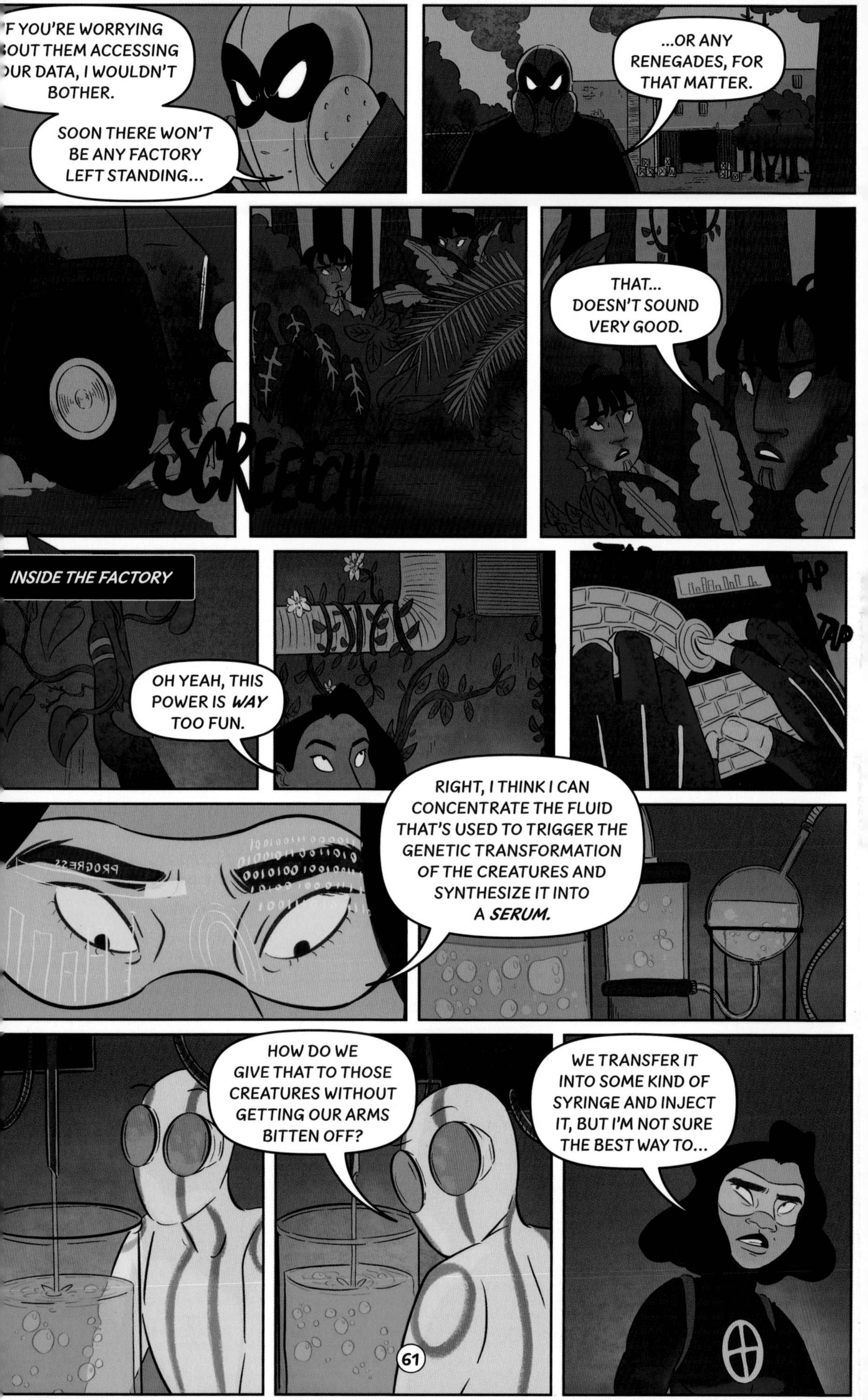

F YOU'RE WORRYING
OUT THEM ACCESSING
UR DATA, I WOULDN'T BOTHER.
SOON THERE WON'T BE ANY FACTORY LEFT STANDING...
...OR ANY RENEGADES, FOR THAT MATTER.
SCREECH!
THAT... DOESN'T SOUND VERY GOOD.
INSIDE THE FACTORY
OH YEAH, THIS POWER IS WAY TOO FUN.
TAP
TAP
RIGHT, I THINK I CAN CONCENTRATE THE FLUID THAT'S USED TO TRIGGER THE GENETIC TRANSFORMATION OF THE CREATURES AND SYNTHESIZE IT INTO A SERUM.
HOW DO WE GIVE THAT TO THOSE CREATURES WITHOUT GETTING OUR ARMS BITTEN OFF?
WE TRANSFER IT INTO SOME KIND OF SYRINGE AND INJECT IT, BUT I'M NOT SURE THE BEST WAY TO...

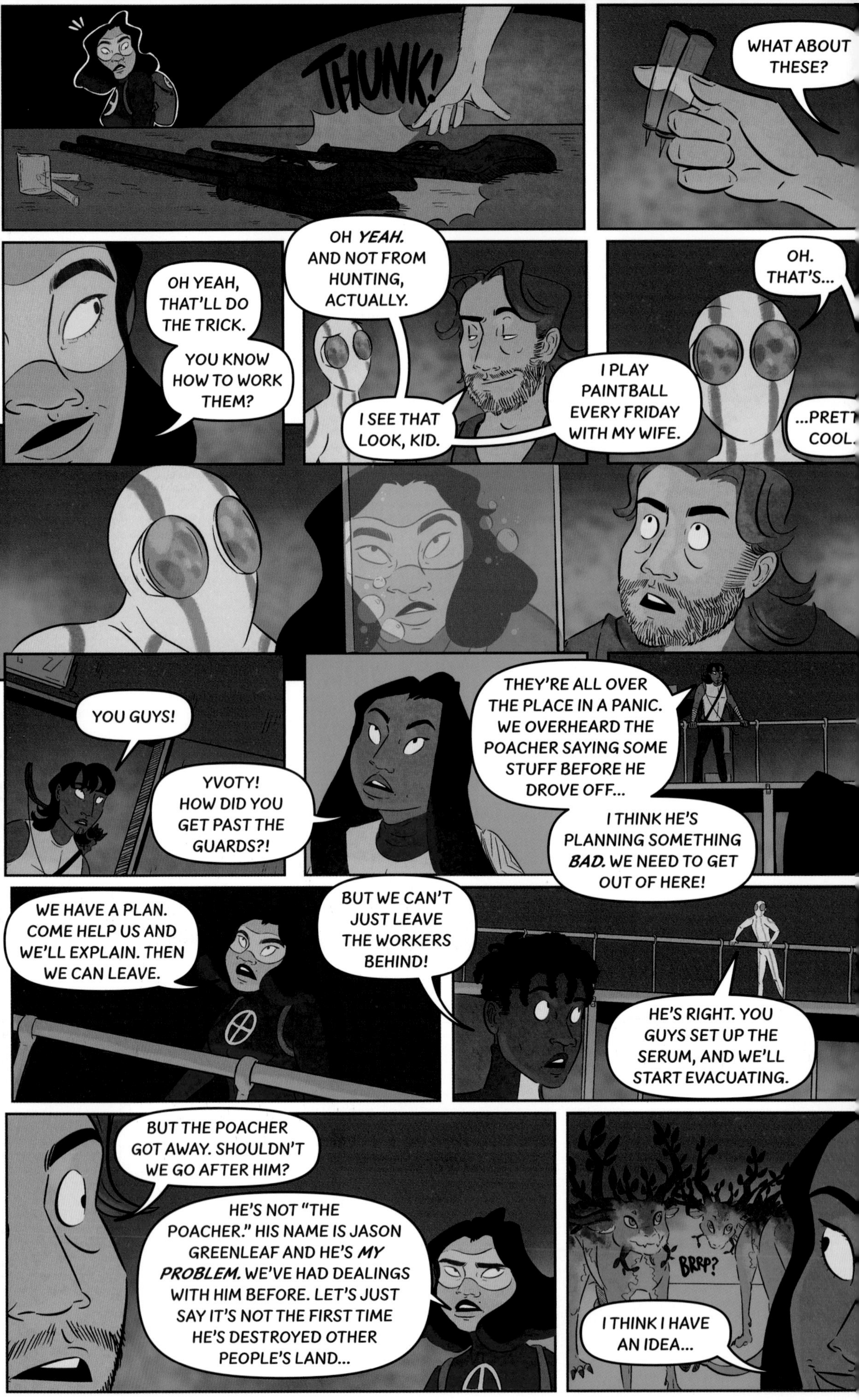
THUNK!
WHAT ABOUT THESE?
OH YEAH, THAT'LL DO THE TRICK.
YOU KNOW HOW TO WORK THEM?
OH YEAH. AND NOT FROM HUNTING, ACTUALLY.
I SEE THAT LOOK, KID.
I PLAY PAINTBALL EVERY FRIDAY WITH MY WIFE.
OH. THAT'S...
...PRETT COOL.
YOU GUYS!
YVOTY! HOW DID YOU GET PAST THE GUARDS?!
THEY'RE ALL OVER THE PLACE IN A PANIC. WE OVERHEARD THE POACHER SAYING SOME STUFF BEFORE HE DROVE OFF...
I THINK HE'S PLANNING SOMETHING BAD. WE NEED TO GET OUT OF HERE!
WE HAVE A PLAN. COME HELP US AND WE'LL EXPLAIN. THEN WE CAN LEAVE.
BUT WE CAN'T JUST LEAVE THE WORKERS BEHIND!
HE'S RIGHT. YOU GUYS SET UP THE SERUM, AND WE'LL START EVACUATING.
BUT THE POACHER GOT AWAY. SHOULDN'T WE GO AFTER HIM?
HE'S NOT "THE POACHER." HIS NAME IS JASON GREENLEAF AND HE'S MY PROBLEM. WE'VE HAD DEALINGS WITH HIM BEFORE. LET'S JUST SAY IT'S NOT THE FIRST TIME HE'S DESTROYED OTHER PEOPLE'S LAND...
BRRP?
I THINK I HAVE AN IDEA...

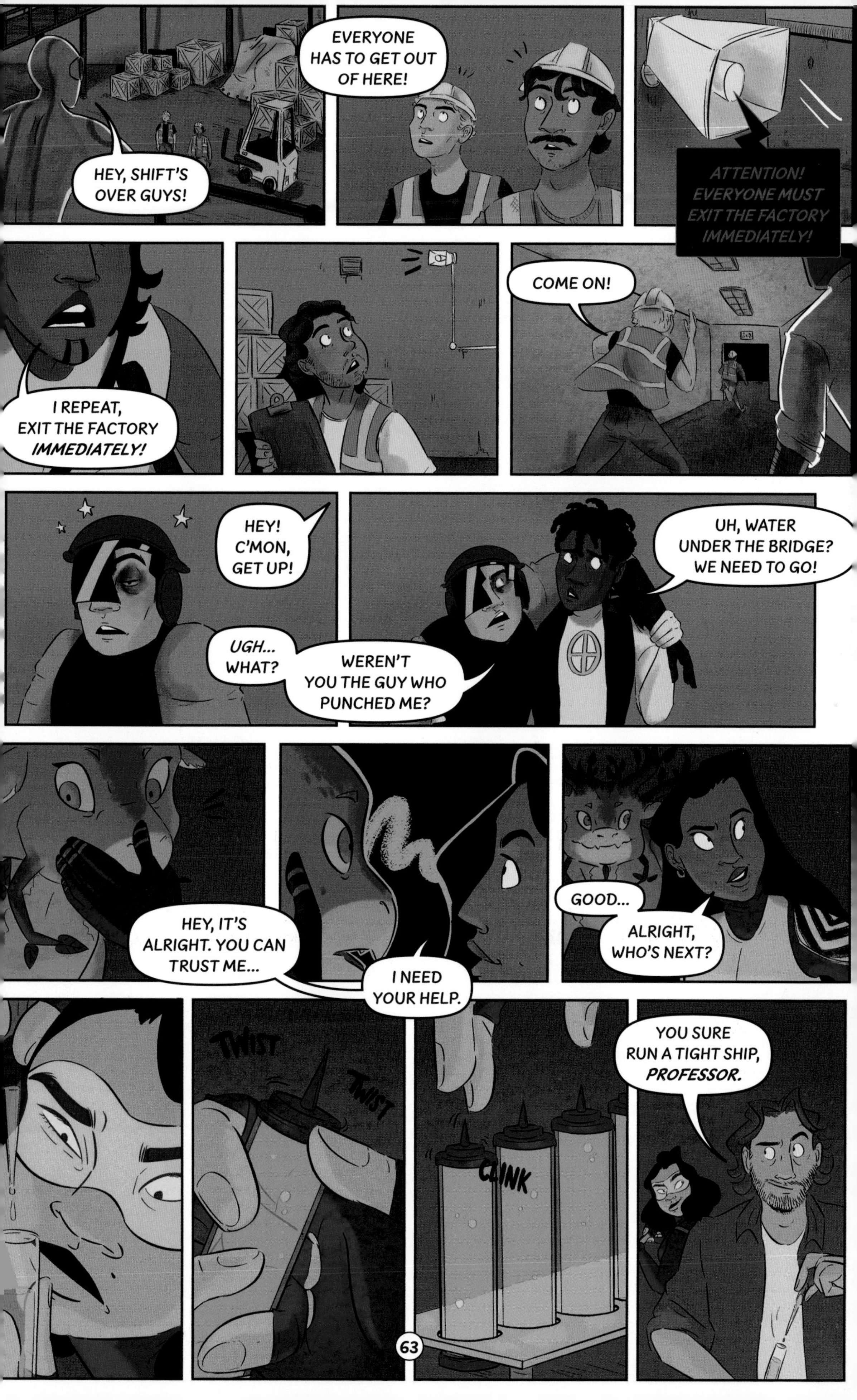
HEY, SHIFT'S OVER GUYS!
EVERYONE HAS TO GET OUT OF HERE!
ATTENTION! EVERYONE MUST EXIT THE FACTORY IMMEDIATELY!
I REPEAT, EXIT THE FACTORY *IMMEDIATELY!*
COME ON!
HEY! C'MON, GET UP!
UGH... WHAT?
WEREN'T YOU THE GUY WHO PUNCHED ME?
UH, WATER UNDER THE BRIDGE? WE NEED TO GO!
HEY, IT'S ALRIGHT. YOU CAN TRUST ME...
I NEED YOUR HELP.
GOOD...
ALRIGHT, WHO'S NEXT?
TWIST
TWIST
CLINK
YOU SURE RUN A TIGHT SHIP, *PROFESSOR.*

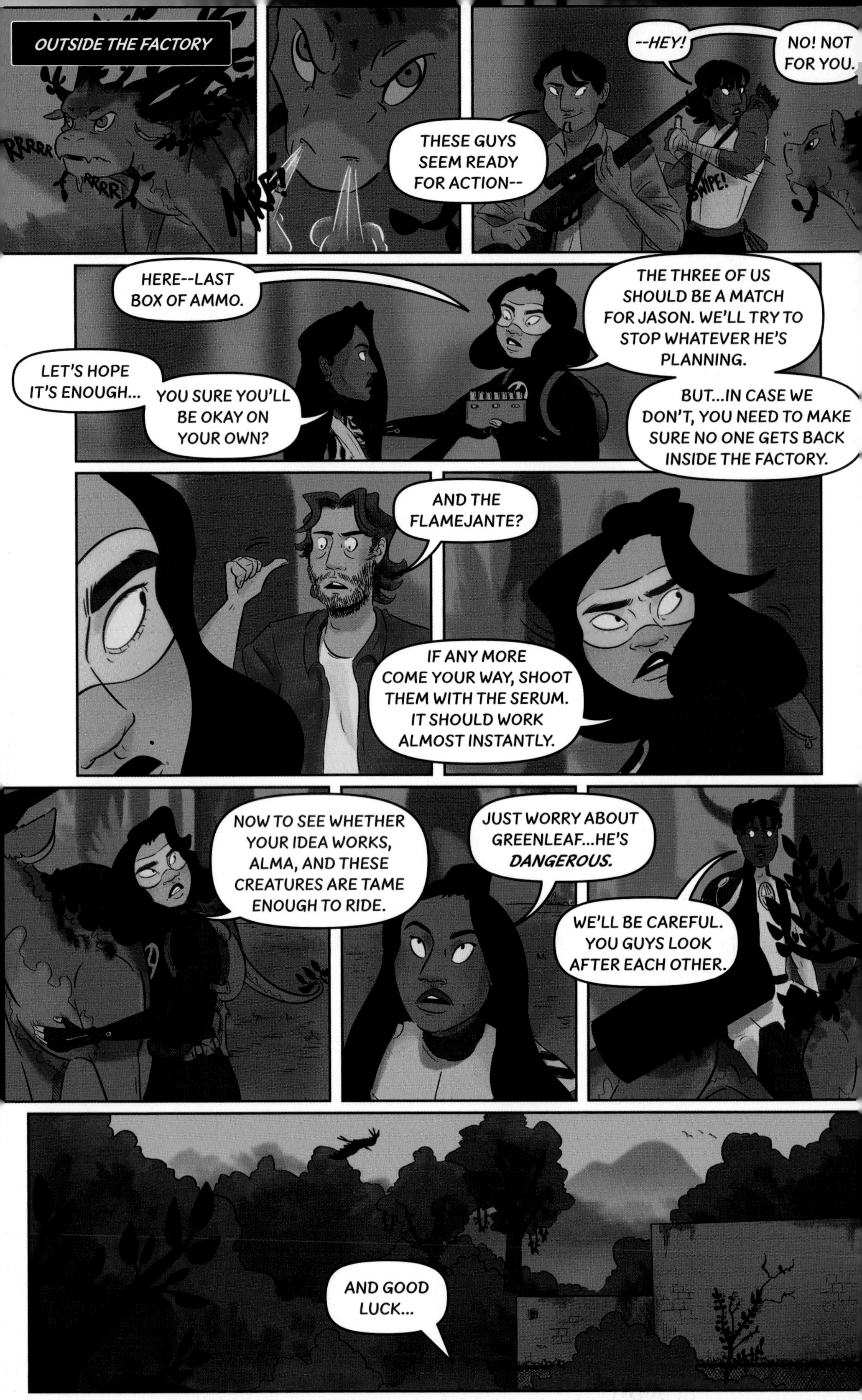
OUTSIDE THE FACTORY
RRRRR
RRRR
MRRF!
THESE GUYS SEEM READY FOR ACTION--
--HEY!
NO! NOT FOR YOU.
SWIPE!
HERE--LAST BOX OF AMMO.
THE THREE OF US SHOULD BE A MATCH FOR JASON. WE'LL TRY TO STOP WHATEVER HE'S PLANNING.
LET'S HOPE IT'S ENOUGH...
YOU SURE YOU'LL BE OKAY ON YOUR OWN?
BUT...IN CASE WE DON'T, YOU NEED TO MAKE SURE NO ONE GETS BACK INSIDE THE FACTORY.
AND THE FLAMEJANTE?
IF ANY MORE COME YOUR WAY, SHOOT THEM WITH THE SERUM. IT SHOULD WORK ALMOST INSTANTLY.
NOW TO SEE WHETHER YOUR IDEA WORKS, ALMA, AND THESE CREATURES ARE TAME ENOUGH TO RIDE.
JUST WORRY ABOUT GREENLEAF...HE'S *DANGEROUS.*
WE'LL BE CAREFUL. YOU GUYS LOOK AFTER EACH OTHER.
AND GOOD LUCK...

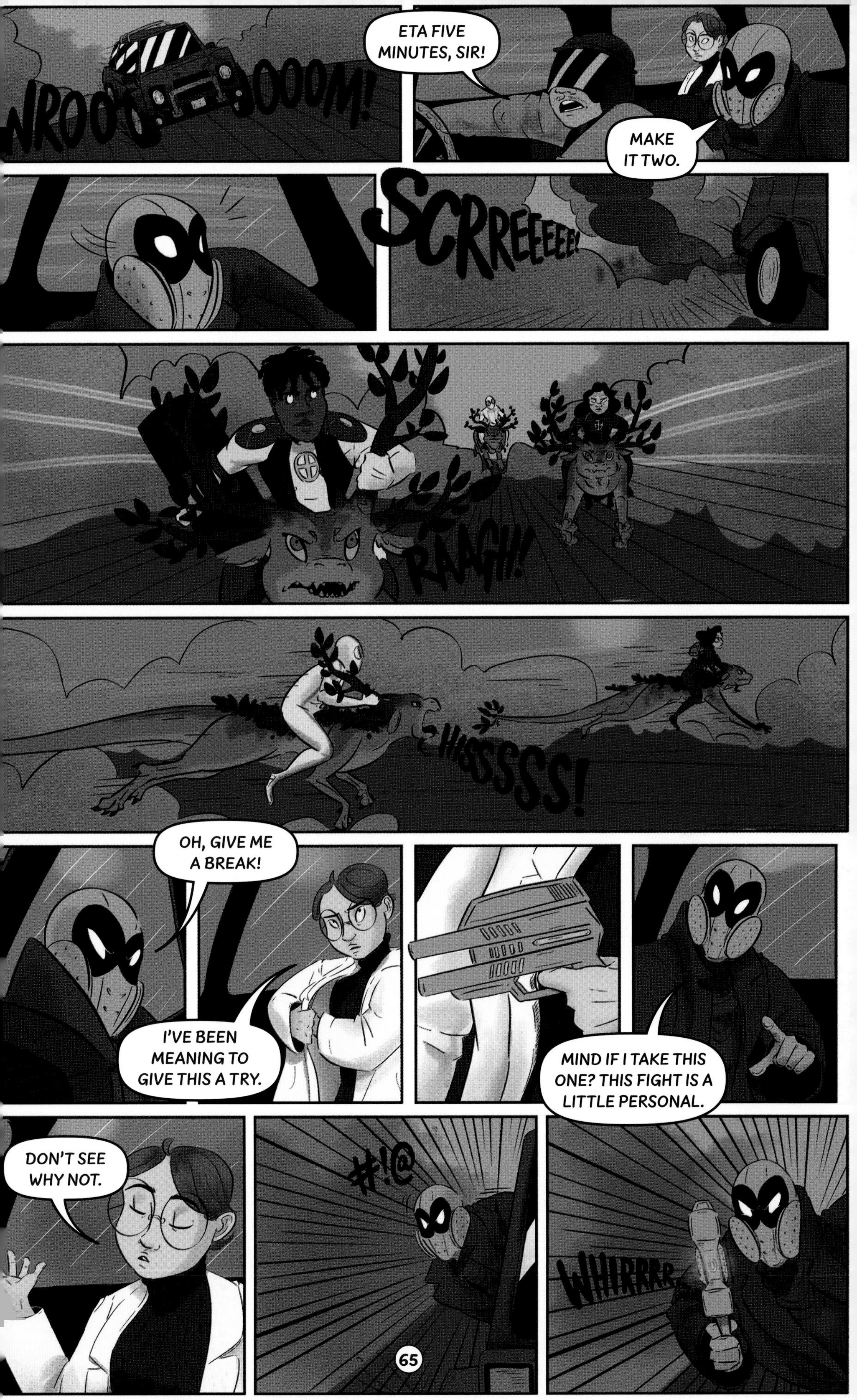
WROOOOOOOOM!
ETA FIVE MINUTES, SIR!
MAKE IT TWO.
SCRREEEEEE!
RAAGH!!
HISSSSS!
OH, GIVE ME A BREAK!
I'VE BEEN MEANING TO GIVE THIS A TRY.
MIND IF I TAKE THIS ONE? THIS FIGHT IS A LITTLE PERSONAL.
DON'T SEE WHY NOT.
#!@
WHIRRRR

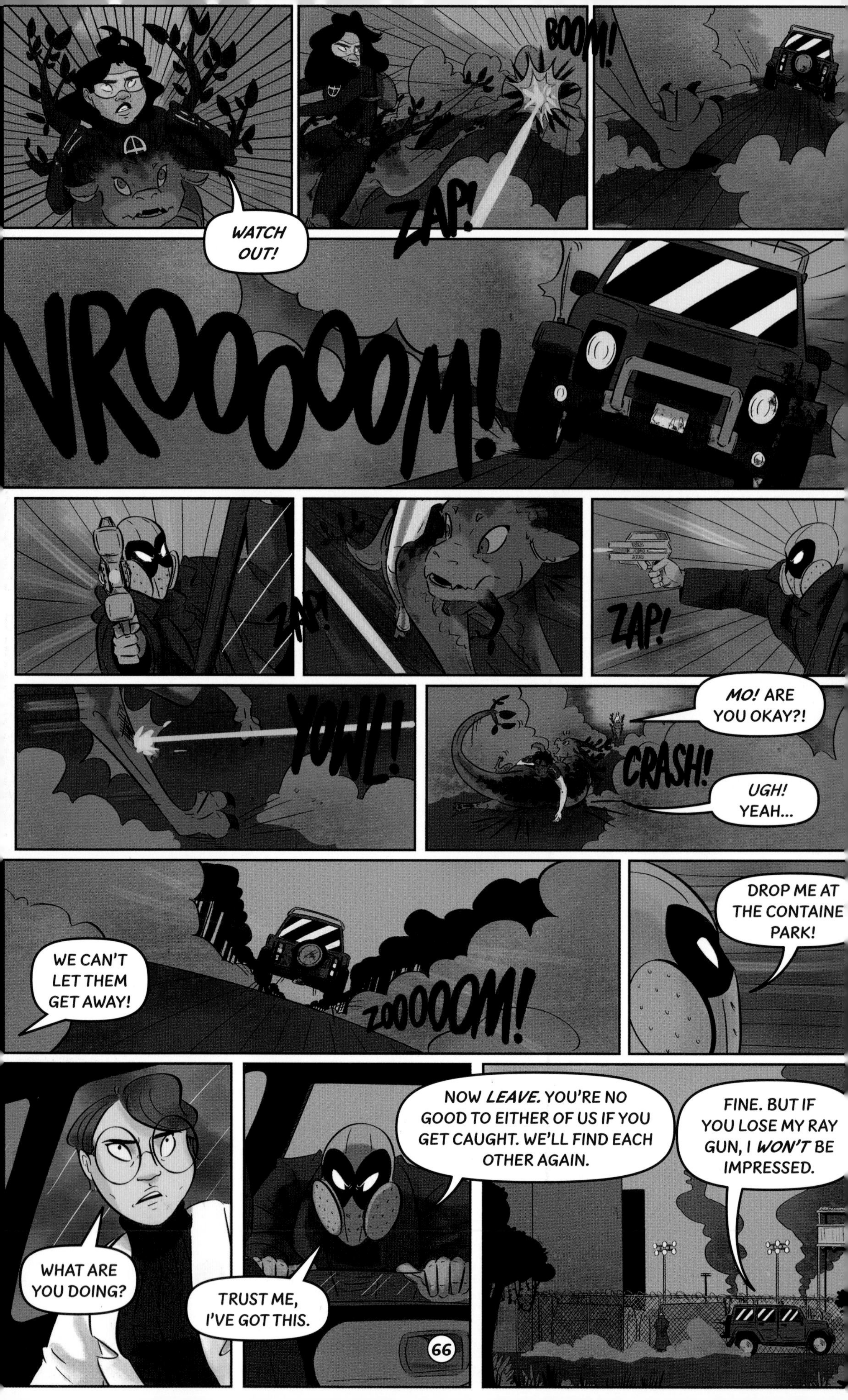
BOOM!
WATCH OUT!
ZAP!
VROOOOOM!
ZAP!
ZAP!
YOWL!
MO! ARE YOU OKAY?!
CRASH!
UGH! YEAH...
WE CAN'T LET THEM GET AWAY!
ZOOOOOM!
DROP ME AT THE CONTAINE PARK!
WHAT ARE YOU DOING?
TRUST ME, I'VE GOT THIS.
NOW *LEAVE.* YOU'RE NO GOOD TO EITHER OF US IF YOU GET CAUGHT. WE'LL FIND EACH OTHER AGAIN.
FINE. BUT IF YOU LOSE MY RAY GUN, I *WON'T* BE IMPRESSED.

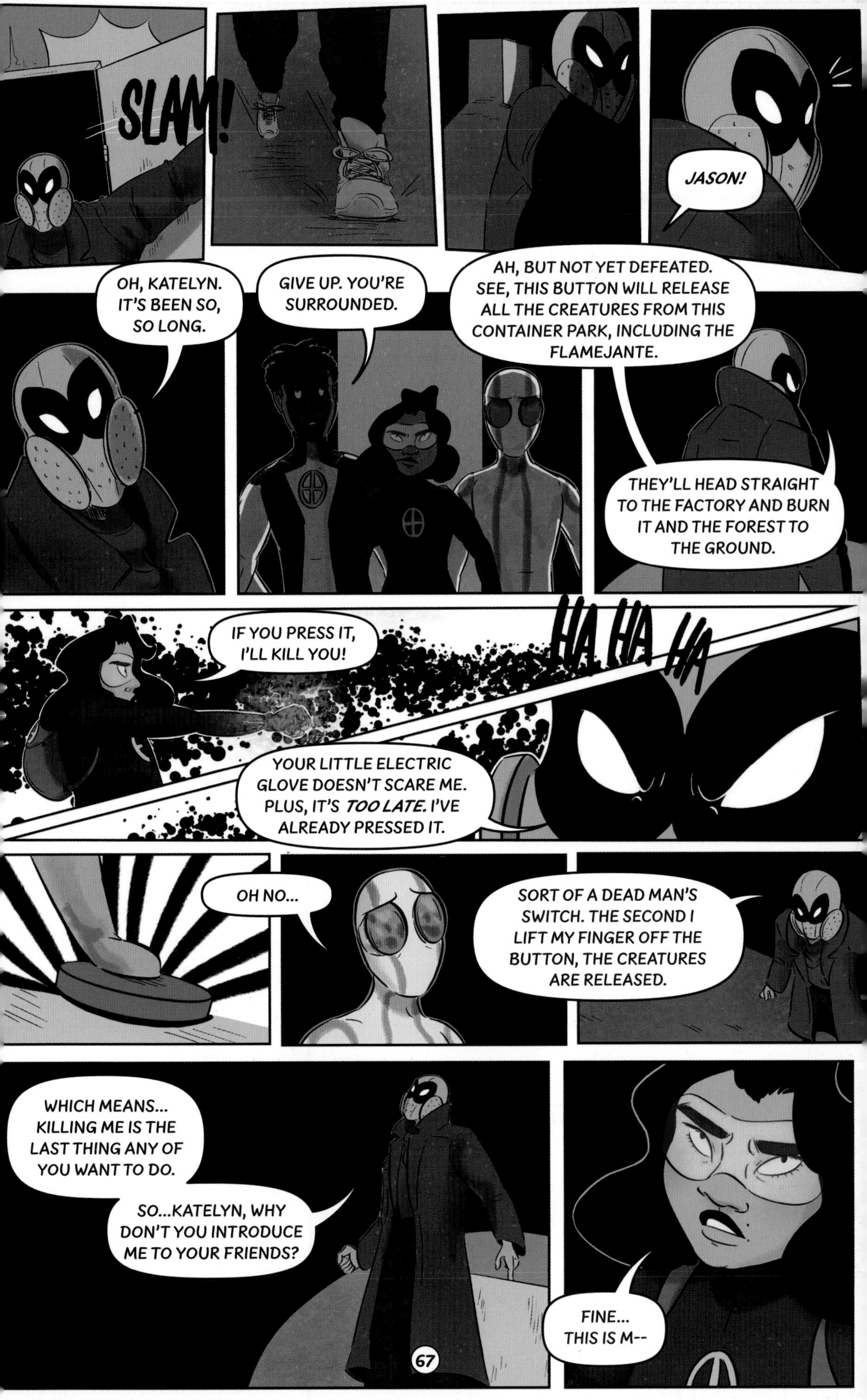

SLAM!
JASON!
OH, KATELYN. IT'S BEEN SO, SO LONG.
GIVE UP. YOU'RE SURROUNDED.
AH, BUT NOT YET DEFEATED. SEE, THIS BUTTON WILL RELEASE ALL THE CREATURES FROM THIS CONTAINER PARK, INCLUDING THE FLAMEJANTE.
THEY'LL HEAD STRAIGHT TO THE FACTORY AND BURN IT AND THE FOREST TO THE GROUND.
IF YOU PRESS IT, I'LL KILL YOU!
HA HA HA
YOUR LITTLE ELECTRIC GLOVE DOESN'T SCARE ME. PLUS, IT'S *TOO LATE.* I'VE ALREADY PRESSED IT.
OH NO...
SORT OF A DEAD MAN'S SWITCH. THE SECOND I LIFT MY FINGER OFF THE BUTTON, THE CREATURES ARE RELEASED.
WHICH MEANS... KILLING ME IS THE LAST THING ANY OF YOU WANT TO DO.
SO...KATELYN, WHY DON'T YOU INTRODUCE ME TO YOUR FRIENDS?
FINE... THIS IS M--

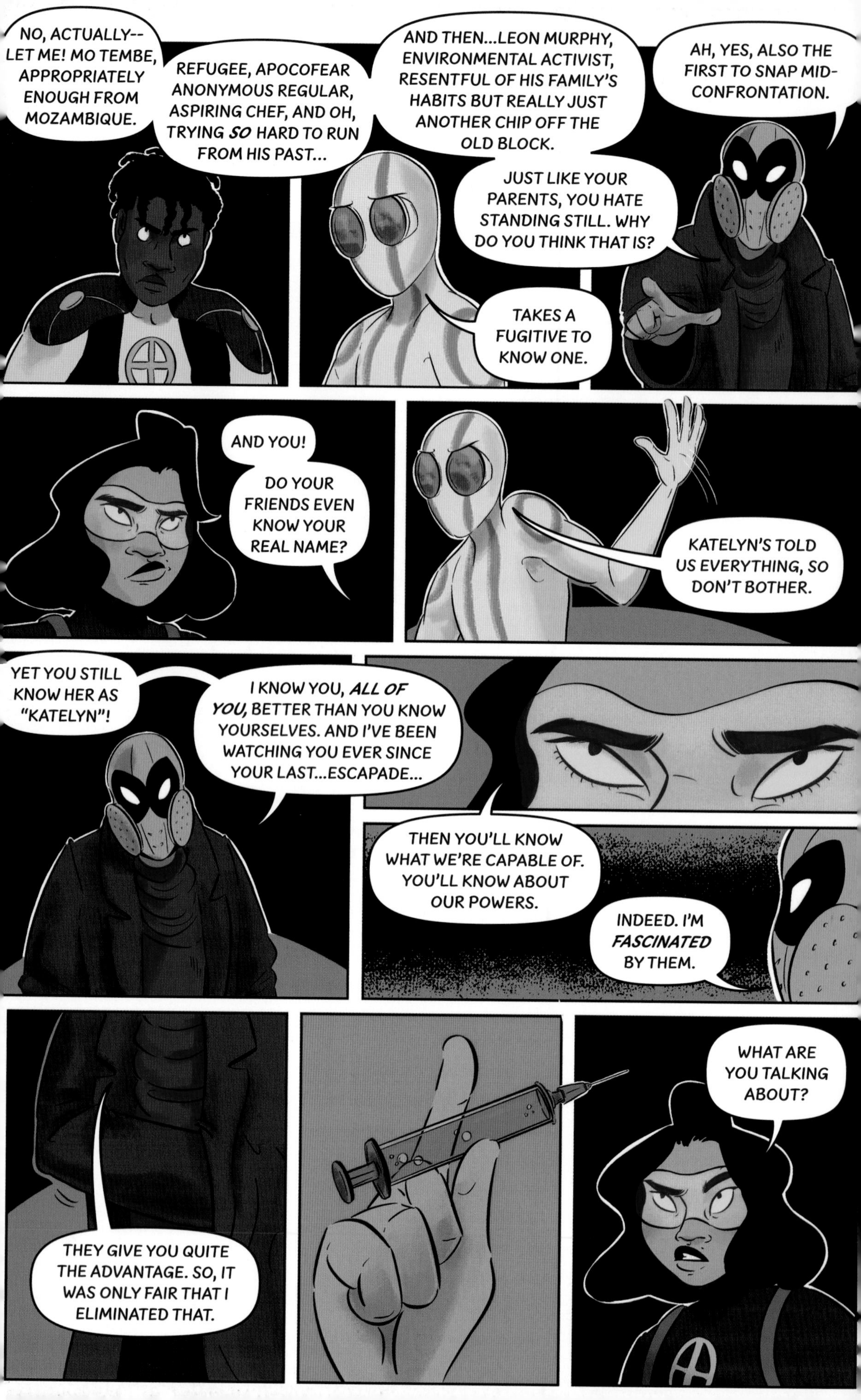
NO, ACTUALLY-- LET ME! MO TEMBE, APPROPRIATELY ENOUGH FROM MOZAMBIQUE.
REFUGEE, APOCOFEAR ANONYMOUS REGULAR, ASPIRING CHEF, AND OH, TRYING *SO* HARD TO RUN FROM HIS PAST...
AND THEN...LEON MURPHY, ENVIRONMENTAL ACTIVIST, RESENTFUL OF HIS FAMILY'S HABITS BUT REALLY JUST ANOTHER CHIP OFF THE OLD BLOCK.
JUST LIKE YOUR PARENTS, YOU HATE STANDING STILL. WHY DO YOU THINK THAT IS?
TAKES A FUGITIVE TO KNOW ONE.
AH, YES, ALSO THE FIRST TO SNAP MID-CONFRONTATION.
AND YOU!
DO YOUR FRIENDS EVEN KNOW YOUR REAL NAME?
KATELYN'S TOLD US EVERYTHING, SO DON'T BOTHER.
YET YOU STILL KNOW HER AS "KATELYN"!
I KNOW YOU, *ALL OF YOU,* BETTER THAN YOU KNOW YOURSELVES. AND I'VE BEEN WATCHING YOU EVER SINCE YOUR LAST...ESCAPADE...
THEN YOU'LL KNOW WHAT WE'RE CAPABLE OF. YOU'LL KNOW ABOUT OUR POWERS.
INDEED. I'M *FASCINATED* BY THEM.
THEY GIVE YOU QUITE THE ADVANTAGE. SO, IT WAS ONLY FAIR THAT I ELIMINATED THAT.
WHAT ARE YOU TALKING ABOUT?

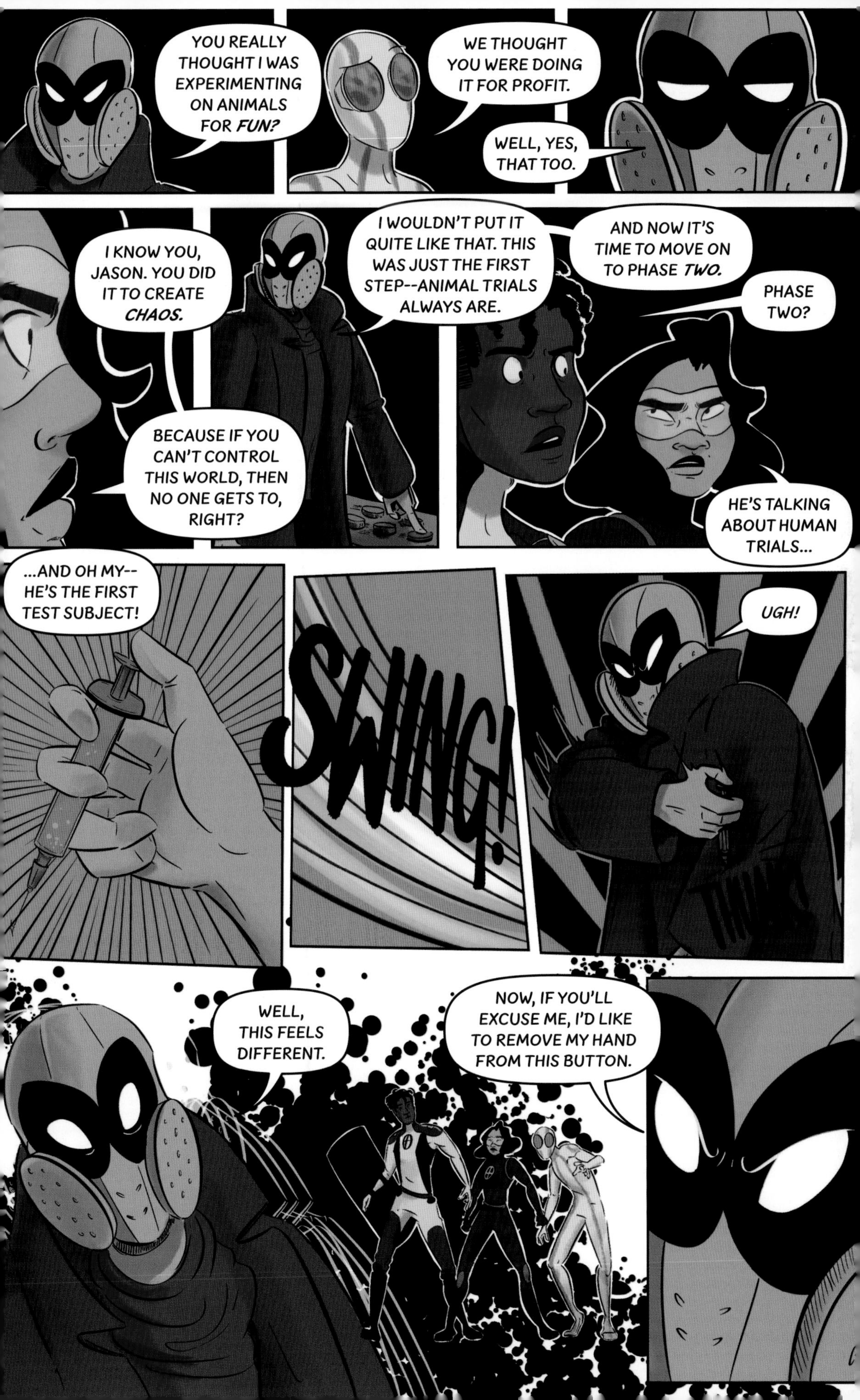
YOU REALLY THOUGHT I WAS EXPERIMENTING ON ANIMALS FOR *FUN?*
WE THOUGHT YOU WERE DOING IT FOR PROFIT.
WELL, YES, THAT TOO.
I KNOW YOU, JASON. YOU DID IT TO CREATE *CHAOS.*
BECAUSE IF YOU CAN'T CONTROL THIS WORLD, THEN NO ONE GETS TO, RIGHT?
I WOULDN'T PUT IT QUITE LIKE THAT. THIS WAS JUST THE FIRST STEP--ANIMAL TRIALS ALWAYS ARE.
AND NOW IT'S TIME TO MOVE ON TO PHASE *TWO.*
PHASE TWO?
HE'S TALKING ABOUT HUMAN TRIALS...
...AND OH MY-- HE'S THE FIRST TEST SUBJECT!
SWING!
UGH!
THUNK
WELL, THIS FEELS DIFFERENT.
NOW, IF YOU'LL EXCUSE ME, I'D LIKE TO REMOVE MY HAND FROM THIS BUTTON.

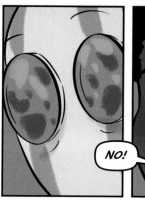

NO!

BEEP!

GROOOOWL!

CONTAINER DOORS OPENING!

HISSsss...

GRRR

RAAHH!

GRUUGH!

BRR!

BEEP!

SCREEEEEEE!

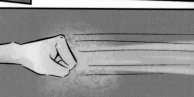

UGH!

HMM, THAT DID STING A BIT.

W-WHAT?

THAT, MY FRIEND, IS WHAT WE CALL "LEVELING THE PLAYING FIELD."

NOW, YOU ALL HAVE TWO OPTIONS. YOU CAN STAY HERE AND FIGHT ME, FAIR AND SQUARE, OR YOU CAN GO BACK TO THE FACTORY AND SAVE YOUR FRIENDS. BUT YOU CAN'T DO BOTH.

YOU MIGHT BE ABLE TO BEAT ME, BUT IT WILL BE AT THE COST OF YOUR FRIENDS' *LIVES.* AND YOU MIGHT BE ABLE TO SAVE YOUR FRIENDS, BUT IT WILL BE AT THE COST OF MY ESCAPE.

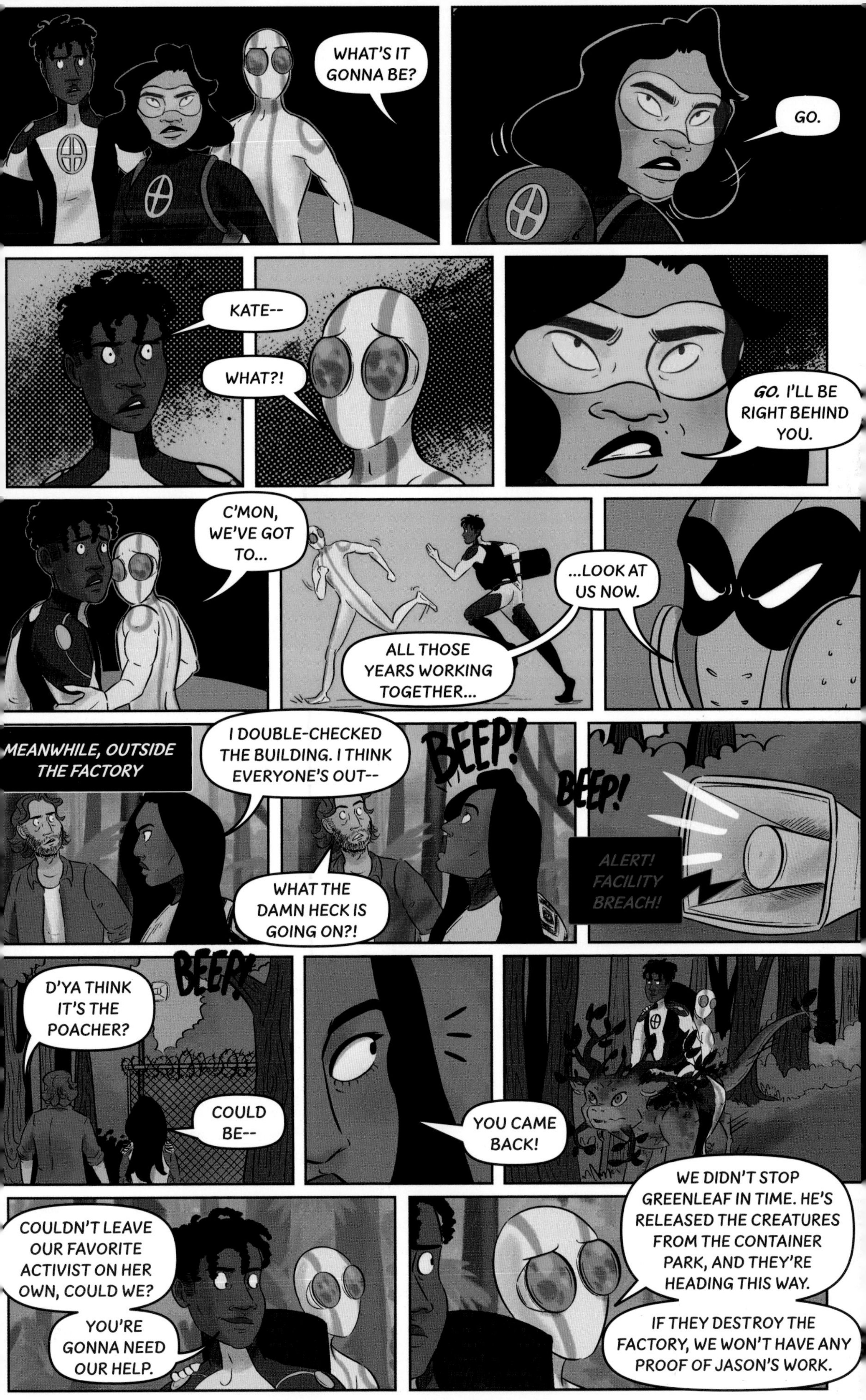
WHAT'S IT GONNA BE?
GO.
KATE--
WHAT?!
GO. I'LL BE RIGHT BEHIND YOU.
C'MON, WE'VE GOT TO...
...LOOK AT US NOW.
ALL THOSE YEARS WORKING TOGETHER...
MEANWHILE, OUTSIDE THE FACTORY
I DOUBLE-CHECKED THE BUILDING. I THINK EVERYONE'S OUT--
BEEP!
WHAT THE DAMN HECK IS GOING ON?!
BEEP!
ALERT! FACILITY BREACH!
D'YA THINK IT'S THE POACHER?
BEEP!
COULD BE--
YOU CAME BACK!
COULDN'T LEAVE OUR FAVORITE ACTIVIST ON HER OWN, COULD WE?
YOU'RE GONNA NEED OUR HELP.
WE DIDN'T STOP GREENLEAF IN TIME. HE'S RELEASED THE CREATURES FROM THE CONTAINER PARK, AND THEY'RE HEADING THIS WAY.
IF THEY DESTROY THE FACTORY, WE WON'T HAVE ANY PROOF OF JASON'S WORK.

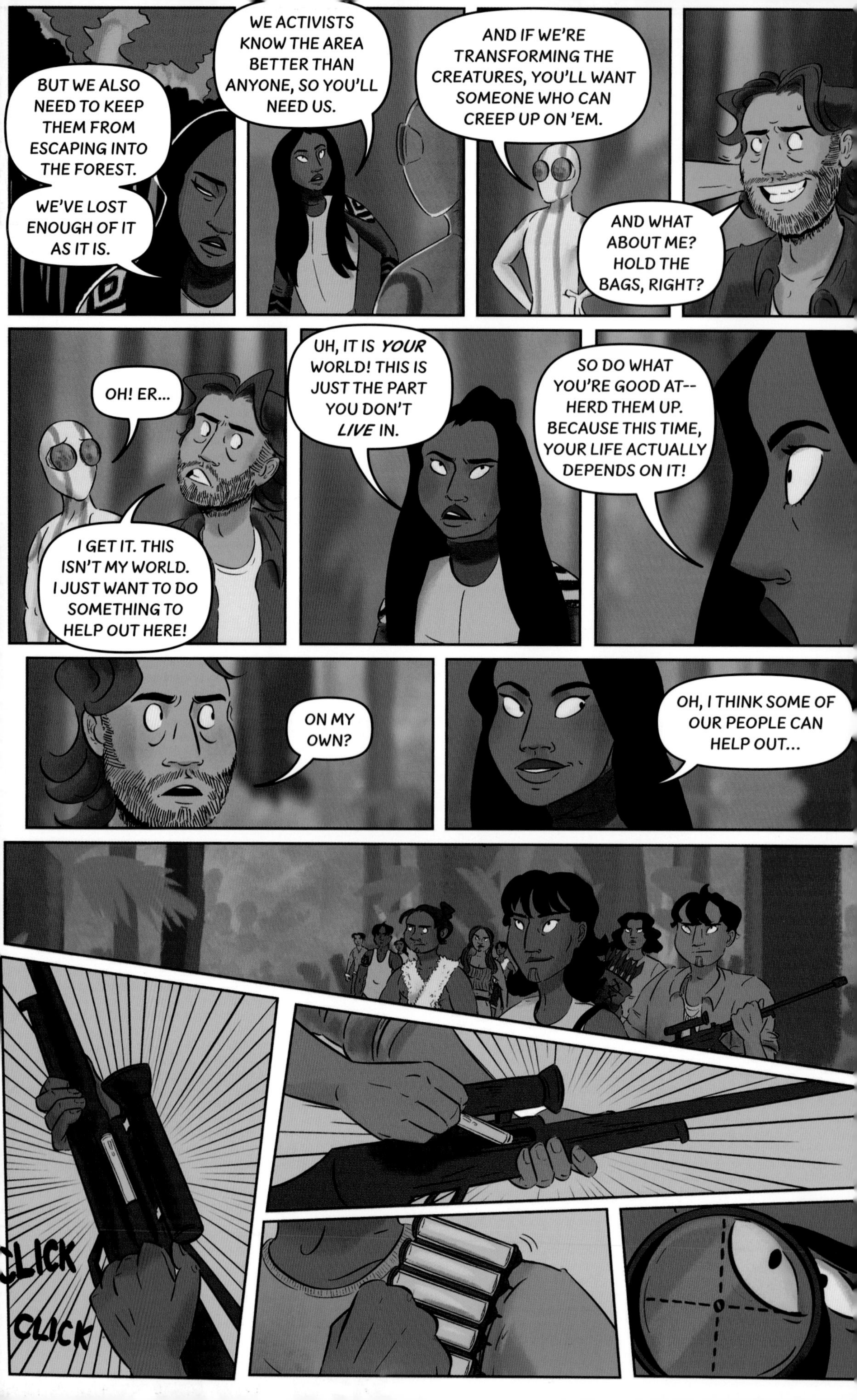
BUT WE ALSO NEED TO KEEP THEM FROM ESCAPING INTO THE FOREST.
WE'VE LOST ENOUGH OF IT AS IT IS.
WE ACTIVISTS KNOW THE AREA BETTER THAN ANYONE, SO YOU'LL NEED US.
AND IF WE'RE TRANSFORMING THE CREATURES, YOU'LL WANT SOMEONE WHO CAN CREEP UP ON 'EM.
AND WHAT ABOUT ME? HOLD THE BAGS, RIGHT?
OH! ER...
I GET IT. THIS ISN'T MY WORLD. I JUST WANT TO DO SOMETHING TO HELP OUT HERE!
UH, IT IS *YOUR* WORLD! THIS IS JUST THE PART YOU DON'T *LIVE* IN.
SO DO WHAT YOU'RE GOOD AT-- HERD THEM UP. BECAUSE THIS TIME, YOUR LIFE ACTUALLY DEPENDS ON IT!
ON MY OWN?
OH, I THINK SOME OF OUR PEOPLE CAN HELP OUT...
CLICK
CLICK

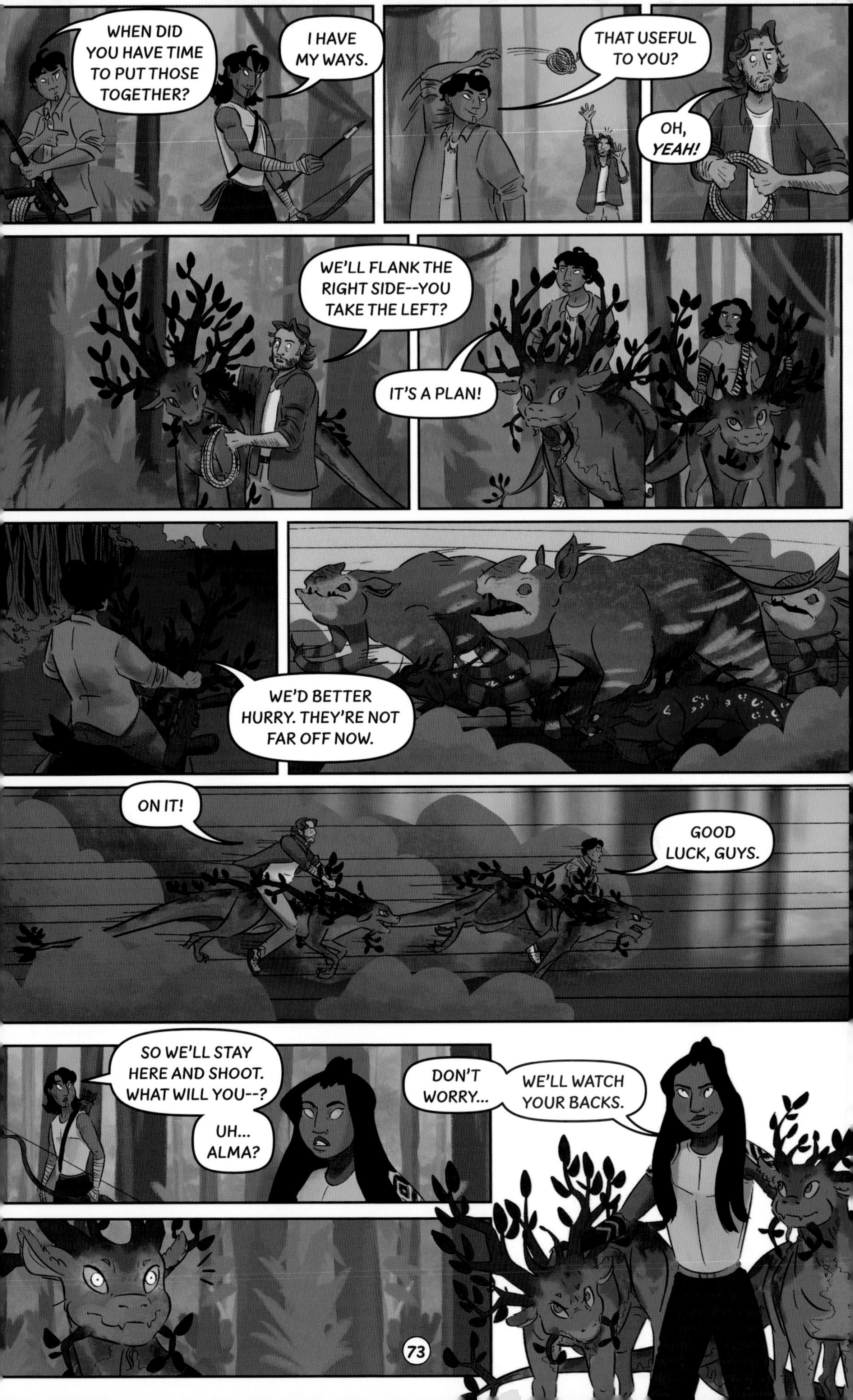

WHEN DID YOU HAVE TIME TO PUT THOSE TOGETHER?
I HAVE MY WAYS.
THAT USEFUL TO YOU?
OH, *YEAH!*
WE'LL FLANK THE RIGHT SIDE--YOU TAKE THE LEFT?
IT'S A PLAN!
WE'D BETTER HURRY. THEY'RE NOT FAR OFF NOW.
ON IT!
GOOD LUCK, GUYS.
SO WE'LL STAY HERE AND SHOOT. WHAT WILL YOU--?
UH... ALMA?
DON'T WORRY...
WE'LL WATCH YOUR BACKS.

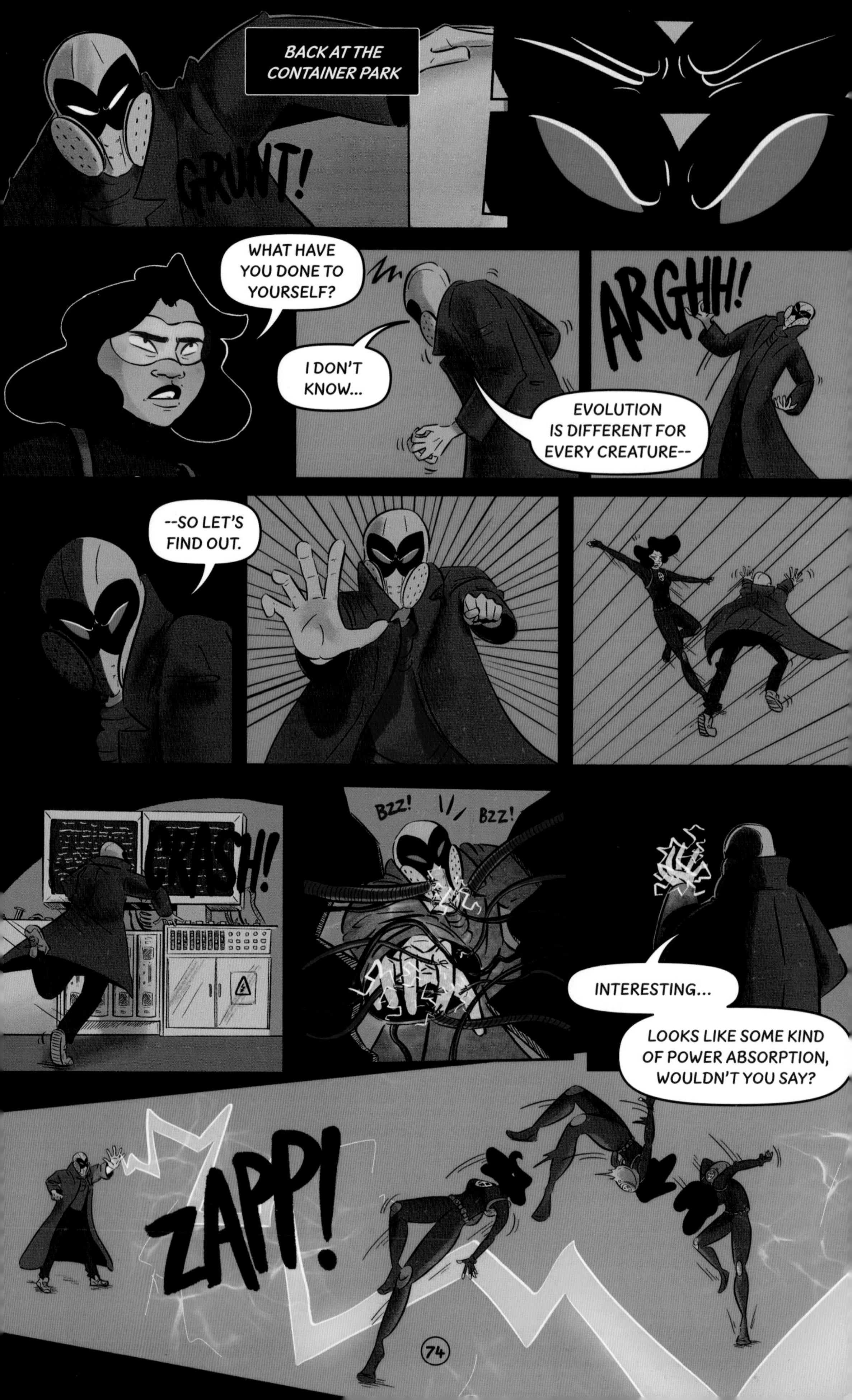
BACK AT THE CONTAINER PARK
GRUNT!
WHAT HAVE YOU DONE TO YOURSELF?
I DON'T KNOW...
EVOLUTION IS DIFFERENT FOR EVERY CREATURE--
ARGHH!
--SO LET'S FIND OUT.
CRASH!
BZZ!
BZZ!
INTERESTING...
LOOKS LIKE SOME KIND OF POWER ABSORPTION, WOULDN'T YOU SAY?
ZAPP!

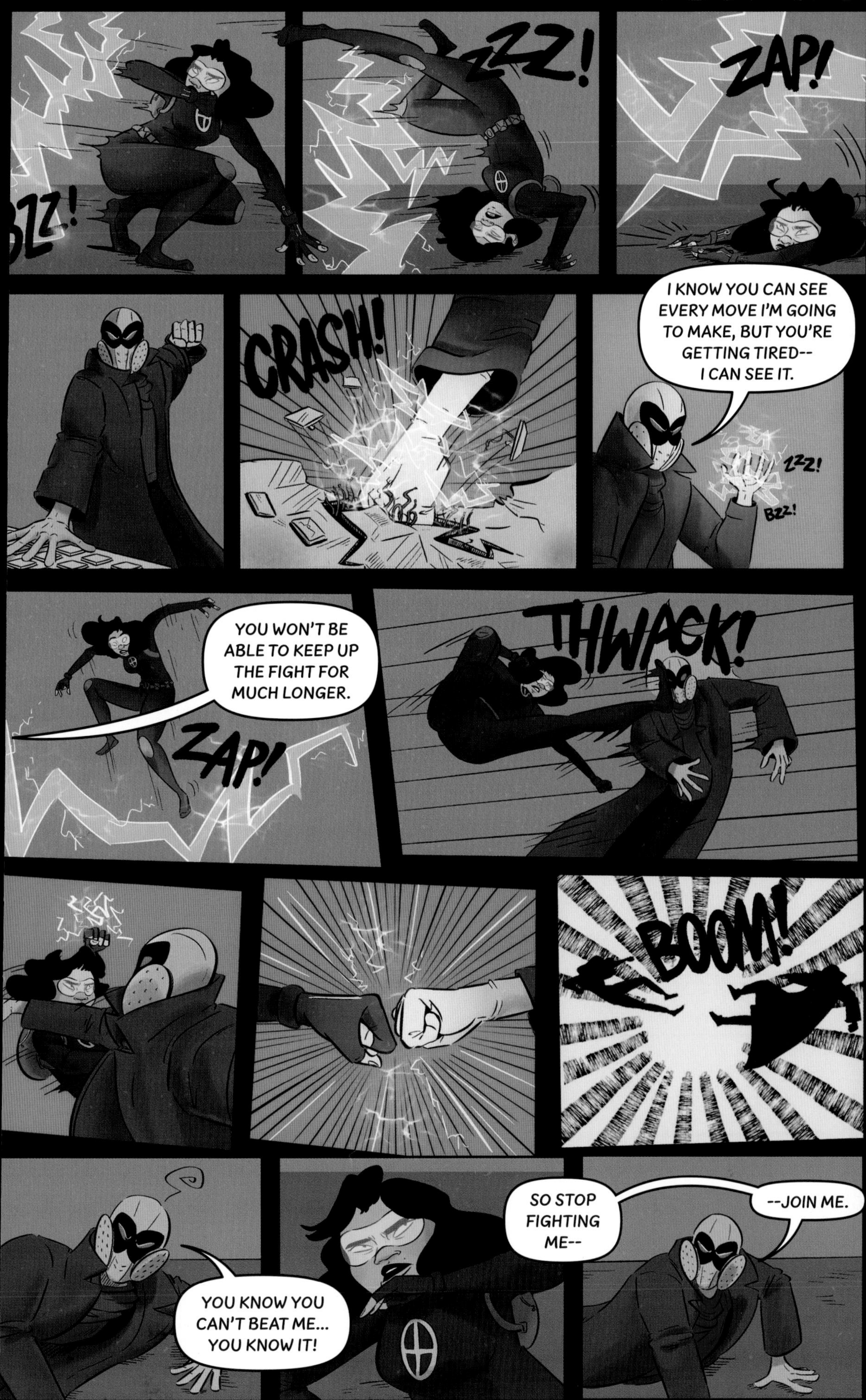
BZZ!
ZZZZ!
ZAP!
CRASH!
I KNOW YOU CAN SEE EVERY MOVE I'M GOING TO MAKE, BUT YOU'RE GETTING TIRED-- I CAN SEE IT.
ZZZ!
BZZ!
YOU WON'T BE ABLE TO KEEP UP THE FIGHT FOR MUCH LONGER.
ZAP!
THWACK!
BOOM!
YOU KNOW YOU CAN'T BEAT ME... YOU KNOW IT!
SO STOP FIGHTING ME--
--JOIN ME.

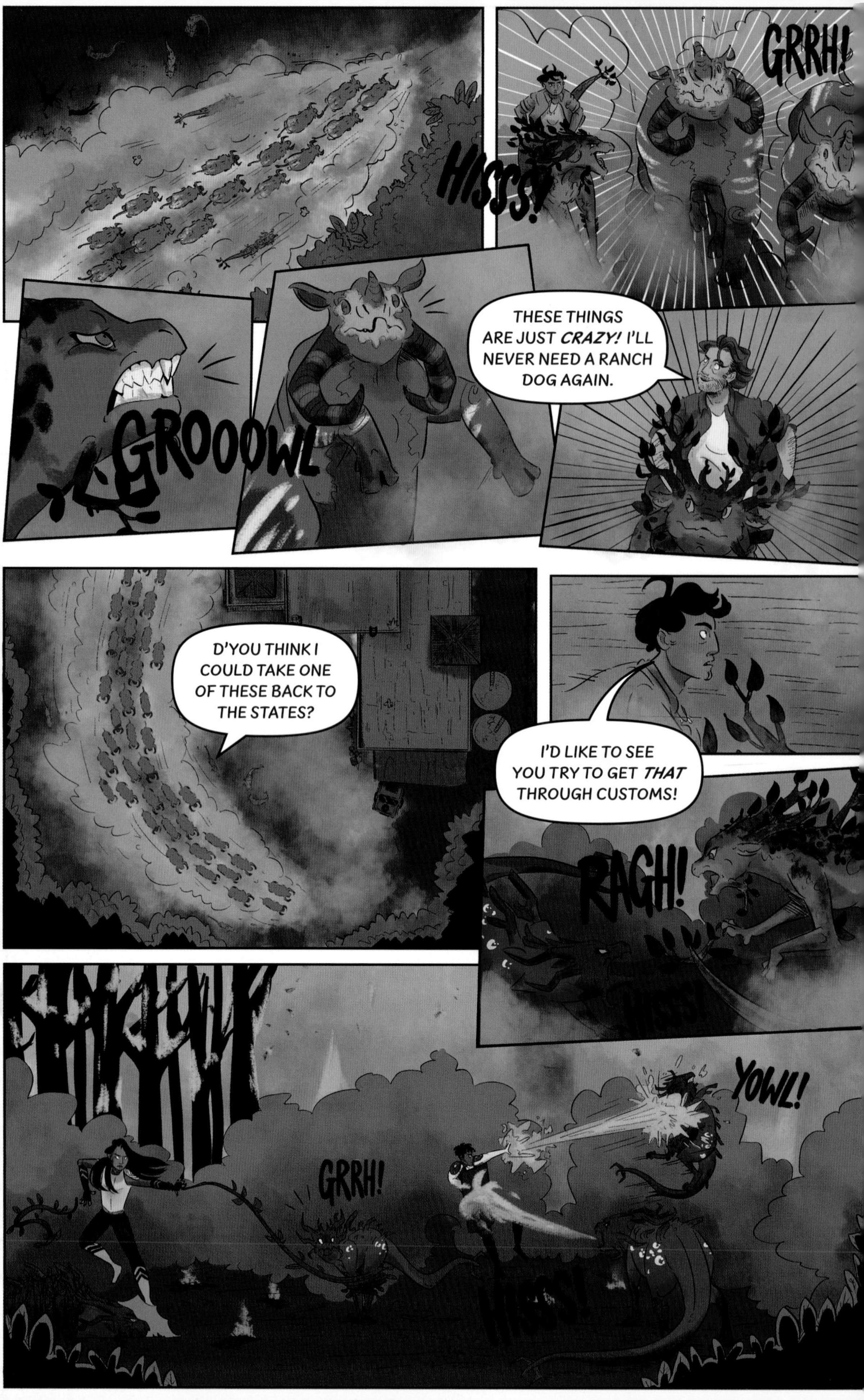

HISSS!
GRRH!
GROOOWL
THESE THINGS ARE JUST *CRAZY!* I'LL NEVER NEED A RANCH DOG AGAIN.
D'YOU THINK I COULD TAKE ONE OF THESE BACK TO THE STATES?
I'D LIKE TO SEE YOU TRY TO GET *THAT* THROUGH CUSTOMS!
RAGH!
YOWL!
GRRH!

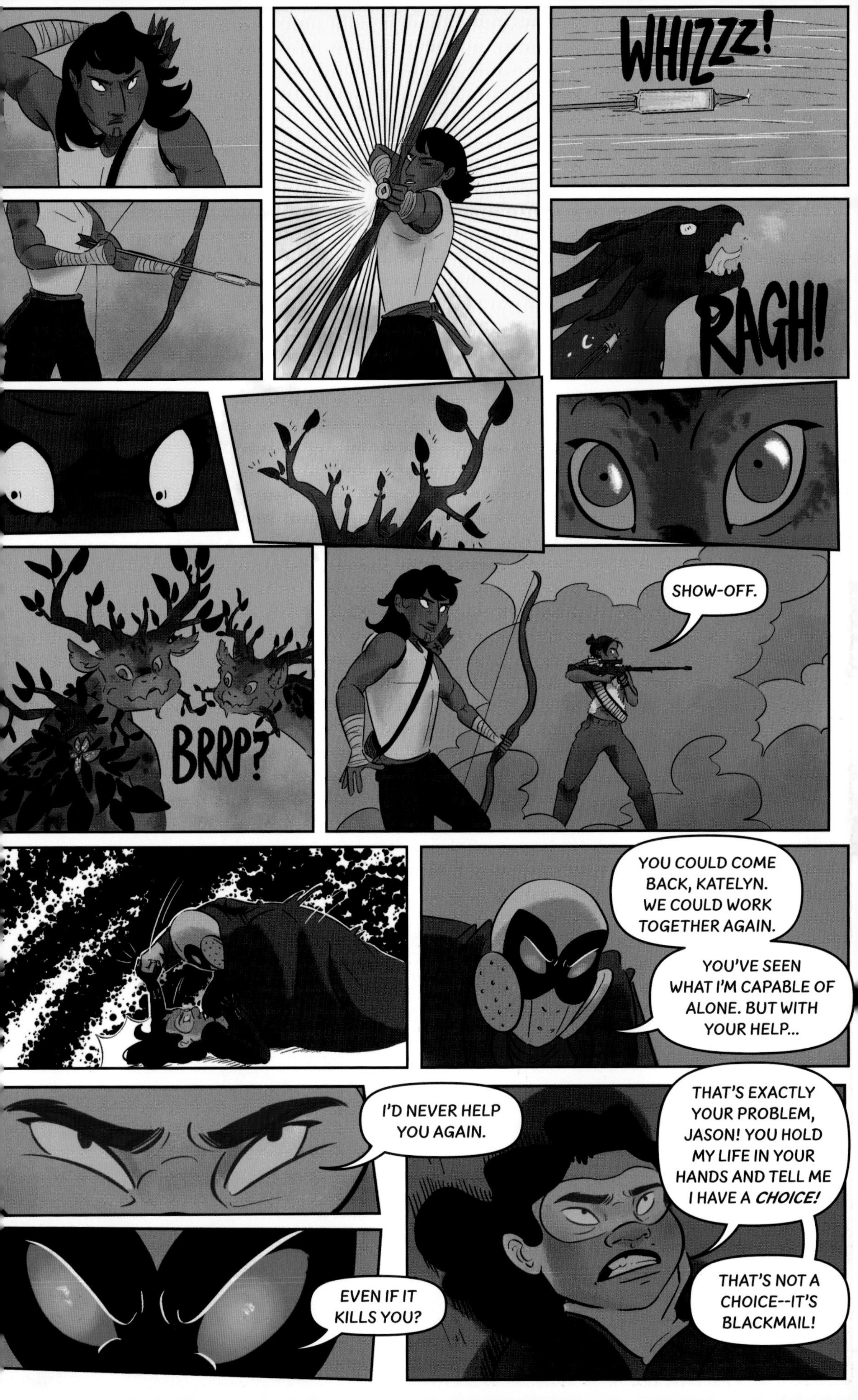
WHIZZZ!
RAGH!
BRRP?
SHOW-OFF.
YOU COULD COME BACK, KATELYN. WE COULD WORK TOGETHER AGAIN.
YOU'VE SEEN WHAT I'M CAPABLE OF ALONE. BUT WITH YOUR HELP...
I'D NEVER HELP YOU AGAIN.
EVEN IF IT KILLS YOU?
THAT'S EXACTLY YOUR PROBLEM, JASON! YOU HOLD MY LIFE IN YOUR HANDS AND TELL ME I HAVE A CHOICE!
THAT'S NOT A CHOICE--IT'S BLACKMAIL!

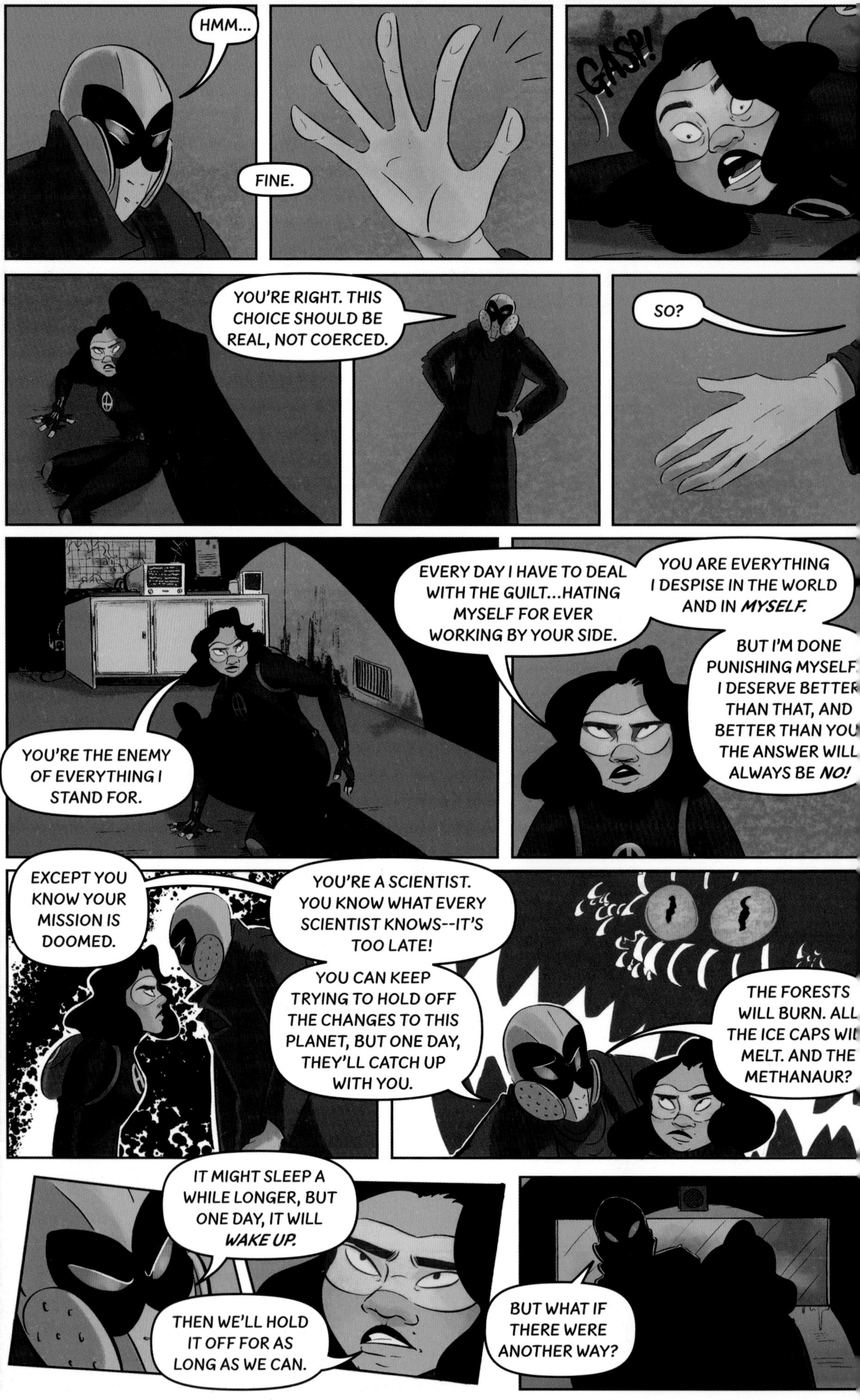
HMM...
FINE.
GASP!
YOU'RE RIGHT. THIS CHOICE SHOULD BE REAL, NOT COERCED.
SO?
YOU'RE THE ENEMY OF EVERYTHING I STAND FOR.
EVERY DAY I HAVE TO DEAL WITH THE GUILT...HATING MYSELF FOR EVER WORKING BY YOUR SIDE.
YOU ARE EVERYTHING I DESPISE IN THE WORLD AND IN *MYSELF.*
BUT I'M DONE PUNISHING MYSELF. I DESERVE BETTER THAN THAT, AND BETTER THAN YOU. THE ANSWER WILL ALWAYS BE *NO!*
EXCEPT YOU KNOW YOUR MISSION IS DOOMED.
YOU'RE A SCIENTIST. YOU KNOW WHAT EVERY SCIENTIST KNOWS--IT'S TOO LATE!
YOU CAN KEEP TRYING TO HOLD OFF THE CHANGES TO THIS PLANET, BUT ONE DAY, THEY'LL CATCH UP WITH YOU.
THE FORESTS WILL BURN. ALL THE ICE CAPS WILL MELT. AND THE METHANAUR?
IT MIGHT SLEEP A WHILE LONGER, BUT ONE DAY, IT WILL *WAKE UP.*
THEN WE'LL HOLD IT OFF FOR AS LONG AS WE CAN.
BUT WHAT IF THERE WERE ANOTHER WAY?

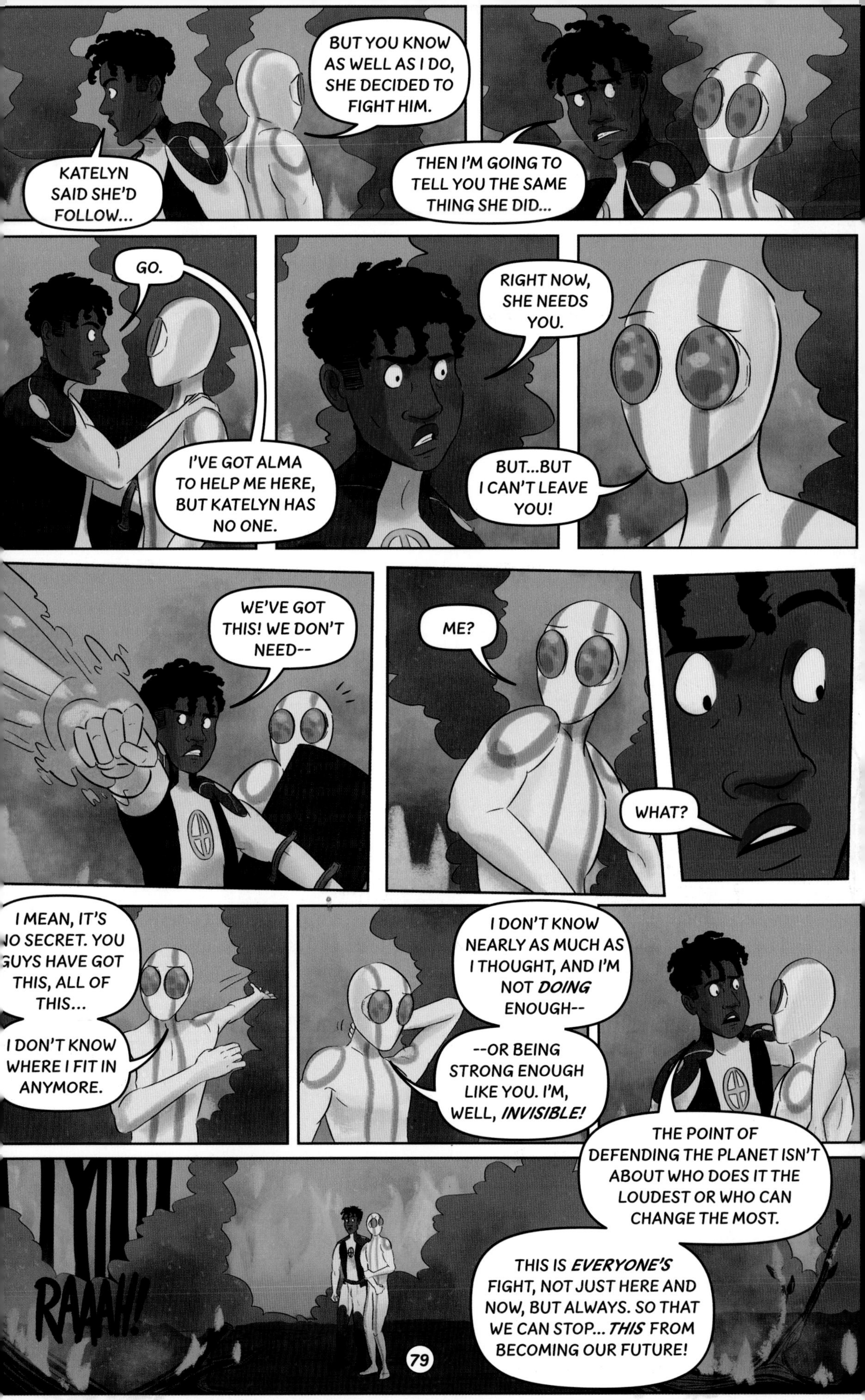
KATELYN SAID SHE'D FOLLOW...
BUT YOU KNOW AS WELL AS I DO, SHE DECIDED TO FIGHT HIM.
THEN I'M GOING TO TELL YOU THE SAME THING SHE DID...
GO.
I'VE GOT ALMA TO HELP ME HERE, BUT KATELYN HAS NO ONE.
RIGHT NOW, SHE NEEDS YOU.
BUT...BUT I CAN'T LEAVE YOU!
WE'VE GOT THIS! WE DON'T NEED--
ME?
WHAT?
I MEAN, IT'S NO SECRET. YOU GUYS HAVE GOT THIS, ALL OF THIS...
I DON'T KNOW WHERE I FIT IN ANYMORE.
I DON'T KNOW NEARLY AS MUCH AS I THOUGHT, AND I'M NOT *DOING* ENOUGH--
--OR BEING STRONG ENOUGH LIKE YOU. I'M, WELL, *INVISIBLE!*
THE POINT OF DEFENDING THE PLANET ISN'T ABOUT WHO DOES IT THE LOUDEST OR WHO CAN CHANGE THE MOST.
THIS IS *EVERYONE'S* FIGHT, NOT JUST HERE AND NOW, BUT ALWAYS. SO THAT WE CAN STOP... *THIS* FROM BECOMING OUR FUTURE!
RAAAH!

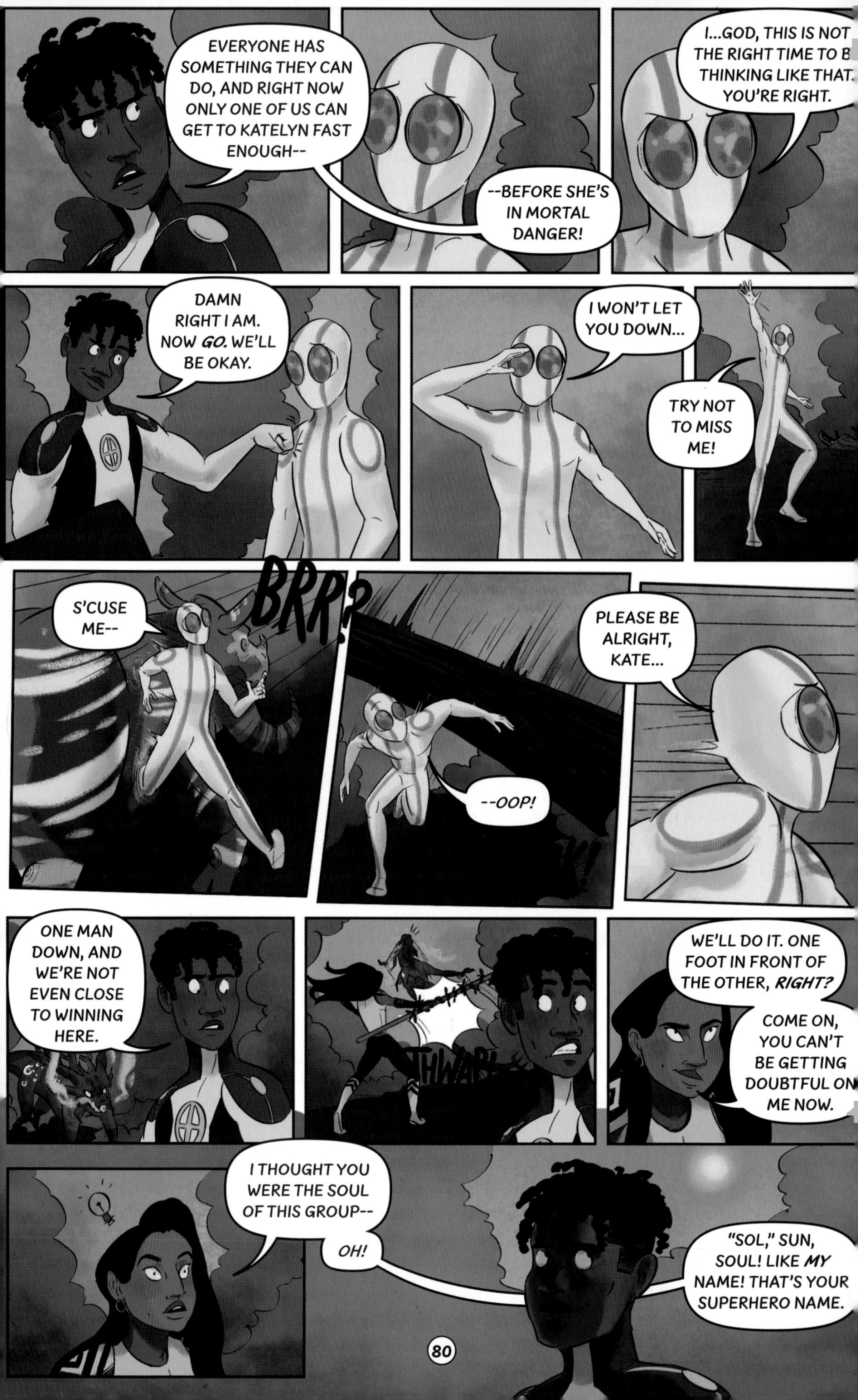
EVERYONE HAS SOMETHING THEY CAN DO, AND RIGHT NOW ONLY ONE OF US CAN GET TO KATELYN FAST ENOUGH--
--BEFORE SHE'S IN MORTAL DANGER!
I...GOD, THIS IS NOT THE RIGHT TIME TO B THINKING LIKE THAT. YOU'RE RIGHT.
DAMN RIGHT I AM. NOW GO. WE'LL BE OKAY.
I WON'T LET YOU DOWN...
TRY NOT TO MISS ME!
S'CUSE ME--
BRR?
--OOP!
PLEASE BE ALRIGHT, KATE...
ONE MAN DOWN, AND WE'RE NOT EVEN CLOSE TO WINNING HERE.
WE'LL DO IT. ONE FOOT IN FRONT OF THE OTHER, RIGHT?
COME ON, YOU CAN'T BE GETTING DOUBTFUL ON ME NOW.
I THOUGHT YOU WERE THE SOUL OF THIS GROUP--
OH!
"SOL," SUN, SOUL! LIKE MY NAME! THAT'S YOUR SUPERHERO NAME.

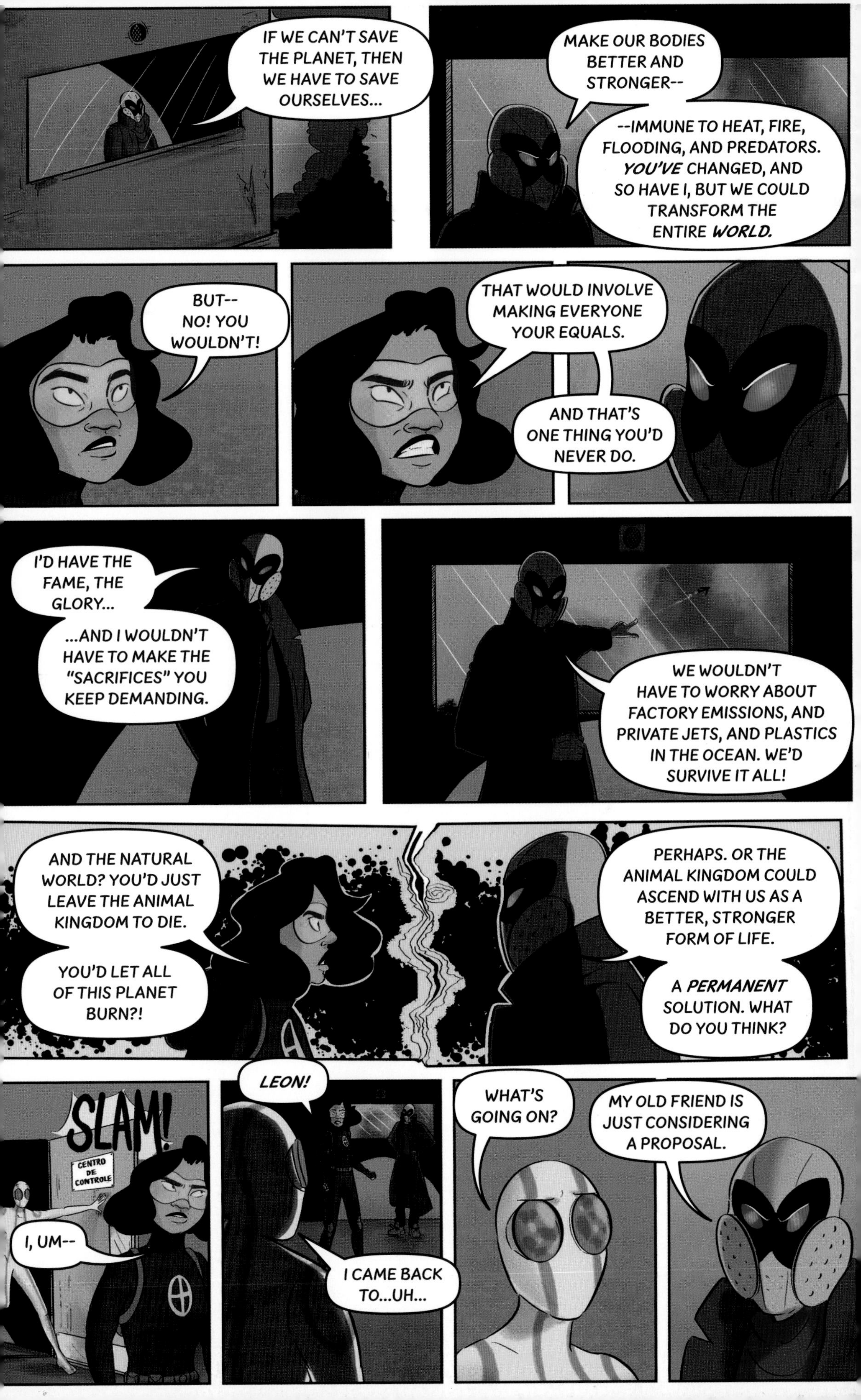
IF WE CAN'T SAVE THE PLANET, THEN WE HAVE TO SAVE OURSELVES...
MAKE OUR BODIES BETTER AND STRONGER--
--IMMUNE TO HEAT, FIRE, FLOODING, AND PREDATORS. YOU'VE CHANGED, AND SO HAVE I, BUT WE COULD TRANSFORM THE ENTIRE WORLD.
BUT-- NO! YOU WOULDN'T!
THAT WOULD INVOLVE MAKING EVERYONE YOUR EQUALS.
AND THAT'S ONE THING YOU'D NEVER DO.
I'D HAVE THE FAME, THE GLORY...
...AND I WOULDN'T HAVE TO MAKE THE "SACRIFICES" YOU KEEP DEMANDING.
WE WOULDN'T HAVE TO WORRY ABOUT FACTORY EMISSIONS, AND PRIVATE JETS, AND PLASTICS IN THE OCEAN. WE'D SURVIVE IT ALL!
AND THE NATURAL WORLD? YOU'D JUST LEAVE THE ANIMAL KINGDOM TO DIE.
YOU'D LET ALL OF THIS PLANET BURN?!
PERHAPS. OR THE ANIMAL KINGDOM COULD ASCEND WITH US AS A BETTER, STRONGER FORM OF LIFE.
A PERMANENT SOLUTION. WHAT DO YOU THINK?
SLAM!
CENTRO DE CONTROLE
I, UM--
LEON!
I CAME BACK TO...UH...
WHAT'S GOING ON?
MY OLD FRIEND IS JUST CONSIDERING A PROPOSAL.

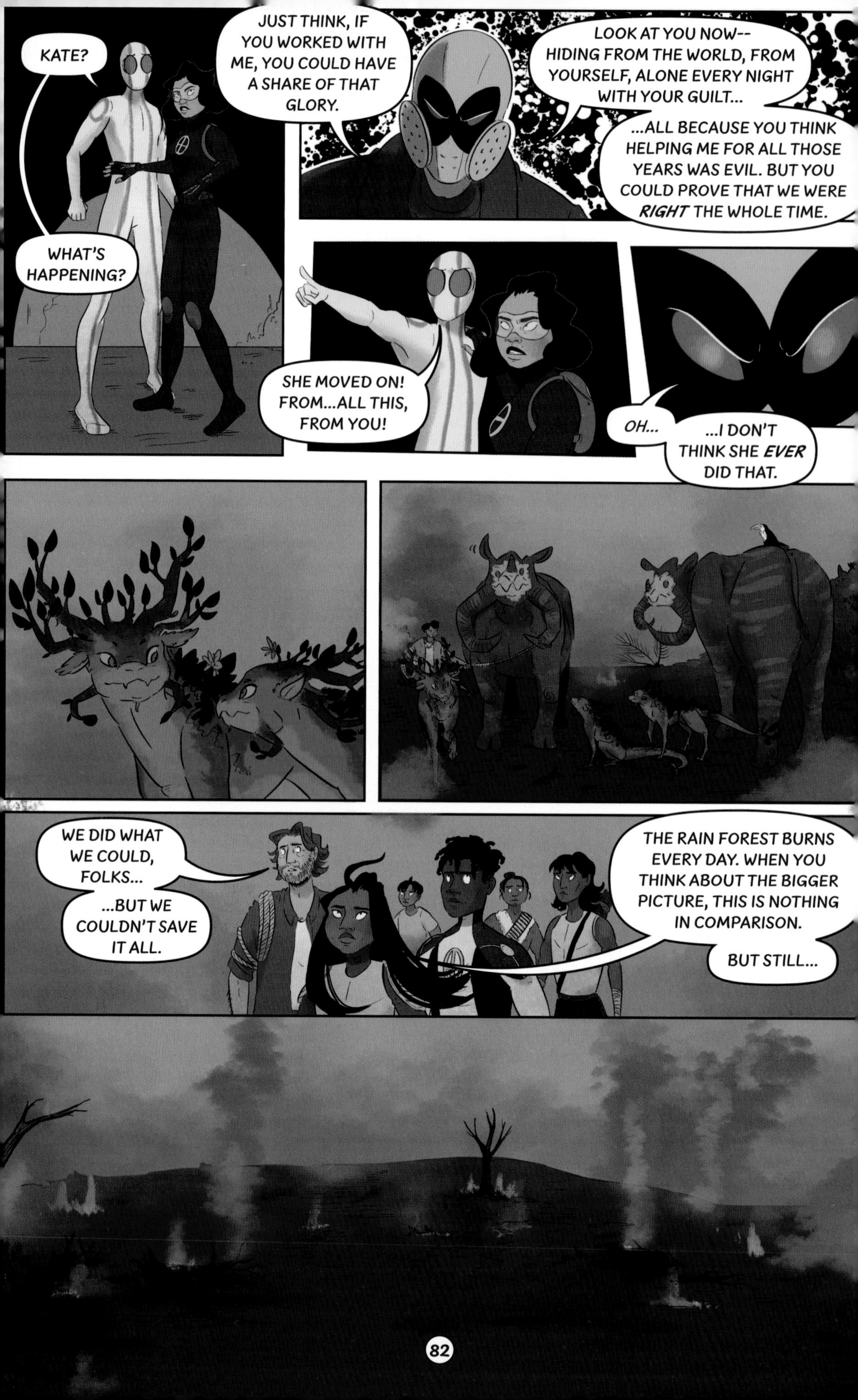
KATE?
WHAT'S HAPPENING?
JUST THINK, IF YOU WORKED WITH ME, YOU COULD HAVE A SHARE OF THAT GLORY.
LOOK AT YOU NOW-- HIDING FROM THE WORLD, FROM YOURSELF, ALONE EVERY NIGHT WITH YOUR GUILT...
...ALL BECAUSE YOU THINK HELPING ME FOR ALL THOSE YEARS WAS EVIL. BUT YOU COULD PROVE THAT WE WERE *RIGHT* THE WHOLE TIME.
SHE MOVED ON! FROM...ALL THIS, FROM YOU!
OH...
...I DON'T THINK SHE *EVER* DID THAT.
WE DID WHAT WE COULD, FOLKS...
...BUT WE COULDN'T SAVE IT ALL.
THE RAIN FOREST BURNS EVERY DAY. WHEN YOU THINK ABOUT THE BIGGER PICTURE, THIS IS NOTHING IN COMPARISON.
BUT STILL...

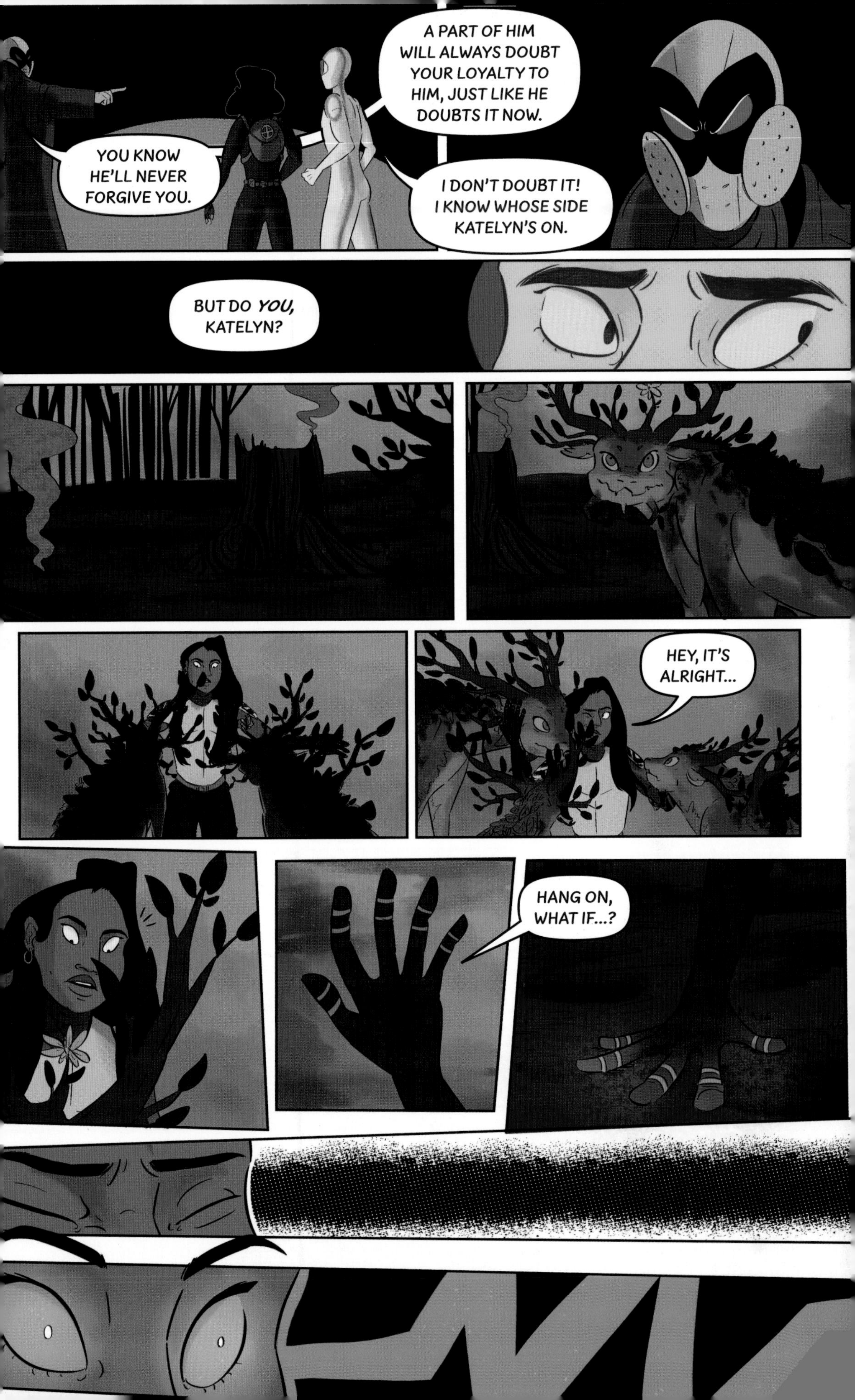
A PART OF HIM WILL ALWAYS DOUBT YOUR LOYALTY TO HIM, JUST LIKE HE DOUBTS IT NOW.
YOU KNOW HE'LL NEVER FORGIVE YOU.
I DON'T DOUBT IT! I KNOW WHOSE SIDE KATELYN'S ON.
BUT DO *YOU*, KATELYN?
HEY, IT'S ALRIGHT...
HANG ON, WHAT IF...?

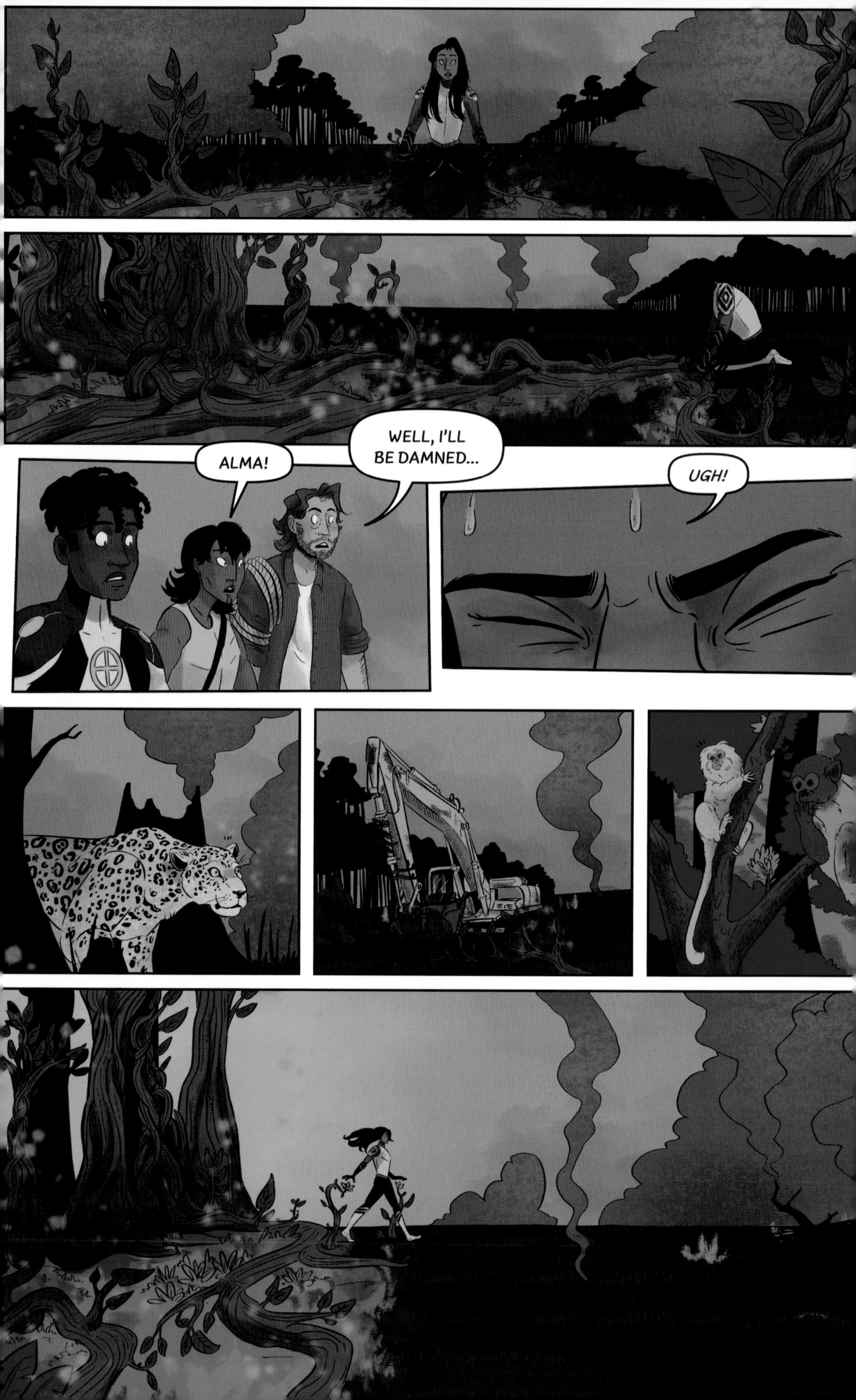
ALMA!
WELL, I'LL BE DAMNED...
UGH!

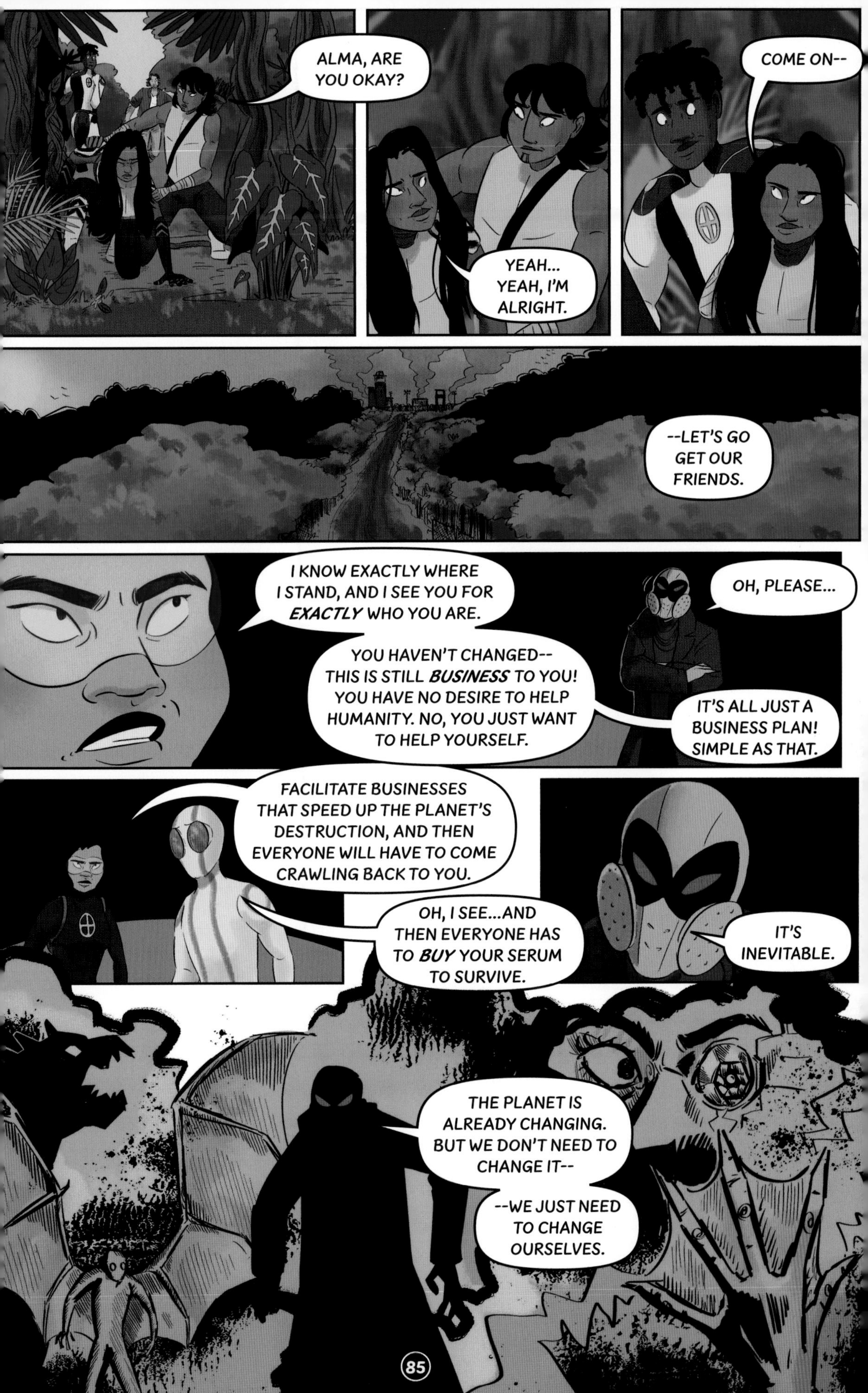
ALMA, ARE YOU OKAY?
YEAH... YEAH, I'M ALRIGHT.
COME ON--
--LET'S GO GET OUR FRIENDS.
I KNOW EXACTLY WHERE I STAND, AND I SEE YOU FOR *EXACTLY* WHO YOU ARE.
OH, PLEASE...
YOU HAVEN'T CHANGED-- THIS IS STILL *BUSINESS* TO YOU! YOU HAVE NO DESIRE TO HELP HUMANITY. NO, YOU JUST WANT TO HELP YOURSELF.
IT'S ALL JUST A BUSINESS PLAN! SIMPLE AS THAT.
FACILITATE BUSINESSES THAT SPEED UP THE PLANET'S DESTRUCTION, AND THEN EVERYONE WILL HAVE TO COME CRAWLING BACK TO YOU.
OH, I SEE...AND THEN EVERYONE HAS TO *BUY* YOUR SERUM TO SURVIVE.
IT'S INEVITABLE.
THE PLANET IS ALREADY CHANGING. BUT WE DON'T NEED TO CHANGE IT--
--WE JUST NEED TO CHANGE OURSELVES.

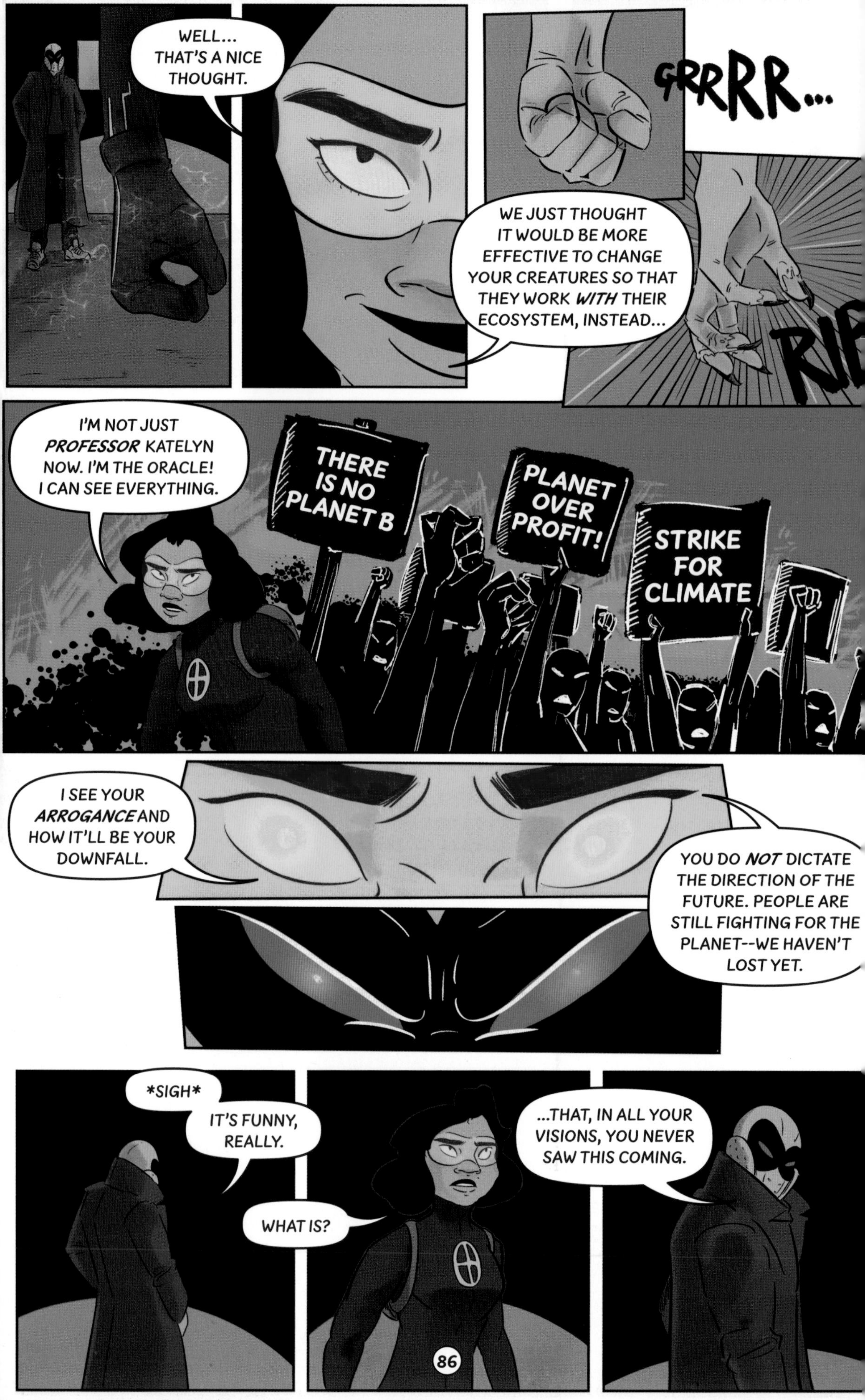
WELL... THAT'S A NICE THOUGHT.
GRRRR...
WE JUST THOUGHT IT WOULD BE MORE EFFECTIVE TO CHANGE YOUR CREATURES SO THAT THEY WORK *WITH* THEIR ECOSYSTEM, INSTEAD...
I'M NOT JUST *PROFESSOR* KATELYN NOW. I'M THE ORACLE! I CAN SEE EVERYTHING.
THERE IS NO PLANET B
PLANET OVER PROFIT!
STRIKE FOR CLIMATE
I SEE YOUR *ARROGANCE* AND HOW IT'LL BE YOUR DOWNFALL.
YOU DO *NOT* DICTATE THE DIRECTION OF THE FUTURE. PEOPLE ARE STILL FIGHTING FOR THE PLANET--WE HAVEN'T LOST YET.
SIGH
IT'S FUNNY, REALLY.
WHAT IS?
...THAT, IN ALL YOUR VISIONS, YOU NEVER SAW THIS COMING.

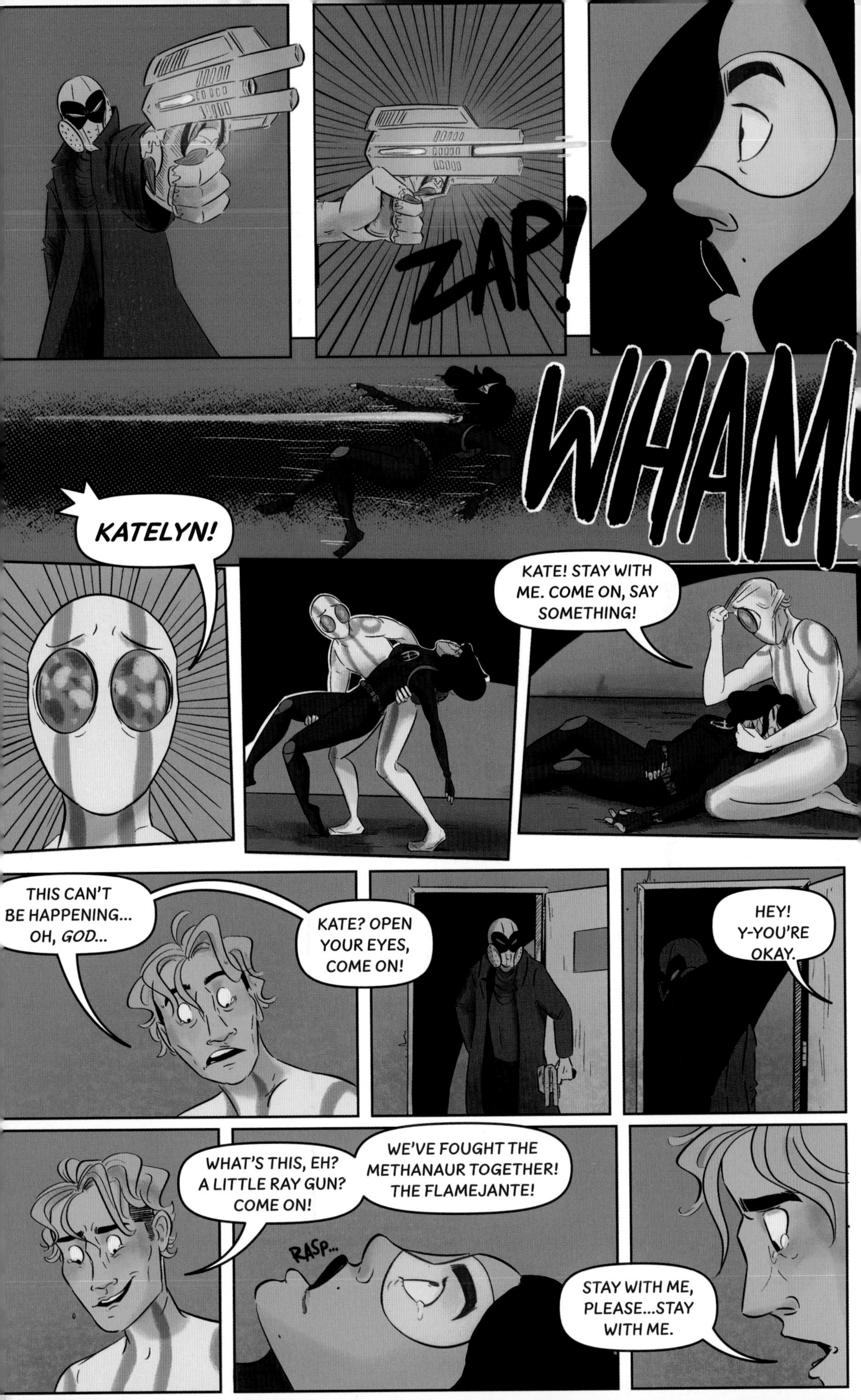
ZAP!
WHAM!
KATELYN!
KATE! STAY WITH ME. COME ON, SAY SOMETHING!
THIS CAN'T BE HAPPENING... OH, *GOD*...
KATE? OPEN YOUR EYES, COME ON!
HEY! Y-YOU'RE OKAY.
WHAT'S THIS, EH? A LITTLE RAY GUN? COME ON!
WE'VE FOUGHT THE METHANAUR TOGETHER! THE FLAMEJANTE!
RASP...
STAY WITH ME, PLEASE...STAY WITH ME.

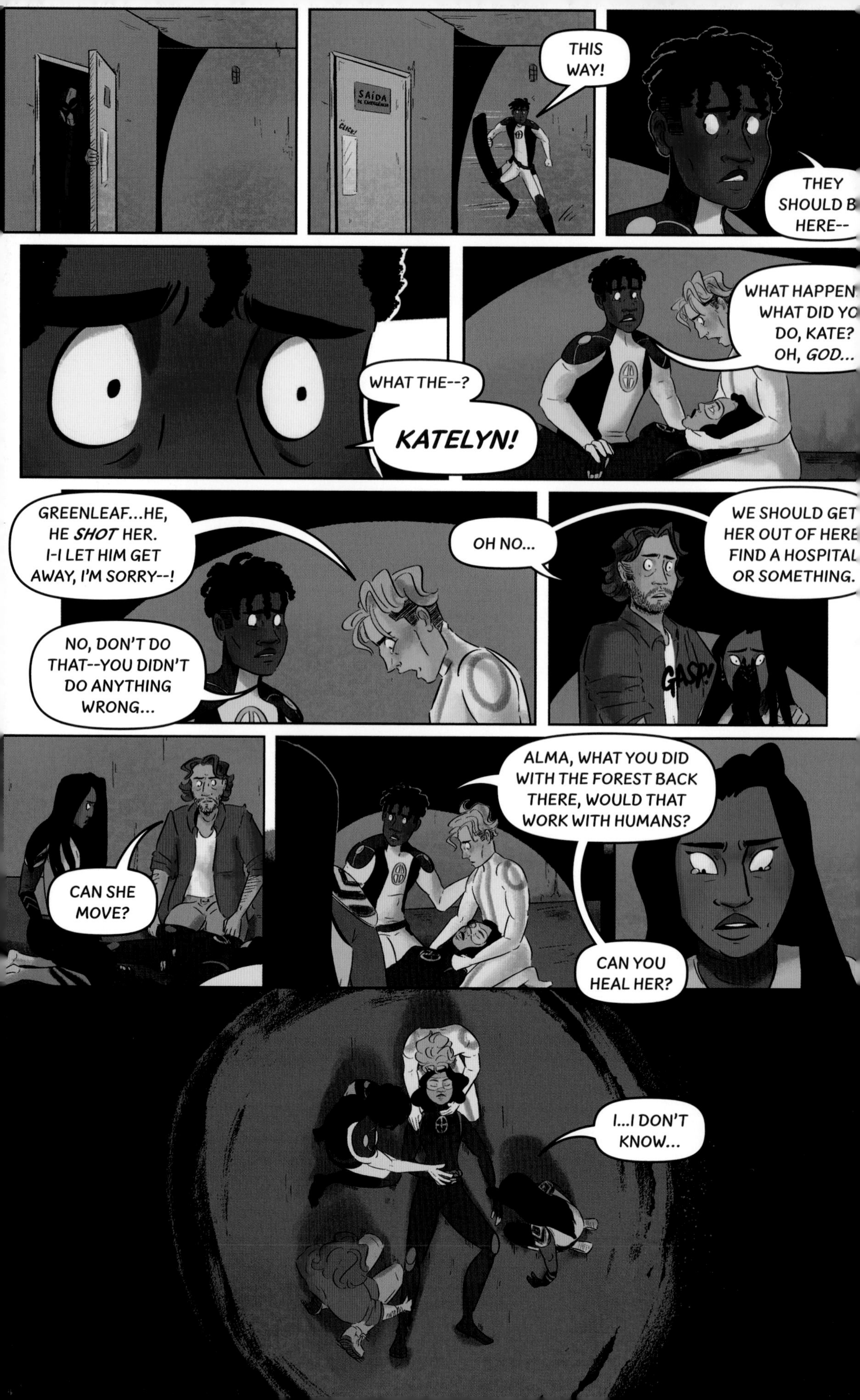
SAÍDA DE EMERGÊNCIA
CLICK!
THIS WAY!
THEY SHOULD B HERE--
WHAT THE--?
KATELYN!
WHAT HAPPEN WHAT DID YO DO, KATE? OH, *GOD*...
GREENLEAF...HE, HE *SHOT* HER. I-I LET HIM GET AWAY, I'M SORRY--!
NO, DON'T DO THAT--YOU DIDN'T DO ANYTHING WRONG...
OH NO...
WE SHOULD GET HER OUT OF HERE FIND A HOSPITAL OR SOMETHING.
GASP!
CAN SHE MOVE?
ALMA, WHAT YOU DID WITH THE FOREST BACK THERE, WOULD THAT WORK WITH HUMANS?
CAN YOU HEAL HER?
I...I DON'T KNOW...

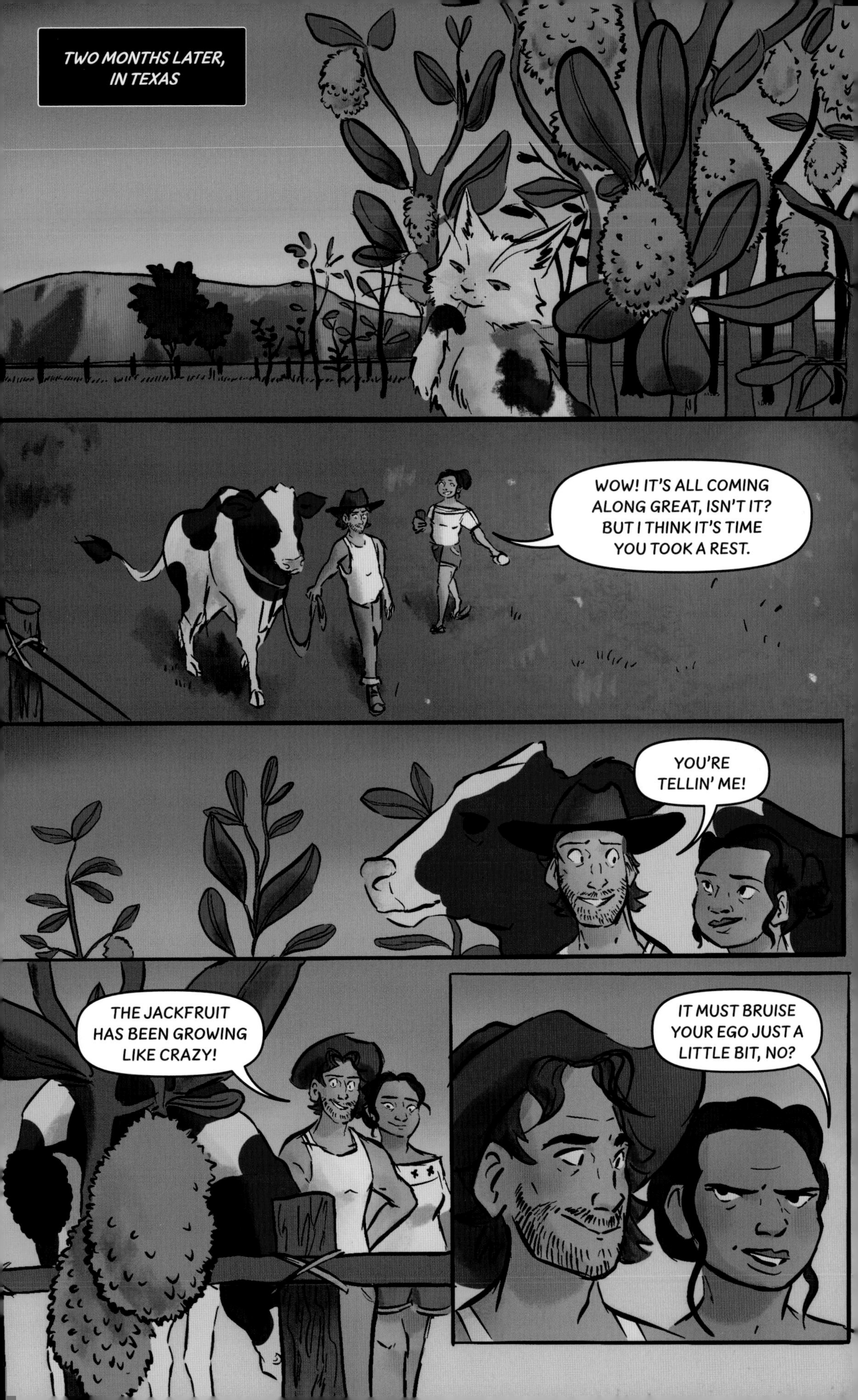
TWO MONTHS LATER, IN TEXAS
WOW! IT'S ALL COMING ALONG GREAT, ISN'T IT? BUT I THINK IT'S TIME YOU TOOK A REST.
YOU'RE TELLIN' ME!
THE JACKFRUIT HAS BEEN GROWING LIKE CRAZY!
IT MUST BRUISE YOUR EGO JUST A LITTLE BIT, NO?

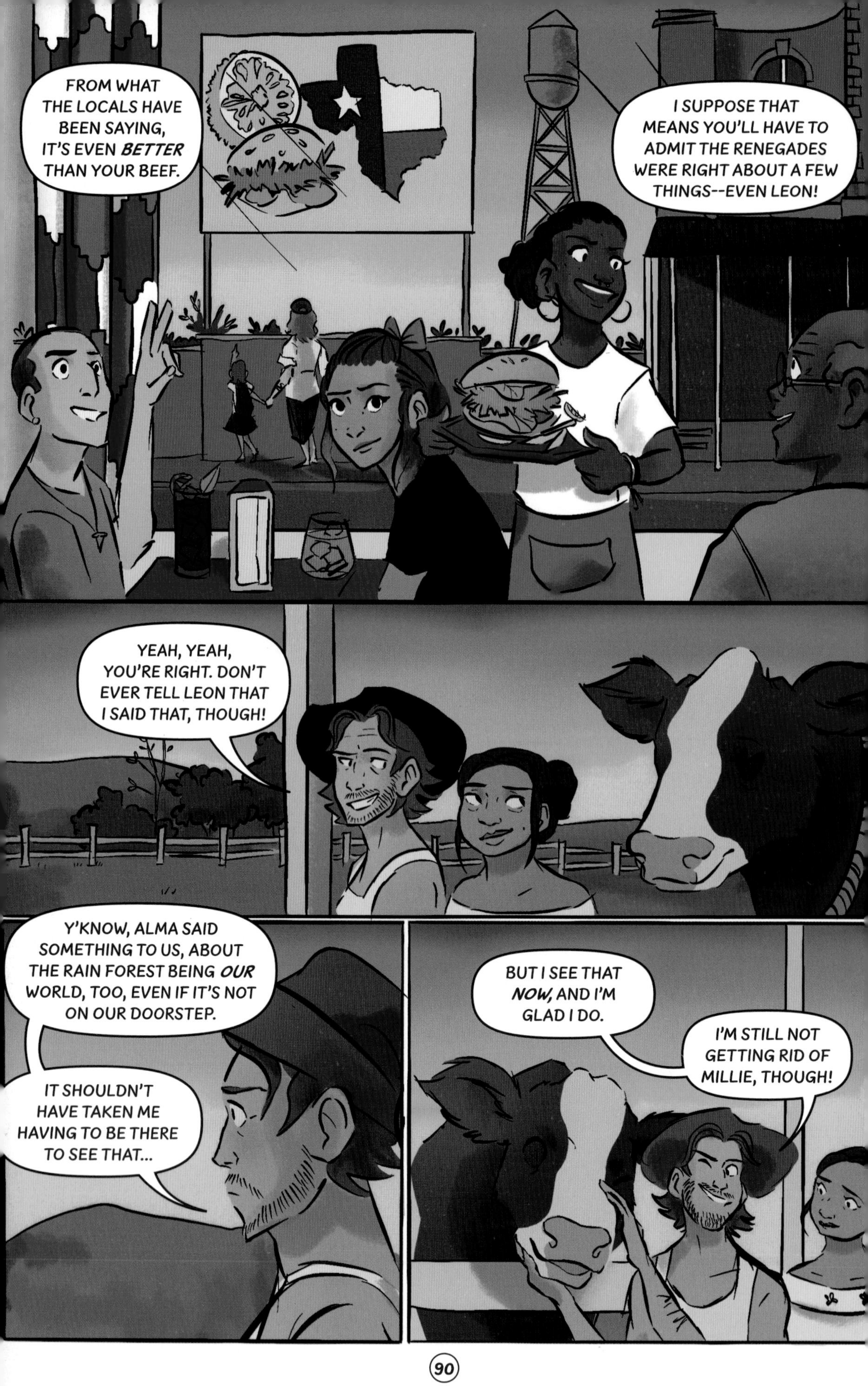
FROM WHAT THE LOCALS HAVE BEEN SAYING, IT'S EVEN *BETTER* THAN YOUR BEEF.
I SUPPOSE THAT MEANS YOU'LL HAVE TO ADMIT THE RENEGADES WERE RIGHT ABOUT A FEW THINGS--EVEN LEON!
YEAH, YEAH, YOU'RE RIGHT. DON'T EVER TELL LEON THAT I SAID THAT, THOUGH!
Y'KNOW, ALMA SAID SOMETHING TO US, ABOUT THE RAIN FOREST BEING *OUR* WORLD, TOO, EVEN IF IT'S NOT ON OUR DOORSTEP.
IT SHOULDN'T HAVE TAKEN ME HAVING TO BE THERE TO SEE THAT...
BUT I SEE THAT *NOW,* AND I'M GLAD I DO.
I'M STILL NOT GETTING RID OF MILLIE, THOUGH!

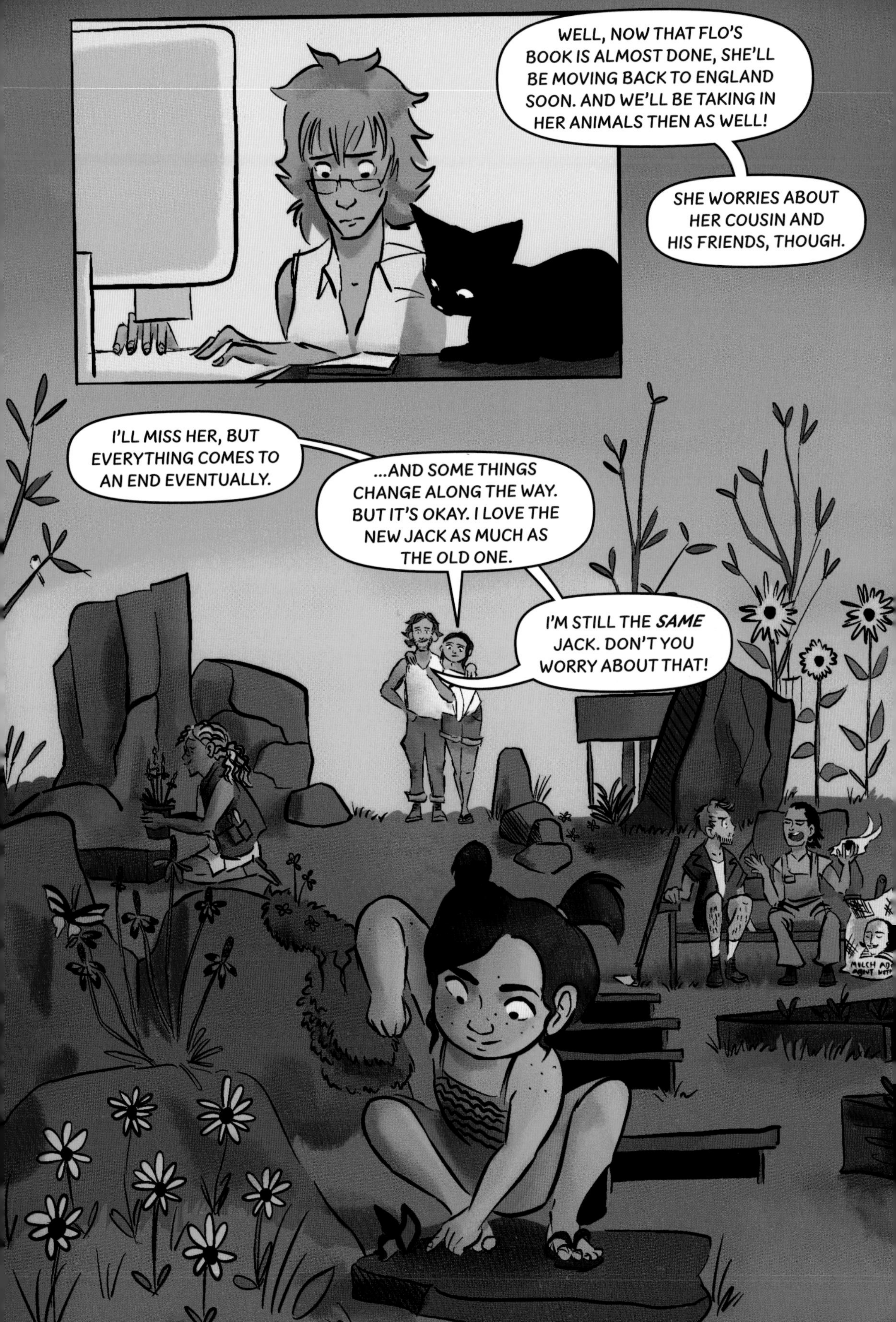

WELL, NOW THAT FLO'S BOOK IS ALMOST DONE, SHE'LL BE MOVING BACK TO ENGLAND SOON. AND WE'LL BE TAKING IN HER ANIMALS THEN AS WELL!
SHE WORRIES ABOUT HER COUSIN AND HIS FRIENDS, THOUGH.
I'LL MISS HER, BUT EVERYTHING COMES TO AN END EVENTUALLY.
...AND SOME THINGS CHANGE ALONG THE WAY. BUT IT'S OKAY. I LOVE THE NEW JACK AS MUCH AS THE OLD ONE.
I'M STILL THE *SAME* JACK. DON'T YOU WORRY ABOUT THAT!

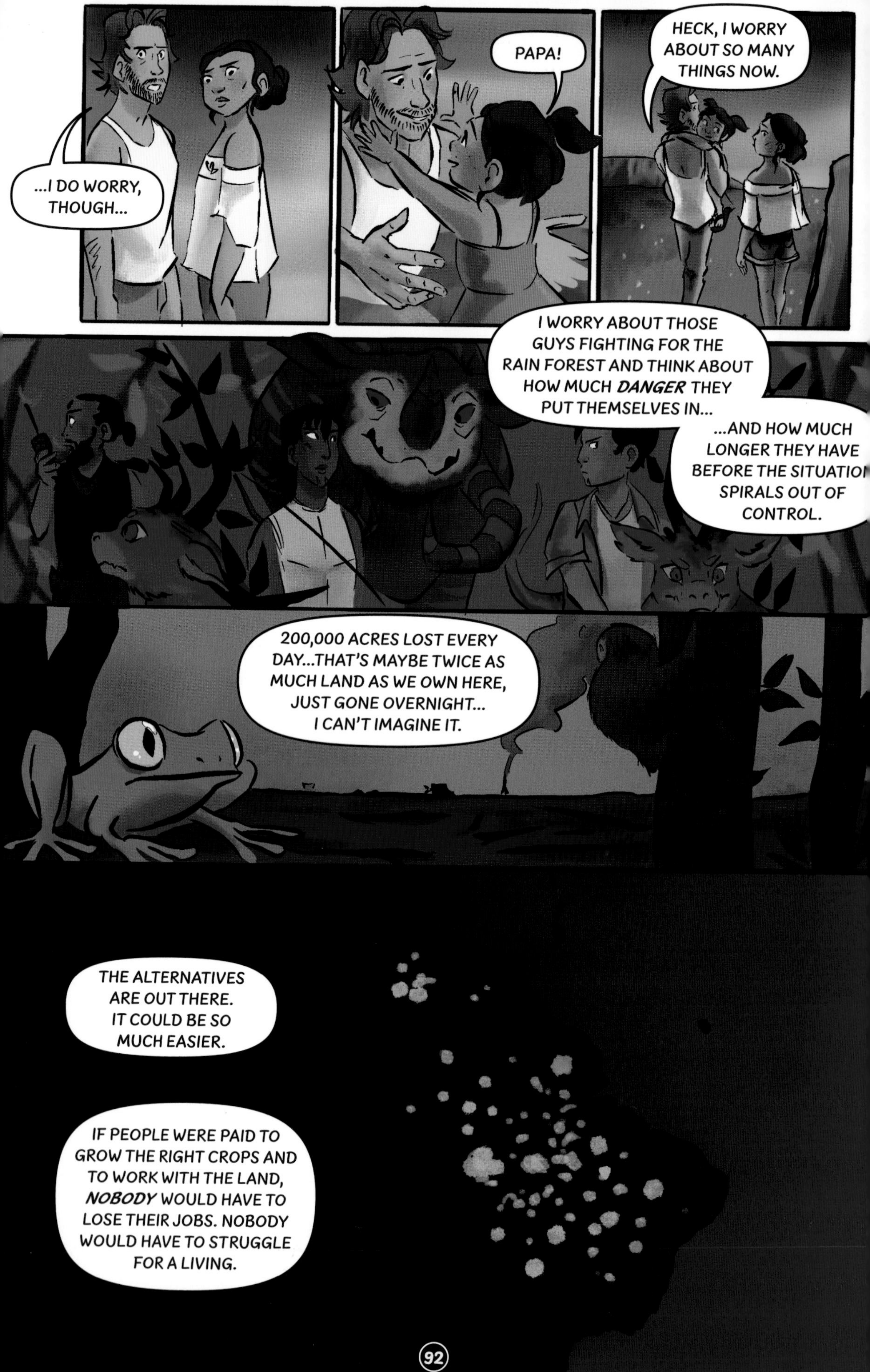

...I DO WORRY, THOUGH...
PAPA!
HECK, I WORRY ABOUT SO MANY THINGS NOW.
I WORRY ABOUT THOSE GUYS FIGHTING FOR THE RAIN FOREST AND THINK ABOUT HOW MUCH *DANGER* THEY PUT THEMSELVES IN...
...AND HOW MUCH LONGER THEY HAVE BEFORE THE SITUATIO SPIRALS OUT OF CONTROL.
200,000 ACRES LOST EVERY DAY...THAT'S MAYBE TWICE AS MUCH LAND AS WE OWN HERE, JUST GONE OVERNIGHT... I CAN'T IMAGINE IT.
THE ALTERNATIVES ARE OUT THERE. IT COULD BE SO MUCH EASIER.
IF PEOPLE WERE PAID TO GROW THE RIGHT CROPS AND TO WORK WITH THE LAND, *NOBODY* WOULD HAVE TO LOSE THEIR JOBS. NOBODY WOULD HAVE TO STRUGGLE FOR A LIVING.

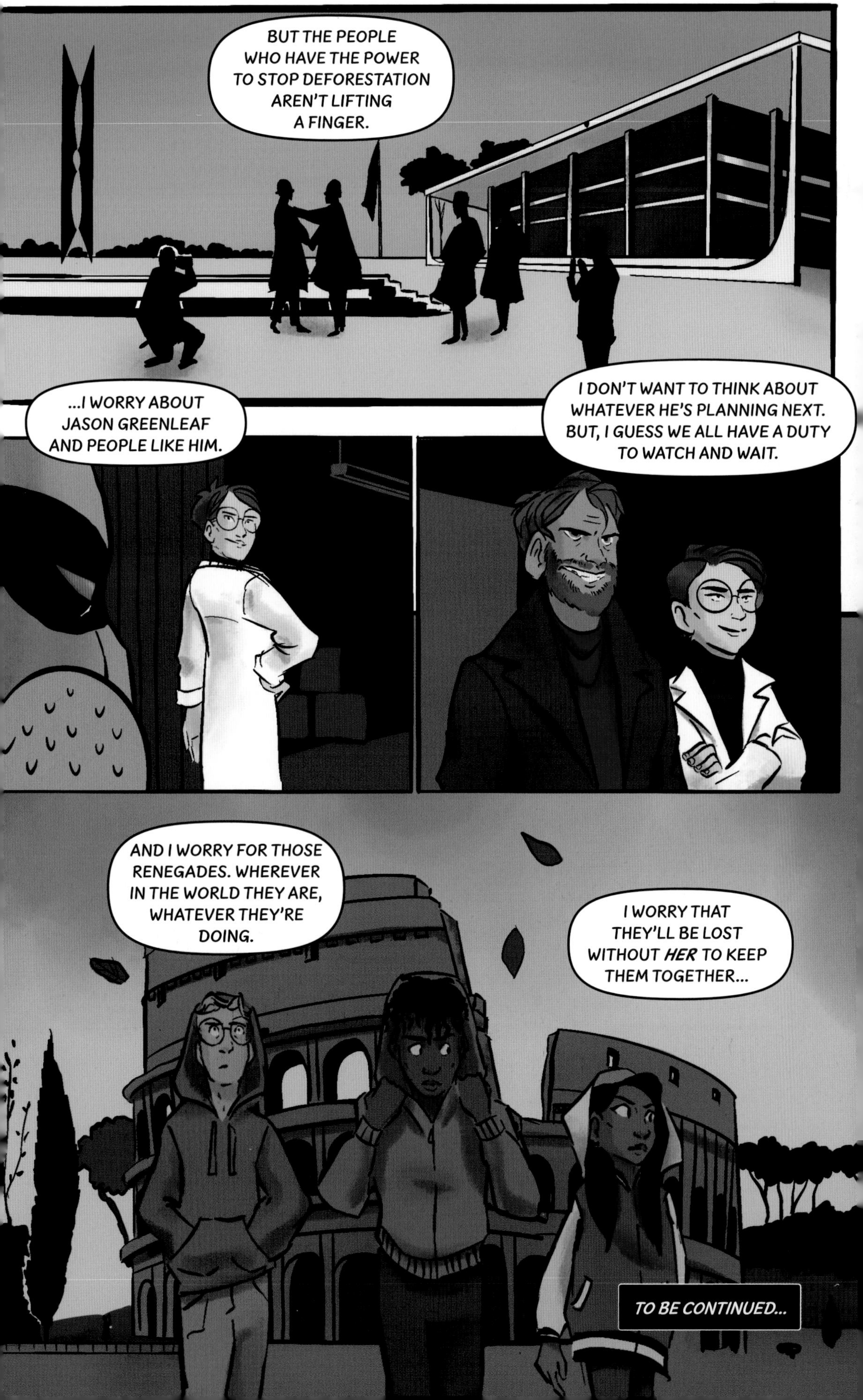
BUT THE PEOPLE WHO HAVE THE POWER TO STOP DEFORESTATION AREN'T LIFTING A FINGER.
...I WORRY ABOUT JASON GREENLEAF AND PEOPLE LIKE HIM.
I DON'T WANT TO THINK ABOUT WHATEVER HE'S PLANNING NEXT. BUT, I GUESS WE ALL HAVE A DUTY TO WATCH AND WAIT.
AND I WORRY FOR THOSE RENEGADES. WHEREVER IN THE WORLD THEY ARE, WHATEVER THEY'RE DOING.
I WORRY THAT THEY'LL BE LOST WITHOUT *HER* TO KEEP THEM TOGETHER...
TO BE CONTINUED...

THE CLIMATE EMERGENCY

WHILE FIRE-BREATHING CREATURES LIKE FLAMEJANTE MIGHT BE A WORK OF FICTION, THE THREAT OF CLIMATE CHANGE IS VERY REAL AND AFFECTS US ALL. TO HAVE ANY CHANCE OF PREVENTING THE PLANET FROM WARMING FURTHER WE NEED TO ACT NOW, SO IT'S IMPORTANT TO UNDERSTAND THE SCIENCE OF CLIMATE CHANGE--THE CAUSES, THE EFFECTS, AND WHAT WE CAN DO ABOUT IT.

WHAT IS CLIMATE CHANGE?

Earth is warmed by a layer of gases in the atmosphere that trap heat from the sun. But many human activities release gases that contribute to this effect, such as carbon dioxide. These gases build up in the atmosphere, trapping more heat, like the glass of a greenhouse, and causing the climate of our planet to warm much faster than usual. This effect is called global warming and has many impacts on Earth's climate, causing sea levels to rise and more extreme weather events to occur.

WHY ARE EARTH'S FORESTS IMPORTANT?

Forests are known as "carbon sinks" because of trees' ability to absorb carbon dioxide from the air. When forests are burned down, not only are carbon sinks lost, but carbon dioxide is released into the atmosphere, adding to the greenhouse effect. Forests, and rain forests especially, are also home to a large proportion of the world's animal and plant species.

DEFORESTATION AND FARMING

Deforestation has increased in recent years, with land being cleared to graze cattle and grow animal feed, and for crops such as soy and palm oil. In Brazil, the actions of big companies and pressures on farmers have caused large parts of the Amazon rainforest to be burnt to make way for agriculture. In July 2019, an area the size of five soccer fields was cleared there every minute.

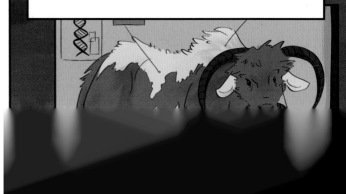

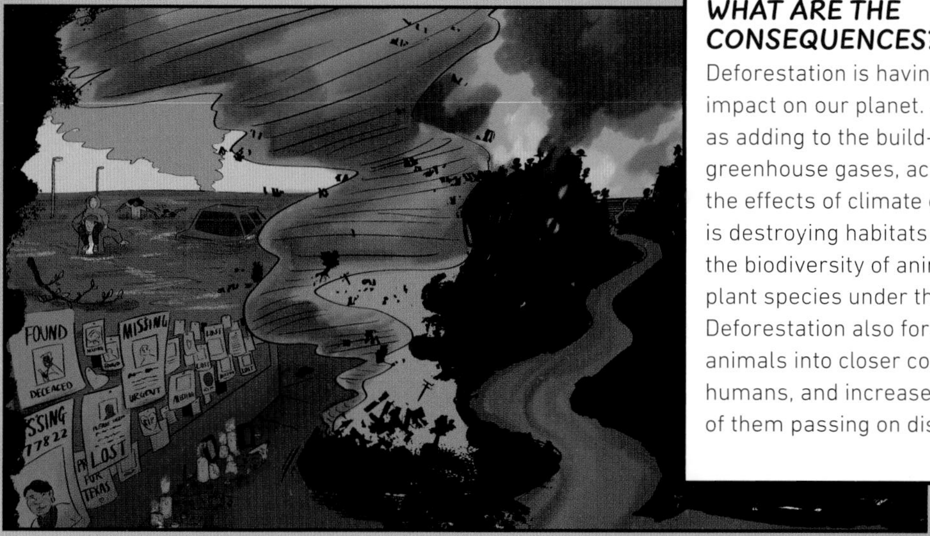
FOUND
MISSING
DECEASED
URGENT
LOST

WHAT ARE THE CONSEQUENCES?

Deforestation is having a major impact on our planet. As well as adding to the build-up of greenhouse gases, accelerating the effects of climate change, it is destroying habitats – putting the biodiversity of animal and plant species under threat. Deforestation also forces animals into closer contact with humans, and increases the risk of them passing on diseases.

DEFENDING THE FOREST

More than 80 per cent of the Earth's biodiversity is protected by indigenous people. Many of these communities have a spiritual relationship with the Earth that has fuelled their activism against land theft and destruction. But the work of ecoactivists can put them into conflict with powerful groups. Influential Lenca and Honduran campaigner Berta Cáceres was assassinated in 2016, and many other activists have been killed.

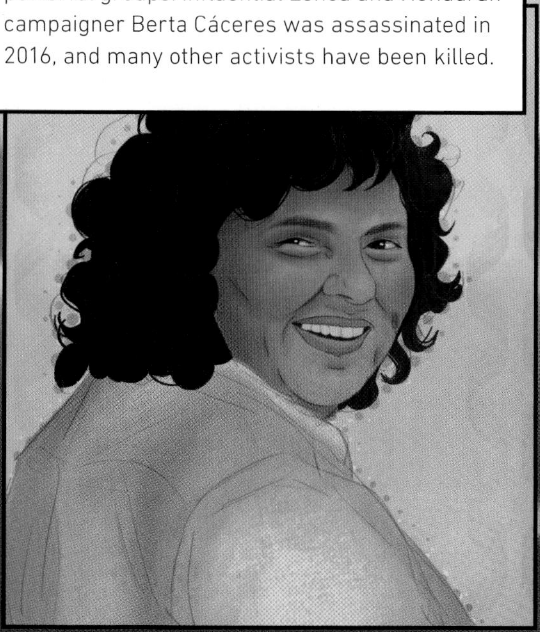

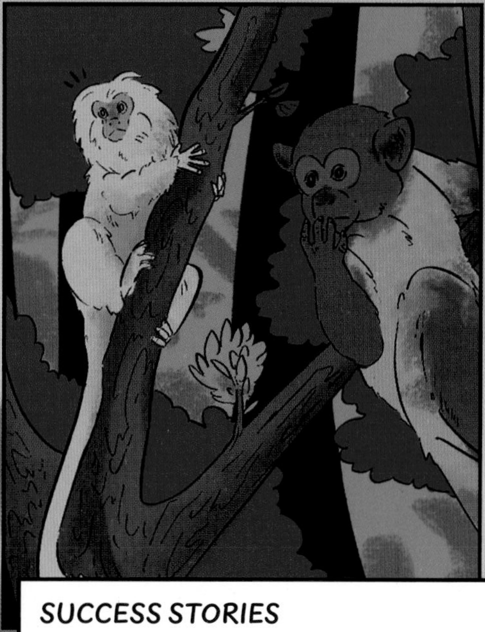

SUCCESS STORIES

It is possible to prevent deforestation, by paying farmers to protect the trees, and developing ecotourism and more ecofriendly types of agriculture and forestry. In one such project in Costa Rica, species like sloths and tree frogs can now live amongst crops like organic pineapple!

WHAT CAN WE DO?

Learning from case studies and the knowledge and practices of many local groups, everyone has the power to urge governments to pass laws to defend the forests, and to push big businesses to farm in a way that respects human rights, and the soil and water we depend on.

MEET THE TEAM

THE RENEGADES COMICS ARE CREATED BY A PASSIONATE TEAM, BROUGHT TOGETHER BY THEIR DRIVE TO PROTECT THE CLIMATE.

HOW TO HELP THE PLANET

As well as pushing for governments to act, there are lots of things we can do to help the planet, such as eating less meat and other foods linked to climate change. Did you know plant-based foods cause less greenhouse gas emissions than many meats? To explore more about topics like these, visit our website down below!

JEREMY BROWN *THE RENEGADES* WAS CO-FOUNDED BY JEREMY WHILE HE STUDIED FOR A MASTER'S IN CLIMATE CHANGE AT KING'S COLLEGE LONDON. IN ADDITION TO DREAMING UP THE CHARACTERS AND STORY ARCS, HE ENJOYS POLITICS AND STAND-UP COMEDY.

KATY JAKEWAY WHILE CREATING *THE RENEGADES*, KATY WAS ALSO STUDYING AT KING'S COLLEGE LONDON. KATY JOINED THE PROJECT IN ITS EARLY DAYS, USING HER PASSION FOR ART AND WRITING TO HELP BRING JEREMY'S INITIAL IDEAS TO LIFE.

DAVID SELBY CO-SCRIPTWRITER OF *THE RENEGADES* AND FELLOW FORMER KING'S COLLEGE LONDON STUDENT, DAVID WAS EAGER TO BUILD ON JEREMY AND KATY'S IDEAS AND HOPES TO SEE THE PROJECT RAISE AWARENESS ABOUT CLIMATE CHANGE.

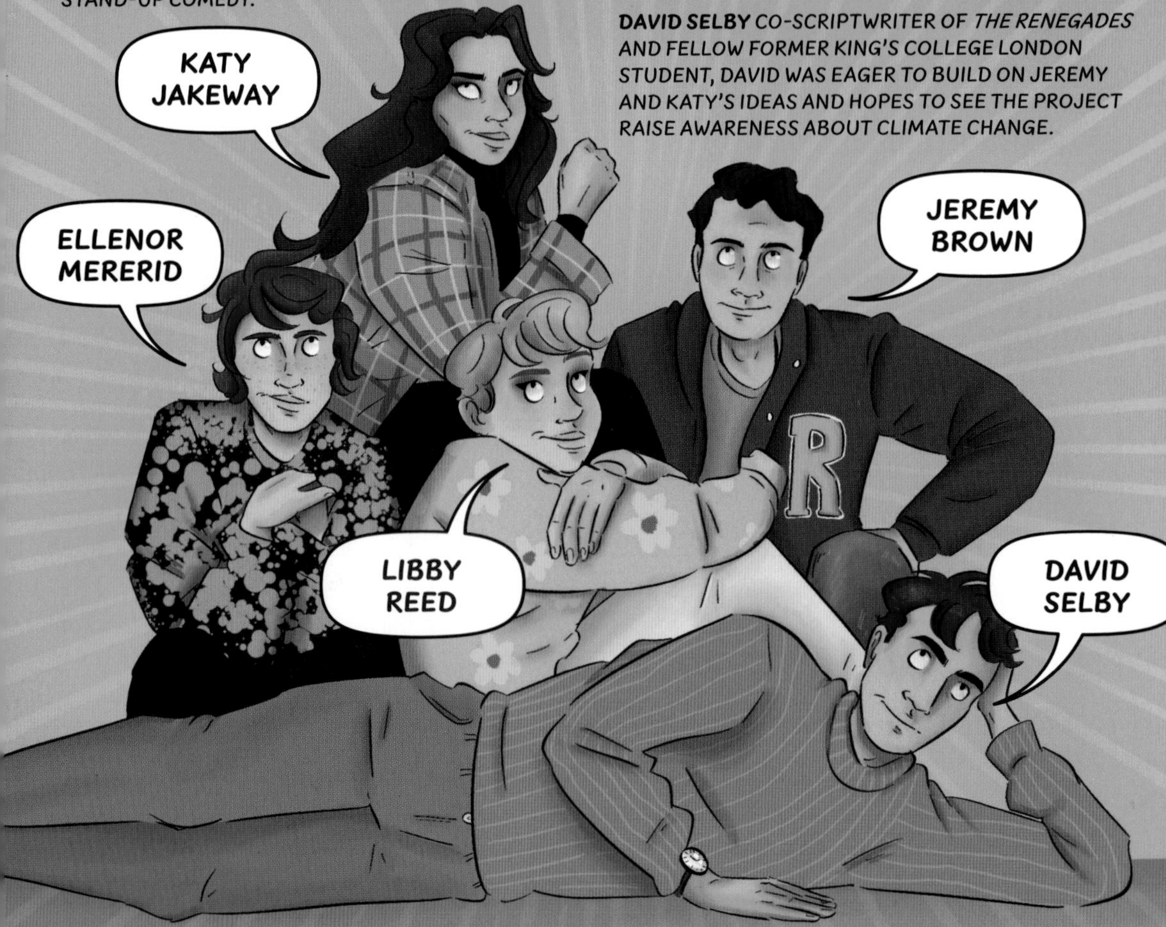
KATY JAKEWAY
ELLENOR MERERID
JEREMY BROWN
LIBBY REED
DAVID SELBY

LIBBY REED LIBBY SPENDS MOST OF HER TIME DRAWING AND MAKING UP STORIES. SHE LOVES ANIMALS, ESPECIALLY REPTILES, AND USES HER ARTWORK TO SHOW THE BEAUTY OF THE NATURAL WORLD.

ELLENOR MERERID ELLENOR IS INSPIRED BY DAVID ATTENBOROUGH AND CHARLES DARWIN—PEOPLE WHO HAVE SHOWN THE MIGHT AND MIRACLE OF OUR PLANET TO MILLIONS OF PEOPLE. ELLENOR LIKES FOLKLORE AND STARGAZING.

ACKNOWLEDGMENTS SPECIAL THANKS TO SUFFOLK FRIEND AND COMIC GEEK MISCHA PEARSON FOR PIONEERING THE GUARDIANS OF THE PLANET (THE PREDECESSOR TO THE RENEGADES). MUCH CREDIT TO CLASSMATES JONATHAN HYDE, TOM HAMBLEY, AND ELIAS YASSIN FOR THEIR GEOGRAPHICAL WISDOM, BOLD ACTIVISM, AND LOYAL FRIENDSHIP, WHICH ALL VERY MUCH HELPED TO SHAPE THE COMIC. THERE ARE TOO MANY TO LIST HERE, BUT A BIG THANK YOU ALSO TO JAMES PORTER, KATE SCHRECKENBERG, GEORGE ADAMSON, ODHRAN LINSEY, MICHAEL BARNARD, PARAS SINGH, AND ALL THE LOVELY CREW AT DK FOR THEIR ENTHUSIASM, PATIENCE, AND COMMITMENT TO PROTECTING THE PLANET THROUGH STORYTELLING. DK WOULD LIKE TO THANK HAZEL BEYNON FOR PROOFREADING.

CHECK OUT OUR WEBSITE **RENEGADESCOMIC.ORG** FOR THE LATEST TIPS ON WHAT YOU CAN DO TO DEFEND THE PLANET YOURSELF!